# SNEAK ATTACK

## NASHVILLE STEEL BOOK ONE

STACEY LYNN

**Sneak Attack**

**Nashville Steel Series**

**Book One**

**Stacey Lynn**

Copyright © 2023 Stacey Lynn

Content Editing: My Brother's Editor

Proofreading: Virginia Tesi Carey, Courtney DeLollis

Cover Design: Shanoff Designs



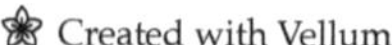 Created with Vellum

# CHAPTER 1
## EDEN

Marysville, Tennessee, population four thousand one hundred and twenty-two.

The green sign welcomed me while the lunch I ate on the road threatened to revolt. There I was, returning to the town I swore I'd never see again.

I swore I could still see the blood staining my hands as they gripped the steering wheel. Sure, it'd been seven years, and no one else could see it, but it was there. A monster inside of me coiled tight, waiting for the moment to strike again.

There was only one person who could bring me back there.

Marley Bickerstaff. The small town's grandma to everyone and the neighbor I met the day my parents' moving truck pulled in across the street from her house.

I owed her a favor for not telling my parents about the night she caught me drinking in Mr. William's barn.

She'd called that favor in, and it was Marley. No one could say no to her, not even me, even though I'd learned how to use that word with rapid frequency since leaving this place.

Hard to argue with her most recent letter, though.

*I'm dying, Eden. Please come stay with me. Let me see you one more time before I leave.*

A lump lodged in my throat as I reached town. Familiar sights dotted Main Street, one of the few ways to get to Marley's home, were as vivid in my memory for the last seven years as they were in person. Few things had changed, but I noticed differences. The laundromat appeared ready to crumble at the next gust of wind, but the lights were still on, and a handful of people were inside. The old hardware store now held a teal and cream sign, curly lettering across the front of a bagel. Some buildings' brick fronts were in desperate need of repair. Others freshly painted.

My palms turned clammy as the diner appeared on the corner. Burgers and milkshakes after football games and sitting outside on tailgates of trucks…memories I had never been able to squash.

It was the middle of a Wednesday. Streets from the hair salon down to the bars had cars lined up out front. I was careful not to focus on anyone who might recognize me, not that the odds were high. My car would keep me anonymous until word got out.

No one would argue with Marley for inviting me back, but I had no doubt they'd save their vindictiveness and their arrows spiked with hatred for when I was alone.

Which meant I might be returning to Marysville for a while, but I'd be returning to town as infrequently as possible. The road curved as I left the small downtown, sharp turns uphill as I turned to the side roads of the hilly farming community twenty miles north of Nashville. My engine roared as the last steep hill had me turning almost one hundred and eighty degrees. I curved past Pheasant Lake with its resort, large enough to help boost the summer economy, small enough that the memories I gathered there in the one year I lived in this town pummeled me. My tires rumbled over the bridge past the bait shop and then it was a sharp left.

That food in my stomach rolled and twisted.

Two more minutes and I'd be back there.

Staring across the street at the home I once lived in.

The home next door that had once held the only boy I'd ever loved.

I couldn't do this.

Wouldn't.

What had I been thinking?

Marley had an entire town of people who would take care of her. She didn't *need* me.

I yanked my car to the side of the road and checked for traffic before cranking it into a three-point turn and headed back to town.

I'd let Marley down. It wouldn't be the first time. I'd call her. She was asking too much. Hell, I'd had this same mental argument for the last nine hours, but now that I was there, I couldn't do it.

My pulse raced and my speeding heart thundered in my ears as I white knuckle gripped the steering wheel back through the tightly wound streets. I turned right before I reached downtown and pulled into the park's parking lot. It hadn't changed a bit.

This was stupid. So very, very stupid. Why in the hell had I come back here?

I never should have left Florida. Never should have agreed to this. I should have gone on and continued talking to Marley through handwritten letters.

No one would want me here. No one would welcome me back into their small town like they'd once done.

Hell, as soon as word got out, I'd probably be run out of town anyway.

*No.*

I reached for my phone. Marley would be upset, but I'd explain.

Movement on the swings at the playground grabbed my attention as I dug through my purse for my phone, and I stilled. Hand wrapped around my screen.

A woman stood nearby, smiling at the boy who pumped his legs fiercely to get as high as he could. The woman brushed hair back and my breath stalled. Their smiles matched, but that was where the similarities ended. From her well-highlighted blonde hair and blue eyes so vividly bright I could never forget them, my jaw unhinged itself as I sat there, hand still holding the phone and frozen as Selma Holden brushed her hair off her shoulders.

*Shit.* Of all the people to see first. I couldn't do this. Could not see her, could not move through the same small town as her again. My phone rang in my hand, startling me. Expecting Marley's call, I was surprised to see another name on my screen.

*Mom.*

I silenced the ringer and stuffed it back into my purse.

Shit. Was my entire past determined to push me today?

Selma said something, laughed and waved for the boy, her son, to hurry up. I should have been shoving my car into reverse and high-tailing it out of Marysville and back to Pensacola as fast as my Toyota could take me there.

But that boy…*Jasper*…Cole's son. Everyone in the entire country knew the story of Cole and Selma and Jasper. Knew Cole's tragic history that had kept him rooted in his hometown. As soon as my parents and I left Marysville and headed south, I'd tried as hard as I could to avoid the mention of his name. It'd worked for a few years. Until Cole Buchanan was drafted to his hometown football team the Nashville Steel after making a name for himself at Vanderbilt University.

Yeah, I needed to *go go go*, but I couldn't.

Because Cole's son, looking so much like him, was flying through the air, landing on hands and feet in the mulch while Selma waited for him to dust himself off. She settled her hand at his upper back and somehow, my feet were forcing me out of the car.

I should have stopped. Should have done all the things I'd already decided I'd do and yet I followed them, past the park and around the corner and with the sun beating down on me, my gray cardigan hugged tightly across my chest, despite the roasting summer heat, and my keys in my hand the only thing I grabbed from the car.

I stayed my distance until the boy screamed, "Dad!"

My keys fell to the pavement and the world around me ceased to exist, narrowed to only the view I had of him taking off down the sidewalk, Cole Buchanan crouching low, arms wide out as the boy jumped into his arms.

Cole Buchanan.

The boy I loved.

The boy who was never mine to love, never mine to have, but we hadn't cared in the end.

Cole Buchanan, hugging his little boy on the sidewalk while Selma, his high school girlfriend's best friend until I swooped in, smiled down at both of them, ruffling his hair.

Cole and Selma had a *son* together.

I'd known it. Of course I had. As soon as Cole was drafted in the first round, his story made national headlines. The boy who'd lost his high school sweetheart in a tragic accident. The boy who gave up his athletic scholarship to play at Vanderbilt so he could stay close to home. The man who had a son his second year of college and stepped up to raise his boy, moved back to his hometown. The man who was drafted to the NFL and *still* stayed living in his hometown, twenty miles north of Nashville.

I'd known it all. Gotten swept away in stories of him for weeks before I managed to pull myself out of the darkness seeping back into my mind.

But seeing it? I staggered back a step and around the corner of the building, where I slammed my back against the harsh brick. It scraped and snagged on my sweater as I furiously blinked away tears, trying to will the vision of what I just saw into a false reality—where Cole was mine. Where Selma minded her own business.

Where Hilary was still alive.

"No. No, no, no." This was worse than all the nightmares I'd had combined. This was worse than the nights I woke up screaming, drenched in sweat and couldn't fall back asleep for days.

This was so much worse—because it was real. And I was viewing it in person, well, hiding behind the building like a lunatic because if Cole and Selma were together like the media so often questioned—

Why in the hell had Marley wanted me to come back and have that thrown in my face?

Why in the hell was I here?

Screw the favor. It'd been years since that night in the barn. She could go ahead and tell my parents. It wasn't like I talked to them anyway.

My chest seized all over again. My hands trembled and my knees shook so hard I slid down the wall, reveling in the scratch along my back. The pain kept me grounded, alert, at least until I fell to my ass, my knees bent in front of me. I pressed my forehead to my knees, closed my eyes, and tried to breathe.

I was safe. I was alive. I had Marley. I had parents who never gave up on me even if I gave up on myself a long time ago. I had a career I loved. The sun was out, brightening the trees around me and the heat pushed through my clothing to remind me my flesh was alive. That my heart still beat.

I grounded myself, focused on all the things that were true and the things I could be thankful for, or at least acknowledge, until the knotted ball of fear and regret loosened in my chest, making breathing easier.

It was only then when I was sure I could stand without falling over, I set my hand on the pavement to push to my feet and a shadow, followed by two hot pink and black athletic shoes, stepped into view.

Selma's presence had been a force in high school, and it had not diminished over the years. If anything, her presence had me trembling all over again, more so when she finally spoke.

"I didn't think you'd have the guts to come back here."

Selma grew up being Hilary's best friend. A third wheel to Cole and Hilary, the town's beloved high school sweetheart couple, the three of them were attached at the hips until I showed up. I hadn't intended to bump her out of the lineup, had never wanted to, but that was….

It happened before I knew she'd despise me for it. Before I ever met her, and I could never make it right no matter how hard I tried to stay away.

That was what Cole and I had been from the moment we met, magnets circling, attached and being yanked apart. By Selma. By Hilary—but considering she'd been Cole's girlfriend, that was her place.

It took effort, more than I thought I had, to stand tall and push off the brick wall. "Marley insisted."

A cop-out. I could have told her I had all the guts to do whatever I wanted, but it was a lie, and I'd promised myself years ago I'd never lie again, regardless of the cost of the truth.

Her beautifully highlighted blonde hair fell past her shoulders as she tilted her head. Selma was gorgeous. Always had been, but where Hilary had that sweet girl next door sweetness to her, Selma's sharp edges and features belonged more on the cover of Vogue.

Certainly not in this small country town.

I was surprised she was still here—but given her and Cole…well, there was a time I would have stayed for him, too.

Almond-shaped eyes narrowed into slits, only highlighting her ocean-blue eyes. "He won't want to see you, and I want you to stay away. From him *and* our son."

My eyes closed as her barb sliced through me as intended.

"I will."

"Yeah, well, I'd believe you, but I don't trust you as far as I can throw you but know this—when he heard you might be returning to town—well, let's just say I know for a fact he won't want to see you either. Ever again."

She turned on her rubber-soled shoes and floated away with grace, leaving me in tatters.

Of course, Cole wouldn't want to see me ever again.

I already knew that.

I just hadn't realized hearing it would hurt so much.

# CHAPTER 2
## COLE

"Jasper! We need to get moving, buddy. Your mom is going to be here any minute."

My son ran at speeds hovering one thousand all day long until it was time to leave our house. Then he trudged through molasses, slow as the day was long. Already I was hating that summer was almost over and school would start. Then he'd be trudging through molasses with lead-weighted boots.

"Bongo needs to go out!" Jasper jumped the last step on the stairs and tried to dodge me, but I reached out, snagging the back of his shirt and pulled him backward where his shoes and bag for his mom's house were by my feet near the front door.

"Shoes on." I ruffled his hair. "Grab your breakfast on the kitchen counter. I'll get Bongo."

Bongo, the one-year-old Golden Retriever Jasper *had* to have. We rescued him three months ago, and I was pretty sure the only reason we did was because of Marley. We'd heard the worst news regarding her diagnosis. Jasper hit me at the wrong time, the wrong day, and Selma doubled down by telling me she'd help when I had to travel.

I'd refused at first, as I did with most of Selma's offers to be closer than she knew I wanted, but that changed the day I came home after a long day of off-season training to the escape artist puppy who'd somehow freed himself from his kennel and tore open the couch cushions. Stuffing had turned my living room into a winter wonderland of fake snow. He'd even somehow managed to upend the coffee table my grandfather and I had built when I was ten. I could barely flip it over by myself, it was so heavy.

How the fifty-pound puppy managed to knock it over, much less escape from his metal kennel that was perfectly locked when I checked it, still made me wonder.

Bongo, who was mostly house trained except for when he got overly excited with any visitor, was at the back door, long, furry and golden tail whipping against the glass as he whined at the leaves blowing in the wind.

*Great.*

I grabbed his leash from the wall next to the door and fought through his fur to get it on, get him outside, frustrated with the dog I was coerced into getting against my will, Jasper's procrastination every morning and the fact that even though it worked, and it was mostly healthy, I had to hand him over to Selma before I went to work almost every day.

Our custody worked easier than most separated parents I knew. She worked nights at a hospital in Nashville four nights a week, working seven to seven. I got Jasper every night she worked. She picked him up on her way home and dropped him off at preschool or one of our parents' houses, leaving me an hour to get ready by myself before I headed to either the practice facility or to the gym in the off-season. We switched off in the evening when Jasper saw his parents who might not be together but still cared about each other—and him —and then, on the weekends, we alternated. Some holidays were done together, depending on whose family was around or if trips were planned, or whether I had a home or away game.

As amicable as it was, saying goodbye to my kid every day knowing he was shipped back and forth to two homes, grated on me daily. The shit of it was, I had the power to fix it...but that meant living with Selma. Marrying her. Committing to her.

And I didn't feel a single urge to do any of that, even if she kept trying.

Like with Bongo.

As predicted, my dog lunged for a leaf, almost yanking me off my feet. I gave him a quick tug.

"Heel."

He refused. On the hunt, I gave him a little lead on the leash.

I'd work on training him better this weekend, my weekend alone.

Hell, maybe I'd forgo handing him off to Selma and put him in doggy daycare like I kept threatening. Maybe a board and train.

The animal could certainly use it.

A knock rapped on the sliding door, and in my peripheral, I caught sight of teal scrubs.

Shit. "Come on, Bongo."

I pulled him back inside, unsurprised that Selma was already there. She never wasted a minute getting to my house, but she didn't usually walk inside like she owned it. Her presence, along with Jasper's procrastination, forced me to suck in a deep breath and clench my mouth shut before I spewed my irritation at her.

It was more than Selma.

*She'd* be back in town today. Maybe already was.

Seven years and I wasn't ready. Not for a minute to run the risk of meeting her on the street.

When I was with Jasper at the park.

Shopping at the grocery store.

Ever since Marley told me she'd asked Eden to return, I'd counted down to this day. Anticipation. Fury. Guilt. It clawed at me, kept me up at night, last night in particular.

It was like I could sense her. Practically smell her again. So much so that it was all I'd been able to do not to stop by Marley's last night, see if a car was there. Keep my ass inside so I didn't go to my parents' house and wander to the one place we always seemed to find each other when we needed each other the most.

"You look like crap." Selma's smile, most likely dazzling to everyone else, was tight.

"Considering you're on day three of your night shifts, I could say the same."

That smile she used to dazzle others dripped with disdain.

So, we got along and cared about each other—that didn't mean I'd ever actually liked her. The only good thing to have come from my lifelong friendship with Selma was Jasper.

"Charming as always."

*You're the one who wants me.*

I bit back the retort. I was on edge from Eden returning, not Selma, and as much as she and I could fight verbally, this wasn't her problem.

"Jasper's almost ready to go. I'm going to take Bongo to the doggy daycare south of town I told you about."

Her brows tugged together with displeasure. When it came to Selma, that was a frequent reaction. Outside the one night we spent together where it wasn't, but even then, it hadn't been pleasurable or passionate—more like comfort food.

Not that I'd ever tell Selma that. I'd end up with her palm print against my cheek.

"That's not necessary. I'm happy to help—"

"I think it is." Necessary. Sometimes Selma grew too comfortable —welcoming herself into my home was only one example.

"Dad!"

"Coming!" I left her gaping after me at the back door and hurried to find Jasper. He was sitting on the bottom stair, shoelaces knotted, and his chin was wobbling. "It's all right, buddy. I've got it."

I crouched down and unknotted the mess he made while my insides went to work doing the exact opposite.

I was finishing the second shoe, and Jasper's near meltdown was forgotten when Selma reached us, Bongo on a leash and kindness back on her face.

"It's no problem, Cole. You—"

I stood and leveled her with a look. "It is, and he's going to the daycare. And you know why."

The leash fell to the floor as her eyes widened. "You've seen her already."

The statement dropped like a bomb while Bongo whined at my legs, sniffing mine and Jasper's shoes, knowing we were leaving, and he was getting a car ride.

"Bongo's going to a daycare?" Jasper asked, but it came at me through a tunnel.

"What do you mean, I've seen her?" My teeth gritted on instinct and my chest burned hot. Too hot. Too tight.

Her lips pressed together, and she glanced at Jasper. Crouched between us, he had his fingers digging deep into Bongo's fur, scratching behind his ears like Bongo loved.

"Yeah, buddy. Bongo's going to make friends. Socialize and stuff. He'll have more fun than sleeping all day."

"Dogs can make friends?"

"You bet they can." I ruffled his dark hair and grinned down at him even if my teeth felt like they might snap in two from grinding them so hard.

My gaze snapped toward Selma completely forgetting…everything. But if she knew…that meant…

Seven years and Eden Barclay was back in town.

"It's obvious," Selma said, and there was a snappish tone to her voice that meant trouble. "She's here. You're already changing things. You said—"

Forget what I said last month when Selma heard what Marley had done and showed up at my house throwing a tantrum about how everything was going to change if Eden returned. I'd tried to reassure her, but shit. What did she expect?

"How do you know she's here?"

"Who are you talking about, Mommy?"

Selma smiled down at her son. Probably the only time she gave a genuine one was to him. "An old friend, honey."

"Friend? Like the kind of friends Bongo will make."

Selma chuckled, and she lifted her eyes to me. "Sure, Jasper. Just like the *dogs* Bongo will make friends with."

My lip curled into a snarl and so help me, if Jasper wasn't there… if I wasn't a gentleman…

No. I'd do nothing either way.

Because Eden left when I needed her most, and the mere reminder still hurt so damn much.

———

It was hours later, after I'd gotten ready for work, after I'd forced myself not to climb in my truck, drive all the way through town to Marley's house to bang on her door. It was after I'd shown up for practice, put in the bare minimum of work because preseason started soon, and this was our last easy week. It was after I'd left the locker room, not bothering to talk to any of my teammates, something I *never did* and had already received a half dozen text messages about, and it was after I'd returned home, forced myself to go to my own house instead of my parents' where I could see her.

Selma had thrown me off my game with a simple, assuming question, which only left me with more of my own I hadn't been able to shake.

What made her think I already saw Eden?

How did she know she was back in town?

And what difference did it make? She wasn't here for me. Hell, if Eden was back and was staying at Marley's request, I doubted she'd ever show her face in town. That would take a strength Eden had never possessed and people could change a lot in seven years, God knew I had, but that meant Eden would have had to grow a whole new personality. I doubted that was possible.

Hell, I wasn't even sure I wanted her to. I'd liked the one she had until it bit me in the ass.

No, I needed to forget she was here. I had a new season coming up, Jasper was starting school soon, and over the last couple of months, Selma's attention toward me was growing to uncomfortable levels.

I had enough female drama in my life, hovering at a breaking point, I certainly didn't need to add more to it.

That was all Eden would give me. Drama. Pain. A dash of hope before she tore it away.

I did not need to lose a whole damn day thinking of two women who at most made me feel the need to have a stockpile of antacids in my truck and my gym locker at the age of twenty-six years old.

"Shit," I muttered and closed my laptop where I'd been paying bills. I needed to run through plays, start watching films for our upcoming game. It might have just been preseason, and we were fortunate to be starting the season with a healthy, veteran lineup, but we'd be going against teams with new coaches and fresh blood. Fresh fire fueling their veins. Every game counted. Every play counted. From the first snap of the ball in our first preseason game to the very last snap, hopefully at the end of the Super Bowl in February. Every single second I was on that field calling a play or on the sidelines cheering on my defense counted to me.

Which was why I shouldn't have been thinking of driving to Marley's. Or to my parents.

And even if I did. What would I do then? Scream at her?

What good would that do?

She made her choice the day she didn't show up for Hilary's funeral, leaving me to deal with the fallout of our decisions and betrayal alone.

She *left* me.

Seven years ago, Eden left town without looking back, leaving me alone to deal with the fallout of our teenage decisions, and yet I could still see her smile, feel the warmth of her touch and the rapid beat of my heart when I sensed her presence.

No...I needed to stay away.

I couldn't be around Eden until I figured out how to protect my heart all over again.

# CHAPTER 3
## EDEN

t had taken me a while to decide to stay yesterday.

I planted my back against the brick wall until well after Selma left and ran through all my options ad nauseam until I finally realized the truth.

If I left now, I'd never heal. I'd never move on, and I'd certainly never trust anyone again. My life would stay as stagnant as the pond in my parents' Missouri backyard, growing moss and algae.

At least from the pictures they sent, since I hadn't seen it yet in person.

Which was probably why I'd finally agreed to come and stayed after my run-in with Selma.

Something had to change, and the only thing left to change was myself.

Marley's raspy voice rattled from her bedroom downstairs, forcing me to roll out of bed.

Sounds of movement in the kitchen had me moving faster. After I finally dragged myself to her door yesterday like a puppy with its tail between its legs, ashamed I'd almost left her, we sat and caught up. It didn't take long before she started yawning. She'd claimed she wasn't tired, but I'd taken over cooking a quick dinner using the ingredients in her stocked fridge before she went to bed.

She'd slept all night.

I woke up feeling like I'd run a marathon in my sleep.

Sliding into my fuzzy white slippers, I grabbed the lightweight gray robe from the back of my door and hurried down the stairs. Marley said she could get dizzy easily, especially before she'd eaten.

The last thing she should be doing was standing on her feet, cooking breakfast over her ancient gas stove.

"I've got breakfast, Marley!" I called out before I reached the bottom of the stairs.

Besides, with her memory failing so quickly she was just as likely to use a cup of sugar instead of flour in the pancakes.

I found her in the kitchen, filling the coffeepot, and for the hundredth time since I walked into her house, I was transported back to a better time—where things never changed, including the crocheted doilies draped over her dark purple couch or the rainbow-colored braided rug that covered her seventies linoleum chipped floor. For certain, if I were to pull up the rug I'd find the missing square in the middle of the kitchen floor, cut up after Cole once dropped a bowl of pickled beets on the floor. No amount of scrubbing with bleach had been able to remove the blood-colored stain.

"Sit. Sit." I guided her to one of the kitchen chairs, dark walnut wood with red and gold striped chair cushions tied to the seats.

"I've been making coffee every morning longer than you've been alive, you know."

"And the doctors said you have to stay off your feet as much as possible which is why I'm here, right?"

A liver-spotted and *cold* hand that seemed to have aged thirty years and not seven patted my hand.

"Yes, yes. I know that. Hard to accept some days, is all."

"Well, now you have me." I squeezed her hand and kissed the top of her head, full of gray hair and curled in a way I knew someone had to be taking her to the salon for her weekly blowout.

Who had stocked her fridge, kept her yard mowed, and the house cleaned was a question I wasn't going to ask.

Cole's parents probably, if they still lived next door. Or even Cole himself.

It didn't even have to be him. Half the town of Marysville would stumble over each other to help a woman who had helped so many.

There'd be hundreds to step up and help, but Cole would have been first in line, his parents right behind him, especially during his off-season.

"I saw some bacon in the fridge last night," I told her as I headed toward the coffeepot. It was faded, more yellow than white and was almost as old as me. It didn't have any of the bells and whistles, like a clock or timer function, anything built in the last fifteen years had. "Do you want some eggs and bacon for breakfast? Toast?"

She coughed, the sound rattling in her chest and reached for a tissue in the center of the table. Boxes of them were now everywhere in her home, always within reaching distance.

I paused while she coughed again and cleared her throat.

"Maybe just some toast this morning. And then you and I can chat."

I tried to think of a hundred ways to avoid this conversation, but I didn't have anything else to do except to sit and talk with her.

"I'm making bacon and eggs for me then," I muttered and turned to her fridge. It was newer. White with a side-by-side refrigerator and freezer that replaced her old yellow one we always teased her about.

"Can't avoid me forever, Eden. Not when you're standing in my kitchen."

"I know."

But I'd sure as hell try for as long as I could.

———

After breakfast, Marley and I headed out to the backyard. She looped her hand through my arm and told me to take a walk with her. I figured my reckoning was coming, but instead, she stayed quiet as we strolled through the path between her trees to the lake out past her acreage.

Marley's home was on a small, no-wake bay on Pheasant Lake. Where the other side of the lake held resorts and the constant hum of lake activity from March to November, this small bay was always gentle. Peaceful.

It was the same now, and the muscles in my shoulders and back that knitted themselves into knots yesterday slowly unfurled as we walked.

Marley must have sensed my need for quiet, because instead of jumping into the conversation I knew she wanted to have, she didn't. We spoke of nothing important and whispered about the weather and fall coming soon. Her favorite parts of fall and which trees turned the best colors. At her first yawn, I guided us back to the house and I was now cleaning the kitchen while she napped in her bedroom.

Cancer. Glioblastoma in her brain that was discovered far too late for any effective surgery, and she was opposed to any chemotherapy to shrink it.

Women so special shouldn't be destroyed so slowly or viciously. On the table, she had a list of doctors, her upcoming appointments, and her medicines all lined up on a lazy Susan with weekly pill organizers ready to be filled. I'd sit down and have her walk me through them when she woke so I could ensure I didn't mess it up, but someone had taken the time to type up an organized spreadsheet and tuck it between the pills.

There was also my own list of things I was working on other than just grocery lists and medicines. I was back to take care of Marley because she didn't have blood relatives remaining, but I still needed to find something to keep me sane.

Which meant hunting down the local humane societies or vet clinics to see if they needed volunteers. I would have to eventually go back to work, but volunteering would do for a while.

My head was down in my phone, pulling up Google Maps listings of all the shelters within fifteen miles, that when a firm knock hit the front door, shaking the glass storm door outside, I barely paused.

I should have.

I should have known better.

I should have realized that a delivery man wouldn't knock on the door or that Marley wouldn't have unannounced visitors.

But I wasn't thinking fast enough for that.

Truth be told, I hadn't done a lot of thinking ever since I agreed to stay with her.

Which was why I opened the door, head still down at my phone, and before I caught a whiff of scent or heard him speak or took notice at all of who was at her door, I already knew it was him.

Cole. His mere presence was enough to have the floor beneath my feet shifting.

"I didn't think you'd have the guts to answer the door or show your face around here ever again."

Seven years.

Seven years since I heard his voice. Since I saw the tortured look in his eyes when I told him I was leaving.

Seven years since I'd seen the man I loved in person and not on a television screen, and that was the first thing he said to me.

Not that I didn't deserve it.

"Marley's sleeping." It was as much of a dismissal as it was a warning.

He stepped into the home like he had every right to be there—and he did—because that was Marley's rule. Everyone was always welcome, and I had no doubt he'd done his fair share of taking care of her over the years.

The move was abrupt. Each swift and steady movement from him jolted me backward until I was grabbing onto the railing for dear life, and Cole was standing in Marley's entryway, glaring at me like I was gum on the bottom of his shoe.

Pretty much the way he looked at me the last time we spoke.

Time had been good to Cole. So had life. That wasn't a surprise, but staring at me then, he sucked the oxygen straight from my lungs and the entire room around us, making my chest seize and my legs turn to jelly.

He wasn't supposed to be here.

He was supposed to not want anything to do with me.

"What do you want, Eden?"

"I'm here to help Marley."

"Bullshit. You stopped giving a shit about her the same as you stopped giving a shit about this town and the destruction you left us all to deal with the second y'all left."

Every word pierced my chest like an arrow dipped in venomous poison.

He was right. About almost all of it.

I had never stopped caring about Marley. She never let me. I'd also never stopped caring about him. Never stopped following his career that wasn't mine to enjoy. Never stopped cheering for his success at Vanderbilt and then with the Steel, even though he was supposed to leave Marysville and go to Tennessee instead.

But that was before we killed his girlfriend.

# CHAPTER 4
## COLE

What in the hell was I doing?

I didn't need to be here. I needed to be around Eden Barclay like I needed to be sacked by a three-hundred-pound defensive lineman. Nothing good would come from being this close to her.

Nothing good would come from her being in town, especially right as my season was starting.

Eden's family flew from town as soon as everything went to shit. She left me to fumble my way through it without the one person who I'd needed the most.

Now she was standing there, gripping that fucking old wrought-iron railing like her life depended on it, stealing all my hatred for her with her simple beauty that'd only gotten better.

This was a mistake.

All of it. Stomping across my parents' front yard as soon as I'd flung my truck into their driveway. Knocking on this door. Stepping inside. Inhaling a light floral scent that shouldn't have had my gut tightening.

"Stay the hell away from us," I told her, and I'd meant me. My family.

She laughed then, cold and brittle, and it whipped across the space between us. "I've already told Selma I would. You're the one here."

"What the hell are you talking about?"

I'd figured Selma had seen her or had spies in the woods out back to see when Eden pulled into town. Those were the only two options for her to accuse me of seeing her this morning.

"She didn't tell you." Eden's words were a whisper, surprised with more than a hint of pain in her voice.

And fuck her for that pain.

"When did you see her?"

"Yesterday. She and Jasper were leaving the park and I..."

She kept talking but it was all muffled as soon as Jasper's name came from her lips. Of course she'd known about him. Hell, the entire country knew Jasper, and our town adopted him as soon as Selma birthed him. If it took a village to raise a child, we had an entire country behind us. I knew exactly what she and everyone else thought, mostly because I let them all believe what they wanted.

Selma had an Instagram page dedicated to happy family pictures. I was never seen with anyone else. The entire country assumed we were together.

It was all fucking fake.

Frankly, it made it easier. I didn't have to worry about women since I'd lost the urge to date long ago. Everyone thought I was some kind of hero for stepping up and claiming my kid, or not thinking I had some meaningless one-night stand.

The media continued to use me as the golden boy with the small-town, down-home morals and values who could throw a football into a receiver under double coverage when it mattered most. It all fit the narrative.

Except it was a lie.

Because I was broken. Battered—and the woman who did most of that damage?

Still looking at me like she was terrified I was going to lose my shit on her any moment.

"This was a bad fucking idea," I grumbled.

For me to have walked over. For her to be in town.

All of it.

Eden and I were always a bad idea. I needed to remember that now more than ever.

I spun on my heels, shoved out of the front door and jogged down Marley's steep incline.

My mom was on their front porch, wearing her standard yellow and white checked apron over a soft pink short-sleeve dress. Dresses. She always wore them unless she was cleaning, and it shouldn't have surprised me for one second she would have heard the peeling of tires into her driveway. She probably smelled the burnt rubber over whatever she was most likely cooking and came out to wait for me.

"Feel better?"

I stomped up the stairs and kissed her cheek. "Not in the least."

"Yeah, you should have known hustling over there like your ass was on fire wasn't gonna get you anywhere. How is she?"

"Marley was sleeping."

"I wasn't asking about Marley." Mom pushed off the railing and opened the door to inside. The fresh scent of recently baked banana bread wafted out of her house, the smell of it lured me in before I realized I was following her.

And yeah…I knew that too.

"Told her she shouldn't be here, and this was all a bad idea."

"I don't know. From what I hear, Eden could use a decent friend in her life."

"What have you heard?"

The Barclays moved to town three weeks before our senior year. Her dad was hired to teach in the business department at Nashville College. It was an interim position and he'd spent Eden's entire senior year of high school keeping feelers open for new jobs, hoping to move to Florida once Eden and I went to Tennessee. He'd done exactly that before moving to Missouri for another position teaching economics a few years back. It was Eden who had vanished into thin air. No social media. No trace of her for as much as I'd searched for two years.

My question proved I'd never stopped thinking of her, hunting for her, even if I wasn't doing deep internet search dives online anymore.

"Nothing really. All I heard when I was at Frank's this morning was her showdown with Selma. It's all town is talking about, what with Selma approaching her on the street and all."

"What?"

Selma *approached* her? Mom had to be wrong. Eden had only said she'd seen them and since she wasn't sporting black eyes or broken limbs when I saw her, I didn't think they'd actually spoken. Although physical violence wasn't Selma's typical arsenal. That came from her words, and I'd seen the power of those firsthand.

"She didn't tell you?" Mom glanced at me, questions in her eyes.

To say my parents loved everyone would be *mostly* true. My parents loved everyone but Irv and Theresa Holden, and any of their offspring—Selma being the first. Some small-town, old rivalry had grown between the families since before I was ever born, back before my dad taught in the same high school he attended. The Buchanan-Holden feud was long known by everyone.

And everyone thought once Selma and I had Jasper, that feud would be over.

How wrong they were.

"Get to the point, Ma. I've had a long day."

"Yes, with showing up at Marley's to yell at Eden after she'd already been yelled at by Selma, and handing your precious boy over to that—"

"Nope. Don't finish that." I didn't care much for Selma, but she *was* the mother of my son. Feud or no feud, crap talking his mom was out of the question and Ma knew it.

"Sorry." She lifted a hand in apology. "I know. That wasn't going to be nice, and I know she loves him and is a great mom. Uncalled for. Just seems Eden sweeps back into town and you two are both acting like kids all over again and it's been less than a day. Time for old wounds to mend is all I'm sayin'."

"That mean you and Irv and Theresa and Dad gonna sit down over sweet tea and cookies and get to it?"

Mom rolled her eyes. "When the smoky mountains tumble is when that'll happen."

"Same."

She knew what I meant. What I was and wasn't saying.

"Difference is, y'all were kids and made mistakes. No harm meant even though tragedy hit. Doesn't mean it can't be made right is all, and I know how hard that was for you. But now that she's back, maybe you can finally put the past to rest." She came to me and settled her soft palm on my arm. Her cool hand was ice to my burning bicep, and I barely resisted a flinch. "I want that for *you* more than anyone else, Cole. It's time."

I yanked my arm away and stepped back. "I need to go pick up Bongo. And stay out of this, Ma. You don't know everything."

"I know more than you think. Always did, and maybe I've kept my mouth shut long enough."

"Please." I scoffed, although the threat sent a tingle of ice pricks at the back of my neck. "You ain't ever kept your mouth shut for anything or anyone and you know it."

I grinned at her, softening the insult while Ma shook her head and tightened her low ponytail. "Love you, Cole. Always will. And Jasper. Selma too in my own way."

The way that meant forced Southern politeness with muttered *bless her hearts* beneath her breath. It was better than it'd once been though, back when Selma learned she was pregnant.

"I know, Ma." I went to her and kissed her cheek before saying my goodbyes.

———

Training camp was always the hardest part of preseason training. I only had Jasper half the time as it was and then giving him up for a full week made my heart seize in a way I never could have predicted before becoming a parent. Fortunately for Jasper, he had a ton of family around to keep him busy when I was working. Not only did his mom and I co-parent well all things considered, but both of us had parents in town. Jasper had an aunt, Selma's sister who lived in Nashville and visited often, and my brother who was in his senior year of college, came home as often as he could from Georgia.

We just got back from camp a week ago and had one week before our first preseason game. I had to spend my time focusing on what was important—the family I'd built since she tore out my heart—and my job. I was twenty-six, still a baby in the league, and while I might have gotten the starter spot with the Steel on a lucky break due to an injury, and then subsequent retirement, of our former quarterback, I'd worked my ass off last year to earn the privilege of keeping that spot.

Last year, our team had lost in our wild card playoff game, the first time Nashville had made the playoffs in five years. There were eyes on us then, since I didn't start until game seven and once I took over we were undefeated the rest of the season. Everyone's expectations were higher this year—the owners, coaches, management, players, and most of all, the fans. The stress heavier. Once I'd taken over last year, there'd been chatter of our team going either way as we struggled to find our balance with a younger roster, and a handful of our defense line retiring. We proved all the critics incorrect, which meant now those same critics expected us to do better, take the team farther. There was a thrum of electricity in the stands at training camp, chatter in the streets when I spent time in Nashville.

The Steel's fans wanted us to have a ring. Wanted us to bring the Super Bowl Championship to their beloved city and they were all relying on me to get the job done.

For the next five to six months, my sole focus needed to remain cemented where it'd been the last five years.

On Jasper and my goals and my job.

The last thing I needed was the distraction of Eden.

Which was why the fact I was huffing and puffing through my workouts was even more frustrating.

"Bruh. What is your problem?" Dawson Butler, our tight end and one of my closest teammates, grunted as he helped spot my bench press. "You've been struggling all day."

"Nothing." I shoved to sit, sweat dripping down the sides of my face and I wiped it off with the hem of my shirt before it hit the scruff of my beard. "An off day."

"You don't have those."

Dawson was big, burly with hair past his shoulders he usually had up in a man-bun while he worked out. Today he'd left it down and it clung to his equally sweaty shirt with the sleeves ripped off. He and I were also drafted together, but while I had to wait until my time came to earn my starting spot, he was already breaking scoring and receiving records left and right, blowing guys who had been in the league for ten years out of the water with his speed, skill, and ability to hurdle most defenders who tried to dive for him.

He hadn't let any of the success change him though. He was as much of an asshole now, as he was the day we first met.

"Everyone's entitled to them." I grabbed my towel and stood off the bench.

The last thing I was going to talk about was my bad day, or the reason for it. I was supposed to be forgetting her existence.

If only that had worked in the last seven years, it might not be so difficult now.

"Is it Jasper? Selma?"

"Leave it, Butler. It's fine."

I was harsher than intended and didn't bother taking it back or apologizing. Butler was known for being a jerk and not just to his teammates, but to his coaches and media. The man showed up to play, hung out occasionally in small groups with the team when he had to, and then who knew what he did besides live like a hermit.

"You're never like this."

I glared at him, draping the towel over my shoulders. "And you usually don't ask so many damn questions."

He sucked in a breath, lips peeled back like I'd almost hurt him but that was impossible. If Butler had feelings, they were encased behind an iron cage.

"Well screw me for giving a damn about you. You're the steadiest one on this team, always have been. You can have an off day but if something is going on that's distracting you, make sure you get your shit figured out before it affects us next week. That's all."

He shoved past me, straight to the weight bench on the far side of our team's practice facility's gym where Tim Nolan, our safety, and Mason Yeets, a cornerback, were lifting.

He was right. Absolutely he was. But talking about Eden would only dredge up a past I'd long since buried. Everything except the visceral reaction I had when I saw her earlier.

She had the same effect on me as she did the first day I saw her. Crying. Upset. Car broken down on the side of the road two days after that same car pulled into the driveway next door to my parents' house with Wisconsin license plates.

Her tire had blown out and she couldn't get a hold of her dad.

I'd pulled up behind her, all teenage cocky swagger and the moment I knocked on her driver's side door, my future had changed.

Only back then, I had no idea it'd be for the worse, and not the better like I'd instantly imagined.

Across the gym, Dawson shot me a look, an eyebrow raised in question. He clearly wasn't going to hold on to my attitude, and he'd made a point with his. Instead of fixing it, I whipped my towel off my shoulders and headed to the showers. We had film and then practice in an hour anyway. Might as well see if I could get my head in the right frame of mind and working out hadn't done a thing to help.

# CHAPTER 5
## EDEN

Marley bounced along in her old Chevy truck bench seat next to me while I drove. The truck might have been the same old mid nineties boxy truck she had ever since her late husband was alive, but steady as ever. Her purse sat on her lap, arms wrapped around it in a hug. Besides the quiet religious hymnal music playing on the radio, and her sporadic coughing fits, we hadn't spoken much since we left the doctor's office.

Her latest MRI showed her tumors were spreading, and without the chemotherapy she still refused, Marley would only continue to get sicker, faster. Her cancer, a glioblastoma in her brain, needed chemo for any hope of giving her more time with us.

"Maybe you should think about what the doctor said."

"Don't need to, honey, and before you tell me whatever it is he said to you when I gave y'all that moment to talk about me when I wasn't there, that doesn't mean I'm gonna listen this time either."

"But—"

"No buts. I miss Darryl. It's been a long time since I've seen my husband, and I'm ready to go see him again whenever the good Lord has determined it's time for our reunion. There're things I'm gonna do first, stories I need to help finish, but as far as I'm concerned, my ending is coming, and I want to meet Darryl again with a full head of hair."

Well now that she had to bring her faith in God into the conversation, I couldn't exactly argue. "God gives doctors and geniuses the ability and gifts to heal with science as much as faith, Marley."

"Know that, too, and I'm thankful to God for all the science and scientists and medical interventions He gives to people to create and use to heal. But for me, that's not the direction He's leading me in."

"Dr. Vanders mentioned getting you a nurse."

"I have you." She was a woman bound by faith and stubborn as the hills were steep.

"Marley..." I tried gentling my voice. "I'm a vet tech, not a nurse, especially not for what's coming."

I refused to think about what that was, but the doctor had painted a picture and it was the ugliest piece of art I'd ever heard described. What was coming would be a painful torture for everyone and increasing in until the end. Not only would the glioblastoma steal her mind, it'd begin affecting other functions. Limbs. Nerves. It just depended on where it moved to next.

"Then I'll trust you to know the time for that, too. I know what you think." She turned to me, her features set with purpose and peace despite the news we'd heard. "But death is a part of life and I'm not afraid of it. And I'm not pretending this isn't happening, but before I go, it *is* my mission to ensure all the people I love who still walk the earth are happy and healed. I don't need chemotherapy and six more months of living in misery to see my mission fulfilled."

My hands creaked on the steering wheel, sweat making my palms slip. "I am happy, Marley. If that's what this is about...Cole and I... that doesn't exist. Never did."

"Don't lie to me. You'll feel guilty for it once I'm dead."

She turned back to the window while I wanted to slam my head against mine.

I wasn't lying. We might have wanted there to be something, back when we were young and dumb and ignorant to the harsh truths of the world, but we weren't now.

Especially after his visit earlier this week.

Whatever stories she wanted to see finished, and I could imagine what those were, were not going to give her the happy ending she had in mind. Of that much I was certain.

———

There were now two grocery stores in town. An ALDI that had been built at some point in the last seven years, and the local Frank's Grocers. I went there, because even though ALDI had come to town back when I lived there, I vividly remembered the frustration of chain stores and restaurants taking over the small town. It was all anyone's parents and grandparents used to talk about. "Soon we'll be all strip malls and parking lots and there goes the town..." used to be common phrases I'd hear while my parents mingled with others, trying to find their community outside Marysville Presbyterian Church at potlucks after Sunday services.

If I was going to be seen for the first time, visible, in town, it most definitely wasn't going to be in a chain store with a target on my back for more ridicule and head shaking filled with Southern disapproval.

I took Marley to church yesterday, picked her up when I knew she'd be ready to come back home, but until Monday and going to the doctor's office in Nashville with her, hadn't ventured back to town.

Fear of Selma? Hell yes.

Fear of running into Cole or seeing his son again? Absolutely.

But now it was Wednesday afternoon, and I'd been back for almost a week. Kids weren't back in school yet, but would be heading that way soon, but most parents would be at work. It should be a quick in and out trip. While the grocery store was large enough to have everything, it was also small enough you couldn't get lost or linger. Small mercies.

Marley's truck quieted once I parked and turned off the engine. A quick scan of the dozen or so cars in the parking lot didn't look familiar, and while Marysville was close to Nashville, they'd always prided themselves on the small-town feel and lifestyle which meant people didn't trade in their cars and trucks every three years like people did with leases. They drove them until the engines fell out, and then the majority bought used to replace it. Or hell, rebuilt the engine from scratch in their Pawpaw's garage.

Nerves ignited as I entered the store and grabbed a cart. Marley's diet was strict but based on the leftovers I'd thrown away this morning, she wasn't intent on following the doctor's recommendations for that either.

Monday's conversation lingered, and while I'd tried to approach her about it, I'd been shut down. I understood faith and belief in God. I'd been raised in a church my entire life until I left Marysville. I'd always found a peacefulness in the walls of a church building, and I'd had several pastors I enjoyed listening to and learning from. I also understood being ready to go, not wanting to fight.

What I couldn't fathom was a life or world or small town without Marley's stubborn but gentle spirit in it.

Perhaps it was selfish of me to want to keep her here for me, especially when I had no plans to stay, but I wasn't the only one who needed her.

My thoughts drifted to her, the grocery list full of healthy items I actually enjoyed but Marley would scoff her nose at, and I turned the corner of the baking aisle only to pull up to an abrupt stop before I slammed into another.

"Sorry," I apologized and then noticed the dark purple scrubs. So similar to what I saw the other day at the park and head full of short, highlighted blonde hair spun in my direction right before…

"No worries." A woman smiled, and thank goodness, it wasn't Selma. "I was distracted, probably my fault."

This woman's face wasn't only kind, the stitching on her chest made me smile. "Are you a vet?" I nodded at the bright white stitching Boone Farm Animal Hospital.

"I am." She grinned at me. "Dr. Kessick. Nora."

It was fate. Had to be. After the week I had, I desperately needed to be around an animal. Any kind for all I cared. "This is going to make me sound absolutely crazy, but do you need volunteers? Or know someone who does? I'm sorry—" I probably came across like a lunatic. "I'm Eden. Eden Barclay and I'm a vet tech down in Florida, but I'm here for a while, and I've been looking at shelters, but haven't found much luck in any nearby that need more help right now."

"Sure. Makes sense since most of them need a lot of foster parents for animals."

"And I'm not in the place where I can do that right now." Dogs and dog fur and cat fur wouldn't be good for Marley. At least I assumed they wouldn't, but I didn't want to test it either.

"Hmm." Her lips pushed to one side. "Let me think on that. Do you have a way for me to reach out to you, or…wait!" She dug into her purse and pulled out a business card. "Give me a few days. I might know of something but want to check first. Give me a call or shoot me an email, and just ask for me."

"Thank you. Thank you so much."

"Happy to help. I know what it's like to be new in town."

I held my tongue. I was new, but wasn't, and I definitely wasn't going to explain. "Thanks."

"Nice meeting you, Eden. Give me a call and we'll chat, okay?"

"Sounds good." I held on to her card until she moved her own cart around mine and we went our separate directions.

I'd probably made a fool out of myself, but if it could get me sitting with animals it was worth it.

———

It was late. Dark. Crickets and chirping cicadas filled the night as I made my way through Marley's property out to the lake. She was asleep, worn out from the day. While I could probably go to bed and be asleep before my head hit the pillow, memories kept me awake, drove me to grab a bottle of wine, glass and opener, and head to the one place I swore I would never venture to when I returned.

The rock.

Our place.

The huge boulder I'd stumbled upon two days after Cole Buchanan changed my flat tire on the side of the road in the pouring rain only two days after my family moved to Marysville my senior year of high school.

It'd be lit by fireflies and the distant floodlights from Cole's parents' backyard, so I doubted it'd be dark.

I'd avoided looking in that direction when Marley and I walked that way my first morning, but now it was my only focus.

I stumbled over brush and leaves and broken twigs, the path we'd worn down as teenagers was now overgrown and bramble from blackberry bushes—largely overgrown, scraped my skin more than once. The only thing that hadn't changed was the brutal August heat and humidity, still thick and making my skin slick with sweat before I pushed through the path.

Only to realize I wasn't alone.

I'd know the shadow of that bulky figure anywhere as he sat down on the boulder, both feet propped on the front of it, forearms to his knees, head aimed straight toward the lake beyond the small, still perfectly clear swimming beach area Cole's dad had made when Cole and Graham were kids.

He'd filled out over the years, and I'd noticed every part of it— both online, watching him succeed and find a way to fulfill the dreams he'd had since he was a child, and in person. Not like I could miss it when he'd stormed into Marley's house last week.

His anger, the way he'd looked at me and demanded that I stay away had me debating. Turning back would be easiest. Better for us both, but when it came to Cole and me, we'd always played with fire.

"I didn't know you'd be here," I said, alerting him to my presence, but like so often happened, he didn't react.

"I knew you'd come out here at some point."

That almost caused me to stumble. Had he…no…

Cole wouldn't be out here, in the dark, waiting for me, not unless he wanted to yell at me again in private.

"I can leave."

He turned then, and I noticed the water bottle between his hands. He definitely noticed the wine bottle and glass in mine before looking away and back to the water.

"No need."

Except now, I wasn't sure I wanted to stay.

I'd found this rock on accident, days after he changed my tire, that first time we met. I'd gone on a walk to explore the woods, and my parents had let me wander just telling me to make sure my phone kept cell reception. At first, I'd stayed to the edges of the water but then I'd noticed a path behind Marley's house and explored.

It took me straight to this enormous boulder, flat on top, with a perfect view of the lake and rolling hills in the distance. It'd also taken me straight to Cole, who'd been lounging on it, on his back, one arm draped over his face. I'd made a sound, my teenage self surprised to find a boy out there—a *shirtless boy with all those muscles*—and he'd jolted up.

*"I'm sorry. I can leave."*

*"It's all right. How's the car?"*

And that was how we became friends. He scooted over and threw on a shirt, a silent invitation for me to join him. I had, mesmerized by the fact he had the body of a man and the smile of a boy. He asked about Wisconsin, why we moved there—my dad's job at a college in Nashville—and he'd prepared me for starting school at the high school a week later. Told me about the best teachers. The ones everyone groaned at when they saw their names on their schedules. He told me if I brought Mrs. Akers, the front receptionist, a Dr. Pepper and green apple, she'd usually excuse showing up tardy and hand me a pass.

We'd somehow managed to find each other every day after that, him alone, always seemingly brooding or thinking deeply, but when I showed up, that all washed away.

Two days before that first day of school, he'd held my hand, pressed his thumb to my chin and tilted my face toward the brilliant blue sky and his magnificent sapphire eyes and kissed me.

And then I found out about Hilary.

"I'll go." I turned to leave, because Cole at the rock, the place that had become ours, the place where we cried and screamed and laughed and came so close to kissing again but never did, were memories I couldn't allow to resurface.

My back was to him, my feet at about the tree line when Cole called out, shaking the ground beneath as fierce as an avalanche.

"I don't hate you. Never did, but I can't forget either."

I turned to him, the moon and the floodlight from his yard shading most of his face but I'd know his features anywhere, the tenseness in his body. The scowl. The furrow of his dark brows and those lips that were still so damn perfect. Somewhere nearby, a dog barked, breaking me out of the vortex he sucked me into.

"I can't forget either."

He whipped his head back to the lake, shoulders slumped.

I vanished into the dark, got back to Marley's, and drank the bottle of wine before I stumbled to bed.

Nightmares plagued me, but I deserved them, every single one.

# CHAPTER 6
## COLE

*can't forget either."*

I hadn't seen Eden's face when she said the words, but I heard the pain in them. It took me back to all those years ago. I'd always hated to see Eden sad even if I was the cause for most of it. She had no reason to blame herself for what happened. I was the cocky teenage asshole with a full ride to Tennessee ahead of me and my dream of making the NFL within my grasp if I kept working hard. I was the small-town football star with the pretty girl on my arm who I'd cared about but couldn't ever seem to break up with because hurting Hilary was like making a puppy cry.

I was the asshole who'd been so cocky and so used to winning everything I thought I could figure it out. I strung Eden along, unable to stay away and did it while trying to be the good guy, but unlike being the hero on the football field, I was never the hero in our story.

I was the villain and had been from that very day I kissed Eden, knowing I was going to take Hilary back the next day. I didn't cheat on her, not with my kisses or my touches despite how desperately I'd wanted to after we got back together, but the day Eden's family rolled to town, Hilary never had a chance of holding on to my heart.

"Mom!"

Jasper shouted so loud in our booth at the diner he shook the table, almost knocking over our water glasses. I grabbed them, water sloshing over the rims, but I saved the workbook sheets he'd been working on.

Selma was all about him doing schoolwork to prepare for kindergarten. I thought it was insane, but Jasper didn't mind them, so I kept my mouth shut. Sure, it was only writing letters, but he was going to have twelve years of school. Selma didn't need to push too fast.

"Hey darling," Selma called. She headed toward us, where Jasper was now flying out of the booth, and into his mom's arms as she crouched down for him, even though she'd just dropped him at my place a couple hours ago. "Miss you already. Having fun?"

"Yep. Daddy says I get dessert at the creamery after this."

"That's great!" She kissed his head and set him back to his feet to get to hers and grinned at me, the table covered with our food we'd just received. "I hope this is okay," Selma said to me. "I needed to come talk to my dad about some things around the house and thought you two would be here."

I absolutely minded. For more reasons than one being I still hadn't bothered to talk to Selma about whatever she confronted Eden about. Wasn't sure I wanted to either, because it was sure to cause problems, but also because we didn't *do* this.

We co-parented well. We shared holidays and we were always flexible due to both of our schedules, mine especially during the season. But meals together as a happy family and in town for everyone to see?

We'd always avoided this, even if I brought Jasper to his grandparents' diner frequently for dinner so they could spend time with him, too.

"Yes! Mom, see?"

Jasper tugged her into this side of the booth before I could answer, but my silence was enough for Selma.

She flashed me a smile that I was pretty sure was more victorious than sincere and settled down next to our son.

If she was expecting me to ask her what needed to be done around her house, I wouldn't. We definitely didn't do that kind of thing. I wasn't her handyman or the guy she called when the plumbing went haywire.

I'd despise the one night I spent with Selma, would have kicked it from my memory long ago if I could, but it'd also brought me Jasper. If it wasn't for him, I doubted I would have ended up getting my shit back together and focusing on school and the game and my dreams. He was the one who eventually saved me, which meant I could never hate his mom, even on the days I really, *really* wanted to.

I shoved a bite of burger into my mouth and chewed while Jasper did his worksheets and Selma praised him for every perfectly straight or curved line. Together, we made him pause to eat his chicken strips and applesauce and try his vegetables, and by the time dinner was done, I was exhausted from trying to keep a smile I didn't feel on my face.

"There's my little girl and my favorite boy in the world!" Irv's voice was booming loud, always had been, and like my parents didn't think a whole lot of Selma, but I was pretty sure he thought less of me.

Then again, I was the twenty-year-old who knocked up his daughter and then didn't do the right thing and marry her. That didn't even have to do with the hatred he had for my parents, that failing was all on me – like so many other things.

But considering I was the NFL quarterback still living in my hometown and the media thought I wore a halo beneath my helmet, he couldn't say crap about it. Especially since I'd hoped like hell for a contract with the Steel so I could stay close to home. I'd never made that a secret.

I was also the former, emotionally wounded football standout who gave up a full ride to Tennessee for football to stay local and play for Vanderbilt once Hilary died, so in the eyes of the media, I was the angel.

The perfect boy.

No one knew my halo had thorns dripped in blood.

And that was how I kept it, why I kept Selma happy, why I stood and shook Irv's hand hello even while he spit daggers at me through his eyes, and why I kept my mouth shut when Selma posted pics of us on her Instagram, allowing people to think we were together.

Because if the media or fans ever discovered the truth?

That halo would be thrown into fire and burned to ash…my good guy reputation along with it.

———

"You're ready. Good job." Coach Paul Bowles slapped my shoulder and headed off to yell at the receivers.

He was right. I was ready for our first preseason game. I was ready to hopefully bring a championship to Nashville and I was more than ready to lead my team to the playoffs again this year. After going from a team who was typically middle of the pack in our division, to finally making it to the wild card playoff game last year, we were fortunate to have almost all of our best players returning, few traded, and a couple key rookies picked up in the draft. That meant our team was filled with seasoned veterans, men who'd felt the thrill of making the playoffs and were determined to again this year—be better. More powerful. Stronger. More winning—both in our stats and our attitude. Football was equal amount heart and strength and mental capabilities and ever since I'd heard Eden's SUV had rolled back into town, my mental game was off.

Last night's stroll to the boulder because I was craving one more glimpse of her, even as much as I wanted to rail and scream at her, was a mistake.

Too bad I was finding it harder to stay away, especially now I knew, from the pain-filled way she'd said she couldn't forget either, she held as much guilt for what happened as I once did.

The problem was I knew it wasn't our fault.

It was an accident, and it wasn't right Eden was still carrying that blame all these years later.

But how in the hell was I going to make it right?

I might have been ready for our upcoming game, our upcoming season, but I was in no way ready or prepared to deal with Eden. Not like this. Not when she was here for a short time and I didn't want her to leave, still carrying that load again.

"Hey. Did good today." Dawson tugged at the chinstraps of his helmet and released them. "Things better?"

"Like I said before, things are fine."

"Lie to yourself all you want, and me, I get it. It's personal. But just make sure it doesn't show up on Sunday."

"Fuck off, Butler."

So he could read me, knew even when I was playing like I should be, my head wasn't in it. I could lie and say that was fine, I could win this game with my eyes closed, but I'd quit lying to others a long time ago.

Only the truth from that night forward.

"Hey!" I called as he jogged past me, heading for Yeets.

"Yeah?"

"I'll be here. And ready. Promise."

That much I could promise him.

A smirk became visible behind his facemask. "Hell yeah, you will be."

I shook my head and slapped the football. Practice was done, and most of the guys were heading off to the locker rooms but there were a few still on the field, still running routes. Our backup quarterback, Sam Denmark who was a rookie barely younger than me, was throwing passes in case he needed to take the field if the worst happened to me.

That was the wake-up call I needed.

By Sunday morning when I stepped onto this field for our first preseason game at home since losing in the wild card game, my head, heart, and body would be focused on only one thing—bringing the Super Bowl Championship to Nashville. Because no one was taking my starting position, not until, at minimum, I had one of those rings on my finger.

———

"Jasper. Grab Bongo's leash, would ya?"

It was eight, and the sun was still shining, but would be setting soon. Jasper was already in his pajamas, ready for bed, but if Eden was anything like the girl she used to be, she'd be wanting to head back to the boulder if I scared her away last night. Which meant tonight, I'd wait until she was there. Jasper wouldn't mind a sleepover at Grandma and Grandpa's, and it was easier for Selma to get him on their side of town in the morning after work, anyway.

All excuses I'd told myself while we had dinner, I gave him a bath, and played Super Mario Bros together. Mom and Dad wouldn't mind if I showed up unannounced either, although they weren't stupid. Their silent looks I got last night when I showed up for dinner and later declared I was taking a walk said plenty.

"We going for a walk?" The leash dangled in his hand and Bongo's bark was almost as wild with excitement as his tail was thumping against the wall.

"Sleepover at Grandma B's. If you want to."

"Grandma B makes the best cookies!"

Chocolate chip. Sometimes with oatmeal. There wasn't a cookie my mom made Jasper wouldn't inhale, and the first thing he always did when getting there whether it'd been a day or a week was to go and check her cookie jar.

"Only one tonight, though, okay?"

"Grandma will give me two."

I had no doubt she would. Probably let him stay up later than I normally did, too, but since that'd be Selma's problem in the morning, I'd let her handle it.

"We'll see what Grandma says, kiddo. Ready?"

"Yes!"

Bongo barked his excited agreement and ran toward the door, jumping and dancing so fast he smushed up the entryway rug into a pinwheel.

"All right. Let's go then." I grabbed the cooler of beer and wine I'd thrown together while he was changing earlier and snagged my keys off the counter.

Shuffling Jasper and Bongo into my truck and making sure I had everything else we needed for the night, I decided not to examine too long or too hard the bottle of wine I'd grabbed at the store after practice, or the wine opener and glass I was already preparing to take from my mom's kitchen before I headed out.

# CHAPTER 7
## COLE

might not have known Eden anymore, but I hadn't been wrong. I stepped through the tree line of my parents' house, my mom's knowing look saying a whole lot without words and a whole lot I didn't want to hear, before she offered me a blanket before I left in case it was cold.

Please. It was August. The humidity alone would have me sweating in a handful of minutes.

Eden had her hair in a braid, draped over her shoulder and a pink tank top hung in two thin straps over her shoulders. She flinched when I crunched on pine needles that littered the forest's floor but didn't turn back to me.

"For someone who said it was a mistake for me to be coming back here, I didn't expect you to seek me out."

I could have dished out a handful of excuses. That I wasn't here for her. It was a coincidence, but again—I'd quit lying to others.

"Thought we should talk."

Her back straightened at that, and she glanced over her shoulder at me before quickly glancing back to the lake. "Maybe I came out here to be alone."

Probably, but she had to know I'd find her here eventually.

"All right. Then we can have a drink together in silence."

There was a time when Eden hadn't liked to be pushed into doing anything. Not sure if that changed, but I didn't mind a drink in silence.

"Or you can go."

"You want me to?" I had stepped closer, was a dozen or so feet away from her but stopped when I asked the question.

With a sigh that could have made the leaves tremble in the trees, she shrugged. "You can do whatever you want, Cole. You always did."

Now that wasn't fair. There were a lot of things I didn't do that I'd wanted to.

Break up with Hilary and break her heart our senior year of high school. Get a new girlfriend and throw it in Hilary's face every day. Kiss the woman currently sitting on the boulder all those times I'd resisted.

Go to Tennessee with her like we'd planned.

I was no saint or hero, but I'd held back from doing *everything* I wanted.

In this, though, I'd take her suggestion. Considering she might jump off the boulder and bolt back to Marley's if I moved too close, I tossed the blanket Ma sent with me onto the ground and proceeded to open the bottle of wine.

Her gaze was a physical touch against my skin, making it prickle even though I didn't look at her while I uncorked the bottle and poured her a glass.

I handed it to her and grabbed a beer out of the cooler. I was sitting at an angle so I could see her, but mostly focused on the lake. At least that was how I appeared. I tracked every move she made, including watching to see if that glass of wine would be dumped onto my head.

There were things I wanted to say to her. I still wanted to scream and shake her and be pissed she'd left, ran away and left me to handle the fallout of our decisions alone. I'd *needed* her then, more than I needed anyone else, and she bailed. That was a hurt I wasn't anywhere close to being over, but I also had questions for her.

Trying to find the ones to start with was the hard part.

Fortunately, it was Eden who went first. "I took Marley to the doctor the other day."

"Any good news?"

"He said she'll see Christmas if she's lucky."

I closed my eyes at the thought of Marley being gone. And so quickly. This fall would fly by and soon I'd be in the midst of the season, life. At least I'd spent most of the summer with her.

"That's not good news."

"Nope." She popped the *p* and took a drink. "And even if she makes it, she'll hardly be able to enjoy it. She's already starting to forget things. Last week she made a pot of coffee as soon as she woke up. This morning, she stared at it like she'd never seen the thing before."

Damn. That was bad.

"Ma and Dad are here to help if you need it, you know."

"I know."

There was a bite to her words I hadn't expected. But Ma wouldn't be mean to Eden. She'd always liked her.

"Marley loves Christmas." I muttered it more to myself than the devilish little angel sitting in my favorite place, the only girl I'd ever hung out there with. Funny, how I never brought Hilary out here, all those years we were together. Definitely not Selma. Since Eden, the only other person who'd plopped their backside on the boulder with me had been Jasper and Bongo. It was sacred to me, somehow, this place with her where we stole so many moments and had so many arguments and came so close to betraying someone we'd both loved.

"I'll make sure it's special for her then." Eden's voice wobbled and I fought not to go to her, to comfort her.

"The whole town will, I'm sure."

"Great," she muttered under her breath. "Can't wait to see everyone."

She'd thought everyone hated her back then. She'd been wrong then and she was wrong now, but I didn't come here tonight to tell her how she had everything messed up in her head. She'd have to learn that for herself. In truth, the only person who still hated the very mention of her was Selma. But that was because she'd caught on to Eden and me long before graduation night, and I'd always known, ever since Hilary and I started dating as freshman that Selma would have stepped right up to be next in line to date me if Hilary and I hadn't worked out, best friends be damned.

"How are your parents?" I asked instead. Rehashing the past wouldn't help anything.

"They're fine, I guess."

She took a healthy swig of her wine, larger than she had been.

"What's that mean?"

"Means we don't talk much. Dad's still working, somewhere in Missouri now. They do their thing, I do mine."

"Honestly?" They'd been close. She was an only child who said she'd never even wanted a sibling growing up like so many other only kids because her parents had always been cool to hang out with. They definitely were in high school.

Not the kind of cool where they were buying kegs for field parties or anything, but they were fun. Angie could bust out into dance moves that would have the teenage girls joining in and more than one guy in our school had called her a MILF.

"Yup." Another pop of the *p* and she stared off into the lake.

"Where you been then?" Because she didn't just *leave*, she vanished. Here one day and the next, all social media accounts gone. No trace of her. I once found an envelope in Marley's house, in hand-writing I knew had to be Eden's. I was in college then and as soon as Marley wasn't looking, I grabbed it. Flipped it over.

No return address. Nothing. And the card? Handwritten in Eden's scrolling writing thanking Marley for the birthday present and no mention of her life, what she was doing, where she was living, or if she was happy.

God, that'd eaten at me for days. Weeks. The internet search I'd dove into to try to find her had kept me up so late at night I'd missed morning workouts at Vanderbilt and gotten my ass reamed by my coach. In the end, all I'd found was her dad, working at a university in Pensacola. The day Eden left Marysville she became a ghost.

"Florida. Dad got a job there. I stayed with them for a while until they forced me to go to school and then I never went back."

They *forced* her? "What the hell does that mean?"

She stared at me, like she didn't realize what she'd said and then when she did, she shut down. In a second. Any slightly friendly look in her eyes vanished with a blink. Doors slammed shut and Eden just…turned off.

"Thanks for the drink."

She slipped off the boulder, set the glass on the blanket and I was jumping to my feet to stop her, but it all happened so fast. Even with my quick reflexes I was too late.

"What aren't you telling me?"

"The thing is, Cole, is that you don't have the right to demand anything from me. Not conversation. Not details of my life. So maybe stop trying."

Her braid flipped through the air as she spun away from me, but if Eden thought that was true, then she sure as hell had changed a lot more than I'd considered.

"What if I can't? Or don't want to?" Hands to my hips, I shouted it before she reached the tree line. Before she disappeared again.

"Maybe consider realizing I'm not your problem anymore so how about we just try to stay away from each other?"

And then she was gone, before I could shout the truths that were burning my tongue despite how much I tried to deny it to myself.

She wasn't my problem. She'd always been my dream. The only one I had besides football.

———

My dad was on the deck pretending to keep an eye on Bongo when I showed up in the backyard.

"Got everything you needed from that?"

I'd stayed out on the rock for almost an hour, sipping my one beer until it became so warm, I dumped it in the grass.

Dad's question didn't help.

"Not even close." I hustled up the steps of his deck and he clasped his hand onto my shoulder. We were silent. He didn't need to tell me it was stupid to go after her, to wait for her, or to want to talk to her.

Out of all the people in my life, it was my dad who I'd always turned to when life got hard. Yeah, obviously he talked to Mom about it after, but not everything. Not the hardest parts.

So, it was him I'd gone to when Eden left. Him I'd been brutally honest with. Dad knew all the darkest, ugliest parts of me and the only one to truly know the real reasons why I went to Vandy instead of UT.

It was that girl.

The one whose back was always the last thing I saw of her as she walked away from me.

"You got time. Time to set it all to rights."

Always the encourager. "Can't set anything anywhere if I'm always chasing after her."

"Give her a couple days. I'm sure she's still getting settled, getting her feet under her being back. Wanna take the time to listen to some advice I'm sure you don't want to hear?"

Well, when he put it like that…

"Not really." My hands settled to my hips anyway, unmoving from the deck. Dad knew too much to be ignored or brushed aside.

"Saw her at the store the other day. Well, leaving it. The way she hustled and tried to be invisible and the haunted look I saw in her eye as she did told me one thing. She's never let that night go, not like you have. Give her time. She's currently facing nightmares and a past you've long since settled. She hasn't had that—she's been running this whole time."

I'd already figured that part out but hadn't considered what being back here would be like for her. Hell, it'd taken me a full year to drive the road where Hilary died and even then, I'd omitted it for the next six months when I did. "Right. That all?"

"Heard from her parents one time. Few months after."

"What?"

"You were already at Vandy. Didn't want to tell you, not with the way things were for her, but they were having a hard time after leaving, and they were worried for their daughter."

"We were all having a hard time."

Dad nodded. "Prolly so, but from what Angie made it sound like, she was doing pretty bad. Wouldn't get out of bed. Wouldn't stop crying. Wouldn't eat. Lost fifteen pounds in two months, that kind of thing." He sighed, ran a hand across his smoothly shaven cheek and jaw. "Were thinking of hospitalizing for her own health and they… well, they needed some insight is all."

Fifteen pounds? She'd never had that to lose.

My teeth ground together as rage built inside of me, hot and feral as I stared into the dark. That first semester of college had been brutal. My summer was already non-existent since I had to report for summer training and transferring to Vandy made everything more rushed. But I'd *gone.* Done the thing and put one foot in front of another to get through. All the while, every single second of every single day, I thought of her. *Needed* her.

"You should have told me. Gave me their number. I could have…"

"What? Given up your backup plan and your dream to chase her down? I was worried enough about you as it was."

*…I stayed with them for a while until they forced me to go to school…*

So that was what she meant.

I hated it. Every single minute. She might have left me, but I'd had an entire town to help me through the trauma. Help me heal. Hilary's parents alone, who moved after because it was too tough for them to stay, had absolved me of all of it early on. That had helped.

Eden never had any of that, just parents who were probably equally confused as to why everything went sideways in a night.

"At least knowing where she was would have let me stop looking for her."

"Maybe. Maybe so. I'm just sayin' you had a village behind you, she had no one. Can't think that'd be an easy race to win with no one at your back or holding your hand through it. My guess, she's probably different now. Tread carefully."

"Why are you telling me all this now?"

"Because maybe your mom and I miss seeing the light in your eyes you always had when she was around, something that even football doesn't give you. Maybe Jasper, but it was different with her, too. We lost you too, that night, a part of you anyway, and selfishly, we want you back. Want you to have that back."

He slapped my shoulder and headed inside, leaving me alone with my dog, the night, and thoughts of the one and only woman I'd ever loved still stinging with every breath I took.

# CHAPTER 8
## EDEN

Of course, Marley watched Cole's football games. It shouldn't have surprised me when she appeared in the kitchen while I was cooking breakfast, wearing Cole's Steel jersey and his number four in fire engine red taking up most of her torso.

Was it too much to ask she'd forget Cole's football schedule like she'd forgotten how to make coffee?

I'd turned back to the stove, burned my fingertip as bacon grease popped and sizzled while I tried to ignore what that shirt meant was coming for me later in the day.

Football.

Watching Cole Buchanan fire a thirty-yard pass to his wide-open receiver who ran it another thirty yards for a touchdown. On the opening drive of their first preseason game being played at home.

Marley's living room vibrated from the noise as the crowd went ballistic, partly due to Marley's need to have the television turned up as loud as it could go. As soon as she turned the game on, she told me she wanted to feel like she was there. If only I could say the same.

She pointed at the screen when the media had scanned the crowd during pre-game warm-ups, stopping on Cole's family.

"My first home game I'm missin' since he was drafted. Five years. If I'm gonna have to sit in this chair and watch the game I'm doin' it feeling like I'm right there."

Right there meant in the seat next to Jasper. With his noise-canceling headphones on and wearing a miniature version of Marley's jersey, he was almost cuter than when I'd seen him on the street. The chair next to him was taken by Selma, also decked out in Steel gear, but not Cole's jersey. I cringed as I saw her smiling face on the screen and looked away. I might have always disliked her, but if Cole was happy...well, I wish I could say I was the better person and was happy for him. Kate and Dave Buchanan were behind them and every time the cameras scanned the crowd, it felt like they stopped on the four of them and told the story of the hometown hero.

It'd calm down as the season progressed, pick back up if they made the playoffs again.

I knew this, because while I'd sell my soul before admitting it, I'd watched every game over the last five years, too.

When they played Tampa Bay, I'd made the seven-hour trip to attend, to see Cole reach his dreams in person. He'd been a backup then, and I'd been stupidly obsessed with watching him on the sidelines as he stood and cheered for every play despite the lack of chance he'd ever had of going in that game. But that was Cole.

Always the team player, always ready to step in if necessary. Always intense when it came to the game. Seemed he was still that same guy off the field too considering our last conversation I hadn't been able to stop thinking about.

He should have hated me, wanted nothing to do with me except twice he sought me out. Tried to talk.

And both times, I'd run like the coward I still was.

Time marched on, but some things never changed.

———

Cole only played the rest of the first quarter. He didn't score another touchdown, although he helped his team get the ball down to the ten-yard line before Pittsburgh's defense managed to stop them from scoring. Fortunately, the Steel had one of the best kickers in the league and his field goal was easily made. Since it was preseason, most players with secured starting roles took to the bench after the first quarter, allowing back-ups and those the coaches would still have questions about take to the field.

Marley sat in her chair, drinking sweet teas I continued to bring her along with a tray of veggies and hummus she scoffed at.

"It's a football game. I should at least be able to have a hot dog."

They absolutely weren't in her diet plan, but maybe I could find turkey dogs or something. Although she'd probably smother them with cheese and chili and condiments making the healthier option irrelevant.

"Next week," I promised her, and replaced her ignored veggies with pickled okra, crackers, and cheese slices.

"Better," she hmphed, "but not great."

I went back to keeping one eye on the game, while planning our meals for the week. Scribbling hot dogs and frozen pretzels, corn chips, and ingredients for homemade queso onto the list.

Maybe that'd help her feel like she was there.

It was the fourth quarter, Nashville was up by seven, and while preseason games didn't affect a team's regular season standing, a win in the first game, especially at home, helped set the tone of the season. The crowd was electric, on their feet with only four minutes left, although even I knew a lot could happen in those four minutes that could stretch to twenty with timeouts and the two-minute warning, when Pittsburgh's offense threw a pass.

The pass was only ten yards, easily getting them a first down. A defense player for Nashville was right there, went to make the tackle and Pittsburgh's wide receiver dodged at the right moment. Nashville's number ninety-two lost his feet, tripped and went to his knees giving Pittsburgh's receiver an opening.

"No!" Marley gripped the armrests of her chair, leaning forward as far as she could in her chair. "Get him! Take him down! Stop… ugh." Her groan that followed was quieted by the stadium's noise and mayhem as Pittsburgh scored.

Twenty seconds later and the extra point kick was good, leaving the game tied at seventeen with three minutes to go.

The teams lined up for the kick, Nashville's kick returner lining up deep in their territory and as the ball sailed through the air, I found myself bracing my hands at the back of Marley's couch, fingers digging into the cushion.

"Come on," I whispered, and Marley barked out a laugh. "What?"

"You been actin' like you haven't been payin' attention to anything in this game, but I knew you were. You keep holdin' on to my cushions like that and I'm gonna need to get my old sewing kit out."

She was right. My knuckles ached and I shoved off the couch as Nashville's returner was downed at their thirty-yard line.

"I only got into it because you've been yelling so loud, Marley."

"Hmph." She rolled her eyes. "What'd I say about lying to me?"

That I'd regret it when she was gone. Probably true, but I'd add it to my growing list.

Seventy yards to go with a rookie quarterback, Sam Denmark. It wasn't impossible. And all they needed was a field goal, but overtime was looking possible assuming we didn't go three and out.

*We?*

This wasn't my team. At least, not vocally. Fortunately for me, dogs and cats and birds didn't care what I talked about so no one in my life, smallest circle of people possible, as it was, knew I cared about football.

But this wasn't a *we type* moment.

Cole had his family, and I would never be a part of it.

Even if I sometimes still dreamed of the possibility.

———

"Dr. Kessick speaking."

Since the vet I met at the grocery store had included her cell phone on her business card and told me to call any time, I didn't feel incredibly guilty for calling her on a Sunday afternoon.

It was the first thing I thought to do to take my mind off Nashville's win and post-game celebration.

I might not have fled to the kitchen, but Selma and Jasper had found Cole on the field after the game and as soon as Selma threw her arms around Cole in a hug that fused their clothing together, I'd needed a distraction other than food.

"Hi Nora, Dr. Kessick, this is Eden calling. We met, well...I ran into you at the grocery store the other day?"

"Yes! Eden. I'm so glad you called, and you caught me at the perfect moment. Do you have a few minutes to talk?"

Absolutely I did. Anything to erase the image of the hug. The way Cole smiled at Jasper when Selma wrapped her arms around him. "Of course."

"Actually...I have a better idea. I'm starving and the last thing I feel like doing right now is cooking. Any chance you'd want to meet up for a quick bite? I know that's strange, but well, I'm new to town and let's just say my chances to hang out with people are pretty slim out here. And I figured since you seemed new...and there's something I'd like to show you."

"Oh." Surprise, tinged with an upcoming decline must have been thick in that one word.

"It's okay." She laughed, chuckled at herself but I was the one who should have been embarrassed. "I'm sorry. Of course, you're probably busy, or have someone."

"I don't." I snapped the words so fast I surprised myself. And wasn't this what I needed? I couldn't rely on Marley for support being in town. And Nora knew *nothing* about me. She was probably the safest person to be seen with. "I'm sorry, you caught me off guard, but well, sure I'd actually love to grab something to eat."

Marley had gone to take a nap right after the game and she'd be sleeping for a few hours. I'd make sure to bring her back something barbecued and dripping with sauce and she'd forgive my veggie and hummus concoction from earlier.

"Only, can we go somewhere other than the diner?" The last people I needed to run into, ever, were Selma's parents.

"Sure. How do you feel about food trucks and beer?"

The beer I could live without, but I'd never yet met a food truck I didn't like.

———

Turned out by food trucks and beer, Nora wanted to meet at a brewery south of downtown Marysville. Off the main strip, Buckin' Brews was immediately noticeable, and barely recognizable.

"The old tack shop and feed store," I muttered, seeing the brown and weathered barn that had once been crumbling and old, appear completely restored. The barn looked like I imagined it would have when it was first built, except as I pulled into the parking lot, the entire back had been transformed. What used to be a dirt lot, huge with room for trucks and horse trailers to pull up behind it, now had a covered patio. The roof rose at an angle, increasing in height and beneath it were rows of long tables, bright yellow metal barstools. Lights were strung every which way over the ceiling and wrapped around the wood beams. A half dozen ceiling fans worked to move the hot, August afternoon air. Thank goodness it was cloudy, keeping the sun from beating down but I sat in my car, both admiring what had been done to the building and saddened by the change in it.

I was never a horse rider. Never spent much time on a farm at all in the year I lived here, but a lot of the classmates I met did, and this was a place they frequented for supplies and feed. They also came to hang out, read magazines and buy books and the candy selection at the store had been topnotch.

"Wow." I blinked, realizing not only had the store gone out of business, but this brewery seemed to be following the trend of being hip and young. Already I could hear music blasting through the speakers. There were several televisions fashioned on two of the covered walls. And food trucks.

Three different food trucks were parked beyond the covered patio out by what looked like a stage set up for live music. The lines for all three were at least five deep and there were still dozens of more people hanging out on the patio.

Damn. Nothing like this was even close to existing seven years ago.

Someone young probably came up with the idea. Someone who wanted to bring the city to Nashville but respected the existing building enough to leave what was left mostly untouched, outside the patio addition.

Nerves swarm in my gut as I exited the car and tucked my keys into my crossbody bag.

I didn't know who was inside yet, or outside. Marysville was a town every young teen claimed to want to leave, but that wasn't always possible. And dreams didn't always go the way you hoped.

Cole being the classic example. Which meant, inside those walls could be everyone I once knew, friends of Hilary who'd recognize me and kick my butt out at first sight.

At least Selma was in Nashville, and I didn't have to worry about her walking in.

I could do this. I'd been in town over a week and had made a couple trips to Frank's. No one had kicked my ass or slashed my tires yet, and if I really considered it logically—no one had even looked at me twice.

It was entirely possible this meeting with Nora could go just as smooth.

And it wasn't like I had to stay for hours.

A quick bite to eat, a conversation and maybe a drink. Then I'd be back to Marley, warm dinner in hand for her when she woke up.

Pep talk done, I headed toward the front door.

I could do this. I *really* needed to be around some animals.

And soon.

# CHAPTER 9
## EDEN

The inside of Buckin' Brews was as rustic and original as I'd hoped for. Sure, walls had been torn down to open up the space to one massive room. There were glass walls making the brew tanks beyond visible and there was the ordering counter with white subway tile behind it to lighten up the space, but other than that, I could still smell the scent of leather and horses and hay.

"You made it!"

Nora's cry was nearby, and I turned, immediately finding her shoving out of the only line of high back wood booths.

I grinned, unable to help it, and laser focused my eyes on her. As long as she didn't scream my name, everything would be fine. And if I didn't see anyone else, maybe no one would see me.

Fat chance of that but considering the place didn't go up in flames once I crossed the threshold, I was good for now.

As soon as I reached her, we both did that awkward handshake, hug, thing where I held out my hand to shake hers and she lifted her arms to hug me.

We laughed, waved instead, and she slid a menu across to me. "Have you been here yet?"

"No."

"We have to order at the bar, but this is their list of beers and everything else they have. Once we get our drinks, I can show you why I wanted to meet you here, if that's okay."

Curiosity piqued, I scanned the list. I wasn't much of a beer drinker, at least nothing fancier than a Corona in the summertime. Wine and mixed drinks were more my thing, so I flipped their drink menu, found what I was looking for.

"Ready."

"Awesome." Her smile was sweet and soft, and we slid out of the booth. Two women were helping customers down at the other end of the bar, so I figured the wait would be a while.

Half the town's population under forty must have been at this brewery. Made sense. Sunday afternoon. Football. Wasn't much else to do except have a few drinks and play corn hole, which I saw outside. Past the patio were men in T-shirts and khaki shorts lined up and ready to play.

Fortunately, with a quick scan of the place, everyone I saw was unrecognizable. Relief settled over my shoulders, helping me relax.

I didn't know anyone here, and that was a good thing.

"Hey Nate!" Nora called, and I turned right as I went to eat my words.

At least I could, if I could remember how to breathe. Think. Talk.

Nate Beckham. Same blond hair, shorter and styled neatly, sweeping to the side. He'd grown a lot in the last seven years. Hilary's younger brother.

He was sixteen the last time I saw him.

Ravaged.

Screaming at me right before he threw up on his feet.

On my worst nights, those screams still haunted me, as did the look on his face while Cole held him back from running into the street.

"Hey Nora—" His smile faltered, and his jaw hung loose when he saw me.

Recognized me.

"Eden." It was a question, a statement, and a curse rolled into one.

I turned to Nora. "I should go."

"You two know each other? How? I thought..."

"I went to school here for a year. Long time ago. Wasn't here long."

"Tucked tail and ran, right? Not surprised." The venom came from Nate and my knees wobbled and my eyes closed.

Nate Beckham. I hadn't considered for a single second he'd still be in town.

I couldn't bring myself to look at him, and the bar top blurred as I tried to stay standing.

"Um." Nora faltered next to me. Clearly surprised for a myriad of reasons and I couldn't explain.

"What can I get you?" Nate asked, and I was one hundred percent sure he was directing it at her. But then he said my name and it was as equally nasty as the first time.

"Just a water," I mumbled.

There was no way I could drink now. I'd chug the whole bottle and have no way to get back to Marley. Which I probably should be doing. ASAP.

Nora placed her order, something called a Juicy Jay, and when Nate turned his back to grab it for her, she arched two brows in my direction. "That was well, we don't know each other so it's none of my business, but that was heavy."

"Long story, but I left town seven years ago and only came back for one reason. I didn't mean to lie when you assumed I was new to town but considering that's how Nate reacted you should probably know that's how *everyone* in town will react to my presence, if not worse."

"Wow. Well, okay…I get if you want to leave, but can I still show you why I wanted you to come here in the first place? It's outside."

I shouldn't. Nate was opening her beer like he wanted to tear the top off with his teeth and I wouldn't be surprised if he spit in my water, but when he came back, some of the hatred in his familiar blue eyes had softened.

"You here for Marley?"

"Yeah. Listen—"

"How is she?"

"Same. Worse. A little of both."

"Right." He slid the beer toward Nora. "Want me to put it on your tab?"

Because he clearly didn't want us anywhere near him any longer than necessary.

"Sure, Nate. Thanks. I'll pay up next week."

"See you around, doc."

He flashed her a halfhearted grin, ignored me, and as he pushed the metal swinging door open with both hands to disappear into the back, the door slammed into the wood wall, rattling everything.

Yeah. I should probably go.

"Come on," Nora whispered, and tugged my elbow. "I don't need to know that story to know it's not good, and I hate gossip. That's why I work with animals. But you'll like this. At least, I think you might."

Great. Another surprise.

We headed out back. My glass of water warmed instantly from the heat and the smell of food trucks assaulted my senses. But another noise, muffled from the music near the building, but one that always made me smile and my heart tripped over itself echoed in the near distance.

*Dogs.*

"What is this?" I asked, forcing myself to smile and push down the interaction with Nate.

"This is where I think you can help." She swung her arm out to several dog pens. Free standing but locked up into octagon shapes and beneath tents, dozens of dogs and puppies played and barked and jumped all over each other. "This is Waggin' Tails dog rescue. They do rescue events at breweries and pet stores all over. I'd just talked to Sarah, the owner of the rescue, the day before I saw you at the store."

She started walking toward the animals and my hands were itching to dig into all that soft fur. Lab puppies. Pit mix puppies. There were tiny dogs and puppies I knew would grow to be huge dogs. "They're running out of foster homes for dogs to go to, so a lot of the new puppies are being boarded at the BarkTown doggy daycare. But they don't have the employees to watch all these dogs consistently either, so I talked to them."

She smiled at me, and we stopped at a cage where a girl about my age, wearing a lime green top and *Waggin' Tails Dog Rescue* was written in hot pink, spoke to a mom and a girl about ten years old as they held an all-white puppy save for the black spot around his eye.

"I figured if you were interested in volunteering, you could talk to Sarah. She has volunteers with her rescues going in for a couple hours every day to help out at BarkTown, but with school starting soon, they're losing their teenage volunteers."

"You mean, I could sit in a doggy care, play with puppies all day? Sign me up."

This was perfect. I could go in the mornings, afternoons, evenings. I could work it around when Marley needed me, a couple hours every day. Hell, more if they needed it.

As soon as the mom and daughter walked off to the hand sanitizing area, the girl with blue eyes slightly too wide for her face, cheeks flushed from the heat, and hair pulled back and held in place with a claw clip turned to us, recognized Nora, and grinned at both of us.

"Hey there. You made it."

She gave Nora a quick hug and smiled at me. It was an easy smile, carefree, and I thanked my lucky stars I didn't know her. "I'm Sarah. You must be Eden. Nora said she might have someone willing to help us out?"

"Yeah." I bent over one of the cages and scratched a brown and black puppy. Looked like a hound, a German shepherd mix of some sort. Probably some lab in there too. "I'm a vet tech down in Florida. I'm only here for a few months, possibly the end of the year, but I'd love to help with animals in any way I can."

They both looked confused. Rightfully so. "I came back to help an old friend. Marley Bickerstaff?"

"Oh. I'm sorry to hear about your friend. Everyone I've spoken to loves her," Nora said, and I could have lived without the pity on her face. "That's really sweet of you."

"Thanks. She's doing okay, for now." I focused on Sarah. "Nora said you need help at the doggy daycare place? I can come in every day, around Marley's schedule. She's sick, but..."

"Everyone knows who Marley is, Eden." Sarah's grin was kind, now sad and it didn't seem right for such a sweet-looking girl to look so sad.

Props to me for being the one to do it.

"How about I go grab us something to eat and you and Sarah can talk? Sound okay?"

Sounded divine, considering no way was my ass going back around the building.

I fished out my bank card, told her to grab me something from the taco truck, whatever sounded good to her and was surprised when I turned back to Sarah, Nate was there.

"If you're going to be out here, figured you'd need more water."

He shoved the glass at me like he wanted to punch me, but I took it. "You didn't have to."

"Know that. But I'm being dick and I don't like to be a dick, especially to people who come into my place, unless they ask for it. You haven't asked for it, but I was surprised to see you. So. Water."

He nodded at the glass and stomped away.

"I don't know if I've ever seen Nate look like that. How do you know him?"

"Used to live here. That's all."

The half-truth burned in my throat. She'd find out eventually. Everyone in town would be talking soon now.

The news wouldn't come from me. Not before I'd secured what I needed to.

# CHAPTER 10
## COLE

'll be back in a minute, okay, bud?"

Jasper, sitting at the kitchen table after dinner, mumbled something while slurping ice cream off his spoon.

I took it as an *okay*.

Now that I finally had Selma alone for a couple minutes, we needed to talk because that bullshit she pulled after the game was absolutely not okay. Not only for me, but for Jasper.

I'd seethed through the post-game interviews, still thrown from her affection and then been pissed all over again when I left the locker room, and she was waiting in the hallway with my parents.

They suggested we grill out at my house, so Bongo wouldn't be alone and Selma, all smiles and with Jasper tucked tight to her side, had replied. "Sounds like a great idea."

The hell it was. Based on my mom's eye roll and thinly pressed together lips, she'd thought the same thing I did.

We couldn't tell her no in front of Jasper. She was pushing boundaries lately I didn't appreciate and if you gave Selma an inch, she'd take a full marathon. Manipulating me into spending time with her by using my son as her tool was absolutely never happening again.

"What in the hell was that earlier?" I asked as soon as the front door shut behind me. I made it a rule to never argue with her in front of Jasper.

"What was what?" She was digging through her purse, looking for her keys. Her tone was all nonchalance, but it was all a lie.

Her Nissan Armada had keyless entry and she didn't need them to open her doors or start the car. Last year, when she told me she was thinking of getting a new SUV and her dad was taking her shopping, I'd told her to make sure whatever she bought had that feature. It was easier with Jasper and his school stuff and safer, so she didn't have to be doing exactly what she was doing now—digging through her purse.

"You know exactly what I'm talking about." I stopped walking, waited for her to realize I wasn't next to her anymore and she had to face me.

"It was just a hug, Cole. Maybe you shouldn't read so much into it."

"A hug. You jumping into my arms and wrapping your legs around my waist in the middle of the field, with Jasper right there watching was *just a hug*?"

"So, I was excited. What's the big deal?"

I'd learned long ago Selma's manipulative streak was nasty. Partly because she was so slippery about it. It was the same as the night I was back home over the summer and met her out because she'd claimed to have been missing Hilary and no one except me would understand. Several drinks in, shots offered by her, and I was comforting her in a way that had absolutely nothing to do with Hilary. But I was drunk, definitely still feeling that guilt over Hilary's death, and still thinking of Eden and pissed off for doing it.

When she cuddled up next to me after, and slipped her arm around my waist and whispered, *"We should do this more often. I've missed you,"* while raining soft kisses over my shoulder and my chest, should have been my first clue she'd taken me for a completely different kind of ride.

"The big deal is we don't *do* that, Selma. Ever. It's good for Jasper to see his parents getting along, it's not okay to start making him think we're going to actually be together. It's a good thing for us to be friendly, but that wasn't anything friendly and you know it. It pisses me off and gives everyone the wrong idea."

"Everyone like Eden?"

Ah…and there it was. That nasty tone and the jealous flare in her eyes.

It shouldn't have surprised me.

"The hell?" It was all I could muster. "What is wrong with you?"

"Oh please. Like you can stand right here in front of me and tell me you haven't seen her?"

"It's none of your damn business who I see."

"So, you have. You have seen her." Her spine turned to steel and there was a fire in her eyes I did not appreciate. She was also changing the subject.

"What does me seeing her have anything to do with that crap you pulled today? That shit was photographed. Probably posted everywhere. There's probably chatter somewhere about us together, or some shit."

"Oh. And that's a problem now? You never minded before."

"I minded, Selma. And you know it. And whatever shit you're pulling now, for whatever reason, that ends. Same with posting me anywhere on any of your socials. We aren't together. We never were, and we never will be, and you *know* all of that, so I don't even care what game you're playing. I'm not joining. I'm *done* joining your little games."

If steam was rising from my skull, I didn't care. Selma was always a tough one to handle because she knew too much. And for the most part, we did co-parent Jasper well. It was when she crossed the line where everything went up in smoke. And she'd been doing it more lately.

"Well…you told me, didn't you?"

There was hurt in her voice I didn't believe for a second, but she was still the mother of my child and even if she was faking the pain to manipulate me, it worked.

Damn her.

"What are you doing, Selma? Why this? And why now?"

I worked to soften the hard edges of my tone and it must have worked, because her posture slipped. "Maybe, because I've been thinking. Of Jasper starting school, of not having his parents together. You don't date anyone, Cole. Ever. And I don't want—"

"Don't." I made sure I was kind, despite the bullshit she was shoveling. This wasn't the first time she'd done this. But it would be the last. "Don't finish that. You don't even mean it. You don't want me. Never did. All I've ever been to you is a prize to win and if you're not going to be honest with me, at least be honest with yourself. You tricked me into fucking you that night. You wanted Hilary and I to break up so you could shoot your shot way back then and you only hate Eden because she's the only girl in the world who had a shot with me."

"She will *never* have anything to do with my son, Cole, so maybe end that dream now."

"Ours."

"What?"

"Our son."

"We'll see."

Oh, she fucking did not…I was in front of her before she could blink. At six three, I towered over her five-four frame and I *never* used my size to intimidate a woman. Ever. But she'd gone too far. "Too fucking far. You ever threaten to take my time with my son away from me and you'll regret it."

"Now who's throwing out threats?"

God damn. This woman. She strolled around this town like she owned it and couldn't see how she was a big fish in a very small pond. But I could be the shark, if I needed to.

"Try me. You try to take Jasper from me, and it will be the last thing you do, so help me, God. I will *ruin* you."

Fear sparked in her eyes. Maybe regret. But she washed it away with a blink and stepped back. I figured I'd made my point as she got to her door and opened it, but then she had to throw the bomb at my feet that almost made my head explode straight into the atmosphere.

"I guess we'll see. I'm not the perfect little angel with secrets, Cole. You are, so maybe remember that."

She slammed her door before I could get to her, but it didn't matter.

I was frozen, rooted to my gravel drive. I didn't even flinch when she threw her Armada around and that gravel kicked up, peppering me in the shins and chest.

She'd *never* made that threat before.

And I knew Selma enough to know she'd use it if pushed. Except it wouldn't just be my life that was raked through the media. It'd be Jasper. My family's. Hilary's parents and Nate.

And Eden.

"Fucking hell."

————

Mondays were usually light practice days after games on Sunday. I'd already done a light workout, mostly stretching, some yoga, and time on the bike to stretch out sore muscles and keep them loose for the upcoming week. Off-season for me was more meant for improving athletic endurance and ability but once the season started, my entire focus shifted to maintaining the growth I'd strived for and staying injury free. Which meant a lot of time on a bike or elliptical and stair stepper, and not nearly enough muscle load to help me push out all the anger that lingered after last night's interaction with Selma.

It wasn't uncommon, although infrequent, for her and me to get in a fight, for her to fly off the handle and then apologize a few hours later. Typically, once she calmed down, maybe vented about how big of a selfish asshole I was to her few friends in town over a couple of cocktails or some shit. They'd tell her to knock it off, she knew the score when she got pregnant, and I was at least thankful she had friends in her life willing to speak truth because on the nights she didn't apologize, it was because she went to her parents.

Her mom and dad were always happy to shove the knife into my back. I got it. She was their daughter. I was just the little shit Buchanan boy who took advantage of her in her grief—another lovely story she spun.

She'd gone too far last night, though, because in all the years we fought and I tried to reinforce already firmly set boundaries, she'd never once threatened my custody of Jasper. Granted, we'd never had to go to court or a judge or any shit like that. We worked it out. It changed depending on her schedule, my travel days during the season and our parents were both more than happy to pick up the slack.

It worked.

At least, I thought it did for the most part, but her threats from last night kept echoing in my head, making me lose focus more than once, now especially, when everyone in the team's film room had turned their head in my direction.

"Dude." Butler kicked my shin.

"Sorry Coach."

I figured it was the right thing to say, based on the snickers in the room from my teammates, it wasn't.

"Apology accepted, Buchanan, but what I'd asked you was if there was anything you should have done differently to score in that second possession."

Of course there had been. There was always a way to be better. Do better. Faster. Stronger, a quick step out of the pocket, or a decision to stay in it. I weave to the right instead of left around a defender who was aiming to knock me out at the knees.

Since I hadn't been paying attention, and my screen on the team issued iPad was black, my dumbass decided on, "Ummm. Probably."

Bad. So bad. Like my rookie year when I first showed up and all eyes were on me and I was sweating in my athletic shorts so badly, terrified I'd be called on and say the wrong thing and lose my spot and get sent to practice squad or something even worse—let go completely.

Fortunately for me, Coach Paul Bowles was a good guy and a patient man off the field to all of us.

"Probably is right. How about you turn your brain on and start listening, hmm?"

"You got it, sir." I tapped my screen and swiped the password key to unlock it as he went back over film.

Next to me, Butler leaned in. "You still going to tell me there's nothing going on? You've never been distracted in a meeting."

"Selma shit," I answered back. "And I need a drink after this."

I rarely drank during the week. A couple beers the night after a game maybe, and never on a Monday. This would be the third night I was craving alcohol since Eden's arrival even if today's need wasn't because of her.

"I gotchu. We'll head out after this."

"Good. Just don't expect me to talk."

"No one wants to listen to you bitch and moan about the crazy chick anyway." That came from Davis Hall, our star running back and team's resident unbelievable playmaker and all-around smartass.

I'd usually defend her, but she sure as hell had shown her crazy last night.

I needed to fix it before her threats tumbled into an avalanche.

# CHAPTER 11
## COLE

"Lawyer."

"Definitely call your lawyer."

Dawson and Davis spit the words out at almost the same time and then each chowed down on a fry at the burger joint we decided on for dinner.

They'd spent most of the dinner listening to me tell them about what went down last night with Selma. While neither were fans of her, never really had been, I hadn't expected that to be their first reaction, both deadpanned like they were on the same wavelength, and I was the one with a screw loose.

"We've never needed to bring a lawyer into this."

"Yeah." Dawson shoved his fork in my direction before spearing it into his jalapeño corn salad. "But that's because you weren't yet a pro when you knocked her up and didn't have millions. You were just a man with a dream, and she was getting her nursing degree. Don't get me wrong, it's cool she hasn't come after you for child support yet and you've been able to parent Jasper together, but something's tripped her trigger and a pissed off woman can do a lot of shit to mess with you. Trust me."

I scoffed. "What the hell do you know about pissed off women? You haven't had a woman longer than a week since you hit puberty." It was an exaggeration, but not by much. We entered the league and were drafted in the same year together. Hell, we lived with each other during the team's first training camp and there wasn't anyone on the team I knew more about than Dawson—including his sex life, which he enjoyed boasting about.

Not in details—because he wasn't that big of a dick.

"Exactly. And you know why? Because I saw the shit my mom pulled with my dad and their divorce was *her* fault to begin with. But she saw her moneymaker on the way out the door and that woman turned feral in her pursuits to suck as much money and life out of him as she could before he left."

I was shaking my head. At both the story and the thought of Selma doing that to me. She wouldn't. As soon as the town heard what she was pulling, they'd turn on her. She had to know that.

"Sucks about your mom," Davis mumbled. "Mine's awesome."

"So was mine until my dad caught her in bed with his best friend while Crystal and I were at school."

"Damn. That's harsh. But Selma—" I shook my head. I couldn't see her doing anything that vicious.

"She would. Especially with as pissed as she sounded. So what was it that ticked her off this time? You didn't like her hug or was it because you still refuse to marry her?"

"Both. Neither," I admitted. Dawson and I were friends. Davis was a rookie, but he was more responsible than most and even though he was five years younger than us, fresh out of college, had a maturity about him I sure as hell wouldn't have had if I hadn't become a father by his age.

"It's a girl," I finally admitted. I could trust these guys, and Dawson had already been up my ass about my focus lately.

"I knew it." He shook his head with fatherly disappointment even my own didn't possess.

"Of course it's a girl." Davis stabbed his kale salad with a fork. "It's always a girl. So who is she?"

There was no way to truly explain Eden. She was the girl who stole my heart when it was committed to another. She was the mirage I searched for in every crowded area for years. She was the ghost returned to haunt me all over again.

And she was still the only woman my soul ever truly beat for.

She was also my greatest mistake.

My biggest regret in a number of ways.

"She's Eden." I settled on her name and the weight that came with it and hoped at least Dawson picked up on it.

Davis didn't, but he wasn't the one I got black out drunk with one night and spilled all my darkest truths to my second year in the league after a particularly nasty fight with Selma.

"Eden…" Dawson, who had gone silent, drawled out her name in a way ants crawled down my spine. "*The* Eden?"

"Yeah. She's back in Marysville."

Dawson, typically our quiet grump, pushed his lips out. "Huh. Well, that explains your attitude lately."

Davis's eyes jumped between us. "What am I missing?"

"A brain between your ears and eight inches between your legs." Dawson grinned at him and tossed a fry into his mouth.

"Nice." I barked out a laugh that grabbed the attention of the table next to us.

Tugging down my cap, I made sure I'd spoken quietly. That we'd all been quiet, but we had been. And the people next to us, looking older than us, probably early thirties with a toddler wearing an oversized pink bow in her hair and squirming in her highchair, barely paid us attention.

"Fuck off, Butler," Davis groaned. "I've got plenty of both."

"Sure, kid."

Davis, showing his maturity, rolled his eyes and turned back to me. "So, who's Eden? Or is it just some euphemism for a woman's secret garden?"

"Eupha what?"

"Now who doesn't have a brain," Davis teased Dawson.

I ignored the visual his lovely question gave me about Eden *and* her secret garden as he put it. "Long story. She was friends with us, though. Selma, me…Hilary…"

He was silent a beat. Gaze focused on me in a way that was way too deep for dinner and a burger. "Got it."

He picked up his burger and took a huge bite, acting like he had me all figured out.

If only he'd tell me what it was he'd uncovered.

Davis chewed his burger while I pushed my plate away, suddenly full with an already churning gut.

"You know what you should do?" he asked.

"What?"

"Move to the city. Put some space between you and Selma. You're all still close enough you can take care of Jasper. Hell, down here you're even closer to the hospital so it's not like pick-ups and drop offs would be any different. Y'all's parents can help out still, too. But the distance, even if it's an extra fifteen miles, might help Selma finally learn you're never gonna be with her. Might help you both move on."

"I've moved on."

"You have?"

"Of course I have."

"Then tell me more about Eden."

My lips froze, fused together. No way in hell, especially not there, in public, or that moment.

"Moved on. Like hell you have." He let out a low chuckle that was anything but humorous and went back to his burger.

"Kid does have a point," Dawson said, leaning in and shoving his black hair off his forehead. "And I was wrong. He's only missing the inches, not the brain but moving might not be such a bad idea. Especially with Eden in town."

"If I moved now, Selma would spill *all* the shit. Every last ugly detail."

It was an excuse, although a more plausible one after her last tantrum.

I didn't want to move. I liked still living in Marysville even if I was on the other side of town as my parents. I liked being close to them. I liked raising Jasper in the town where I grew up, and I liked that since everyone knew me, it was rare I was bothered out in public. Hell, I could still go to the brewery on my Sunday bye week if I wanted and watch the games like every other normal person there. I doubted I'd have that in the city, at least at first, and what would that mean for Jasper when he was in school?

"So let her. She does that, she's only going to throw more sympathy your way anyway. Outed by the baby mama because she didn't get a rock. Please. Selma does that and she's digging her own grave."

"Anyone gonna tell me what I'm missing here?" Davis asked.

"When you're old enough to understand, kid." Dawson flashed him a teasing wink and Davis scoffed.

"You're an asshole."

"I wear the title proudly."

"And stop calling me kid."

"When you're older, little buddy."

Davis rolled his eyes and tossed another fry into his mouth.

They'd given me a lot to think about. From the lawyers to moving and even Eden. But, back to Davis's question, only one thing was truly clear.

Who was Eden?

She was my everything.

Now I had to put in the work convincing her.

And that was about as likely to happen as Selma turning into a kind and generous human being.

I was a fighter though, a dreamer, and so far, all the plans I'd set for myself had come true minus one—and I wasn't going to give up on Eden.

Not again.

Not ever.

———

I left the guys at the restaurant when they ordered another round of drinks. It was getting late anyway, and I still had to get Bongo from BarkTown, the doggy daycare I started taking him to last week before Selma dropped off Jasper.

BarkTown boasted of all the amenities your furry family member could ask for, a huge fenced in outside area that included three splash pad areas for dogs to run through water in the blazing summer heat. Lots of shade and a small wading pool. So far, every time I picked up Bongo, he'd tracked mud into my truck, so I started keeping towels in the back seat at all times. Since the weather had been sunny all day, I figured he'd be soaked again, so I grabbed one of the towels out of the truck as a car pulled up next to me.

A guy climbed out of the SUV next to me. Wearing a Steel ball cap and sunglasses, he had hair that flipped out over his ears and waved as he passed me. "Hey, Cole. Good game yesterday."

"Thanks, man."

He grinned and nodded and didn't linger for more conversation.

I was used to being recognized in town, and since I'd grown up here, everyone knew me anyway, but it still never surprised when someone I didn't know complimented my game or said hello. This guy was around my age, maybe a couple years older, and while I never minded stopping to sign something for fans, especially kids, or have a chat with someone on the street, I was thankful this guy didn't linger. Or go full Monday morning quarterback on me.

That usually came after shitty games though, when everyone and their brother and second cousin's step-uncle had something to say about our loss.

Fun days, those were.

Davis's suggestion of me moving to the city rang in my ears. On those days, it'd make more sense, for sure.

A frantic round of barking came through the doors as the guy in front of me opened them and stepped inside. He held it open for me with his arm behind him and I thanked him while we both walked up to the counter.

"Hey Mr. Hancock. They're getting Milo ready for you now."

"Thanks, Suzie." He tapped the counter and stepped back.

I walked up to Suzie, a high schooler who was the youngest of six in her family. One of her five older brothers was in my grade in high school. Her dad was the president of the bank branch where my parents had always done their banking.

"Hey Suz. How's it going today?"

"Busy, Cole. Someone brought in an aggressive dog and didn't let us know beforehand. He went crazy and one got hurt." At the look in my eyes, she shook her head. "Not Bongo. He's fine. Everyone's fine and the injury was minor. Luckily for us, we have a veterinary technician who's doing some volunteer work for us. Good timing because she was able to get the new pup taken care of and calm the dogs down. Only ended up with some minor scratches on her arms, too."

"Damn. Sounds like a day. Everyone's good, now though?"

"Yeah. We separated the dog, it's just fear is all with him, but it would have been nice to be warned. Gave all the dogs some snacks and turned on the hoses out back. So Bongo might be wet."

I held up the towel and smiled. "No worries. I came prepared."

"Awesome. I'll go get Bongo then."

"No need. I've got him right here."

I knew that voice, and out of all the places in all the world the last place I expected to run into Eden was here.

Her hair was disheveled, and she was bent over, petting Bongo while holding on to his collar, attempting to hook his leash to it, so it gave me a second to prepare myself before she realized who Bongo's owner was.

"Hi there—" Eden lifted her head and the rest of her sentence died on her lips, as well as the light from her eyes.

"Eden."

"Cole." My name came out as a breath and she stood up, almost jerking Bongo back with her, but he was faster, stronger, and loved his owner.

He lunged toward me, almost yanking Eden off her feet.

"Hey boy." He jumped, paws to my chest and the leash in Eden's hand was yanked from it, clattered to the floor.

"Sorry!" she cried. "Oh! Shoot."

"It's okay." We both grabbed his leash at the same time. I won, and her hand brushed over mine. Sparks of something ignited the back of my hand, my arm, until I saw all the red, shallow gashes up her arm.

"You were hurt." Bongo was a jumping, frantic mess with his damp black fur flying all over the place. Tongue hanging out, he danced in a circle while I stared at the cuts all over Eden's arm.

*She* was the vet tech?

# CHAPTER 12
## EDEN

Surprisingly enough, after that lovely bomb was dropped, Sarah was still willing to talk to me about volunteering. I figured she heard about Nate's older sister dying in high school, so she didn't ask many questions. I climbed into one of the playpens while we talked and reveled in the soft fur of a pack of abandoned golden retriever puppies climbing all over me, licking my face. The stress I'd felt since arriving in Marysville melted away with each soft swipe of my hands through their scruff when Nora returned with three plates overflowing with tacos. I joined her at a wood table. We ate. Talked about the animals.

Turned out Nora's grandpa, who used to be the town's only vet, passed away in the spring. Since it was her mom's dad, I hadn't realized she took over for Tom Mischler. She moved to town three months prior from Memphis when he left her his vet practice in his will. She wasn't sure she wanted to stay here forever, "but it's not bad, and the slower pace is kind of nice sometimes. Living in downtown Memphis…" She shuddered, ate her taco, and seemed perfectly content to ask me about my life in Florida, but didn't bring up anything from here.

As for me, I'd gone back to Marley's, handed her some BBQ pork from the truck I'd grabbed on my way to the car, and when I told her what I was going to be doing, she'd simply said, "Good. That's good for you."

We watched *Wheel of Fortune* and *Jeopardy* and I had even more fun torturing myself when the local news came on and Cole's face was once again splashed all over the screen before I'd decided the day had been hard enough.

After Marley took her medicine and went to bed, I gorged myself on Netflix, episodes of *The Office* to get my mind off everything wrong in my life and fell asleep on the couch.

Now, while I survived my first day volunteering, BarkTown was absolute madness.

Sarah had warned me that there were so many dogs there right now, a dozen of the rescue's puppies being boarded there due to lack of current foster homes and with the increase in business to the doggy daycare.

I hadn't exactly been prepared for the golden lab to be the cause of so much drama, but as soon as I got him separated from the black boxer mix, he'd attacked without so much as a snarl or warning growl to warn us, the rest of the day went smoothly. My scratches would heal in a day or two, and I was fortunate I wasn't hurt worse. The lab owners came to pick him up, apologizing profusely. It was his first time in a doggy daycare, they knew he wasn't fond of black dogs, but hadn't thought to warn us.

He'd be welcomed back, and the workers would help him socialize safely at a slower pace.

The boxer mix had cuts on his face that would heal, and her owners, while shaken, seemed to be understanding.

It could have gone much worse.

After I got those dogs taken care of, I stayed inside for the rest of the afternoon, playing with the recuse puppies. However, once they all passed out on their beds in a small, sectioned off area inside, I went outside. It was there the beautiful Golden Retriever I'd seen playfully jumping in and out of the splash pads and barking at jets of water blasting into the air had done figure eights between my legs, so excited for the new person he could lavish his attention on. I fell for that dog in a blink. So when Suzie buzzed the back and announced Bongo's owner had arrived, I *had* to meet the owner of this lovely creature who continually insisted I scratched my fingernails in his fur beneath his jaw.

And of course. *Of freaking course* the owner of that precious, beautiful, and precocious pup was none other than Cole.

The universe seemed insistent on throwing us together and if I wasn't so distracted with the worry in Cole's eyes as he focused on my arm, I'd shake my fists and curse the heavens.

"You were hurt." Bongo jumped around him like the maniac he was, and his tail whipped happily back and forth across my knees.

"I'm fine." I stood back, brushed my hands down my arms as if I could cover the scratches. "Job hazard, no big deal."

"Suzie said—" He looked in the direction of the girl working behind the counter and back to me. "So, you're a vet tech now."

Suzie was sweet, and while I'd recognized her last name Paxton immediately, it was obvious she had no idea who I was. She would have been too young seven years ago, just a child, when everything happened, and her brother Paul wasn't close friends with Cole. The town was small enough that we all knew each other, but Paul preferred the company of the marching band and debate club in high school, not the sports jocks. I hadn't bothered to ask her what he was up to now.

I was absolutely not having this conversation in the lobby of Bark-Town while Lance Hancock waited for Milo and Suzie looked on.

"Bongo was really good today. Great dog." I stepped back and dipped back into the indoor play area and smoothed my hands down my face.

I couldn't go anywhere to escape Cole. Obviously, I should have known that, but the animals were supposed to be a reprieve, and now he'd permeate my own peaceful space.

Just freaking *great.*

———

"You're quiet today."

Marley's arm was tucked around mine, her hand on my forearm as we walked the path to the lake.

"Can't a girl enjoy the beauty of God's land in silence?"

"Of course girls can, but you haven't believed in God since I've known you so how about we don't bring Him into it."

"People change." I hadn't. Not in my belief and while I could agree that there was a God out there, somewhere, I never truly believed He cared about the internal workings of my heart or soul or had a direct impact on our lives.

"And don't I know it, but how about you be real with me for a minute as the kids say these days."

I wasn't sure kids still said anything of the sort. "I'd rather talk about the nurse coming next week."

It was time. Or would be soon, and I needed to have everything lined up. Her breathing was heavier, more wheezy, and it wouldn't be long before these daily morning walks we took grew to be too much for her.

"Gah. I'm dying. Slowly. The nurse isn't going to do anything except make me more comfortable while I go, and we both know it."

Damn her annoying peace with her own death.

"Marley—"

"I've been thinking about me and only me for the last twenty years. It's time I do something different."

"You've never thought about yourself a day in your life," I teased her. The woman rivaled Mother Teresa.

"Talk."

It was a command from a dying old lady. She'd warned me she'd force me to talk sometime, and she'd let me avoid it for over a week. Apparently she was done with that because she didn't need to say more for me to know who I was talking about.

"I saw Cole. Yesterday at BarkTown."

"Seems to me you've seen quite a bit of him since you've been back."

"Not of my choosing."

"Perhaps someone's trying to tell you to stop avoiding what you're hiding from then."

I rolled my eyes and thankfully I was not only taller than Marley, but I was looking away from her, so she didn't see me. A schooling from her never felt good, despite how kindly she gave it.

"I came back for you and that's all. I'd prefer if I *didn't* see Cole anymore."

"More lies upon lies, soon you'll be buried so deep beneath them you won't know how to get out."

"Marley—"

"Nope. My turn. I'm older than you and I've lived longer, and I just know more. Life's too short, Eden. It's too short to carry the weight of all that happened and it's too short to not forgive yourself for it. It's too damn short for you to keep runnin' from your problems, not speakin' to your family. You didn't disappoint them, and they love you more than life itself, they just want to know you're okay. Instead, you've spent the last seven years hiding and hunkerin' down with dogs and cats, not letting anyone else in so no one else can hurt you."

"Dogs give me peace. And you're wrong. I've dated."

"Bologna. You ain't dated anyone longer than a few months at a time and we both know you bail if you ever start feeling something. Besides, true peace comes from within, not from fur—no matter how soft it is and how sweet their kisses are."

She pulled her arm from mine and stopped near the water's edge. The sun shone on her face as she tipped it to the sky and in the distance, birds happily chirped.

But she'd hit me with a one-two punch about Cole *and* my strained relationship with my parents, so I wasn't feeling nearly as happy as the birds.

"I love you, child. Loved you since the moment your family moved in across the street, loved you since I walked over to your house with my blueberry jams and you and your mom were so sweet and thankful. You've been good to me, but I wouldn't be being good to you back if I let you keep burying your head in the sand before it's too late."

"I'm not—"

"You are," she snapped and turned to me. Marley was rarely so forceful, her words knocked me back a step. "You're burying and you're hiding and you're not happy and you haven't been and everyone—me and your parents who love you—can see that. Heck, I bet Cole took one look at you and saw the devastation still stamped all over you. It's time to forgive yourself. It's time for you to *live*, and not for me, but because at the very gosh darn bare minimum, it's what Hilary woulda wanted for you, despite everything else."

Ha. Now that was just false. And how dare she…

"Hilary would have wanted to still be *alive*, Marley. And she would have wanted me to be the one who ran in front of that truck."

"For about a day, but don't be foolin' yourself. She was too damn sweet to hold a grudge and she woulda forgiven you both in time. Cole forgave himself, heck, her *family* forgave him. Hilary woulda done it. My question is…why can't you?"

Because I didn't deserve forgiveness. Hilary's if she was capable of giving it, Cole's or her family's or even my own parents.

I struck the match and set it against the kindling. I took that first step. I wasn't some innocent bystander or a naive girl who got swept away with childish emotions.

I lit the match and burned my little world to the ground.

"You don't know everything, Marley."

"I know seven years is long enough. I know in the Bible, God uses the number seven as the number to signify completion. Seven feasts. Seven churches. Seven days to create the world He gave us to enjoy. Lots more examples I can give you. Now, for seven years, you've wallowed and carried a burden that ain't ever been yours to pick up, but you done it. And it's been long enough. It's time to finish killing yourself with it and start something new."

"With Cole," I assumed, and it came out with a bite in my tone, but my nerves were itching beneath my skin and Marley's hits were cutting deeper than the dog scratches slathered with bacitracin on my arm. She was wrong. Dead wrong about a lot of things.

Cole didn't storm into her house that first day, take a look at me, and see my devastation. He looked at me and saw *his* destruction.

He might have been feeling bad about it now, but that didn't mean he'd ever see me any other way.

We'd *always* go back to what started us.

"You and Cole were meant to be, and I knew that long before you two probably considered it. I didn't bring you back here to take care of me and hook up with him if that's what you're thinking. I did it because I knew you needed it. You needed to face your past before you can be free from it, so yeah. It'd be nice if you and Cole could find your way back to each other—"

"We were never together—"

"Not anywhere outside that boulder you two don't think I know anything about, but you were something even if you hid it, and I saw it plain as God's love for me. But fine, you two don't work out, okay. I'll be at peace knowing you're *healed*, precious girl. And that's more important to me than anything."

"You're a stubborn old lady. You know that?"

"I'm a woman who's usually right. Ain't nothing stubborn about it."

God, I loved her.

A dog barked in the distance, growing louder and it didn't take a genius to know who the dog was or who it belonged to.

"Bongo's coming," I muttered.

"Name fits him. Crazy and bounces all day long. And I bet he's not alone, so I'm gonna head back home. You deal with the dog and that owner of his, yeah?"

"I'll walk you."

"No need." She raised a hand and started shuffling away. "Know these woods like the back of my hand." She coughed into said hand and paused.

"Marley—"

"Stop worrying, precious girl. At least about me. You got bigger fish to fry."

By fish she meant dog and quarterback. They appeared through the path, the sun shining on them making Cole look even more like a superhero and Bongo like the crazy bouncing dog Marley called him.

"Marley. Need a hand?" he called out as she shuffled toward the path to her house.

"Not the one who needs help today, Cole, but I'm sure my time will come."

He frowned, full lips pushing out on his tanned face before he chewed on the inside of his cheek and glanced back at me.

"What's that about?" he asked once her silhouette was no longer visible in the trees.

Bongo ran straight to me, and ran circles around my leg, effectively trapping me from escape unless I wanted to trip over him.

"She's putting me in my place, is all."

"What place is that?"

Like I was telling him. If Marley got her way, which I refused to give her, my place would be in the man's lap. Or arms. Or home.

I shuddered at the thought and crossed my arms over my chest. "What are you doing here? Shouldn't you be practicing or something?"

There wasn't a day he didn't. Not in high school and I doubted that changed now.

"Tuesdays are our days off. I usually bring Bongo out here for a swim if it's nice." He whistled, grabbed Bongo's attention and when Cole threw his arm out, finger pointed at the water, Bongo took off like a rocket.

I watched him bound into the water without reservation, only freedom, and for not the first time since I whittled down my social circle to animals, was jealous of that.

"He's a good dog."

Heat, not from the sun, approached my side. It radiated off Cole like he wore a furnace with him wherever he went. I attempted to hold my breath, but it was no use. The scent of him invaded me, slithered through the coldest, darkest parts and warmed me straight to my core.

Damn Cole and the effect he always had on me.

"How's your arm?"

"It's fine." I rubbed my other hand over the scratches and flinched when a sting of pain fired from one of the deeper ones.

His dark, penetrating gaze scanned my gaze like he could—or wanted—to heal my arm with a look. It was fine, only a couple scratches had truly bled, and it was partly my fault for using my arm to separate the dogs instead of my hips in the first place.

"Hmm." We watched Bongo dance in the water, run to the edge and bark, gobble it with his mouth before jumping back in.

I should have left, but that *hmm* kept me rooted to the leaf-covered ground. Because I knew he was thinking, and the sadistic side of me wanted to hear his thoughts. Continue to inhale his sandalwood scent when the breeze kicked up just right.

"I guess you didn't end up getting that art history degree you always wanted, then, huh?"

There it was.

The reminder of the history.

The reminder of the future I ran from.

We'd had it all planned.

He'd break up with Hilary over the summer before he left for the University of Tennessee. I'd follow in the fall. We'd go to college together—and live happily ever after.

"Why are you bringing this up?"

Tears burned my eyes I fought back so he couldn't see. But it was Cole, and when it came to us, we always saw deeper than skin surface.

I should have believed Marley earlier, but I'd never tell her she was right.

He probably *did* see the devastation stamped all over me the first time he saw me, despite not showing it.

"Maybe because it's time."

# CHAPTER 13
## EDEN

Time was a fickle thing. Days dragged on, and then suddenly a week was over. The summer crawled and as soon as fall hit, you blinked, and it was Christmas. The coolest winter months drew on and then it was springtime and sunshine and beach trips, and before you knew it you were complaining about the heat and humidity and another year had flown by.

The years since leaving Marysville had all been the same. Another year and another tally. Another day remembering the havoc I wreaked in a small town that was too good for me.

Had I never stepped foot in this town, had my dad never gotten a job teaching in Nashville, things would have been different.

I would have been different—perhaps I would have ended up happy.

I definitely wouldn't have been standing next to Cole, all those years later, listening to him tell me it was time to talk.

"Maybe too much time has gone by to make any talking worth it."

"Maybe," he agreed. His hands settled at his hips, before falling to his sides and ended up crossed over his chest similar to mine. "Maybe not. Worth it to try, though, isn't it?"

"What's the point?" He had his life here, and I was leaving as soon as my favor to Marley was fulfilled.

"What are you so afraid of?" he shot back. He turned to me, just his head, dipping his chin down. My gaze glued on Bongo, even though I could see Cole out of the corner of my eye. Staring at me with a steely look of determination.

Only I had no idea what he was so determined to get.

"I'm not afraid, Cole—"

"Bullshit."

"Fuck you."

"There she is." He spun then, stepped in front of me, blocking my view of Bongo until the only thing I saw was his chest. His hands at his hips and the corded muscular arms that disappeared beneath his black T-shirt with his team's red emblem emblazoned over his left pectoral. His throat bobbed as he swallowed.

"There's the girl with fire who ignited everyone around her."

That fire he implied I had burned in my veins, forcing my hands to curl into fists to keep calm. He was wrong. The only thing I set on fire was the town's beloved Marysville princess. And I burned her well and good.

I stepped back and he followed, not touching, but close enough he could grab me if he wanted, and I knew his reflexes were quick enough he'd be on me before I saw him move.

"Why are you doing this?" That fire in me sparked and burned out, turned to ice.

He had no right. There was no purpose. His timing was suspect with Marley's earlier warning.

Were they working together?

Heal the poor broken girl…?

I shook the thought away. Marley wouldn't do that to me. She wouldn't break my trust or my confidence like that.

"Because you're hurting, and there's something missing from you. The light in your eyes and the snark you always had that left everyone in tears with laughter."

"And why is it any of your concern? Oh wait—it's not. Leave it, Cole. I'm here for Marley and when her time comes, I'm gone, too."

My chin wobbled at that. Just the thought of the world being without Marley was enough to send me to my knees these days, especially with her easy acceptance of it.

"And I'll call bullshit again. You might have come back for Marley, but you had to know you'd see me. Had to know we'd run into each other. You can't tell me I didn't come back to your mind at all."

"You did. Because I kept trying to figure out how to avoid you."

"Liar."

He lunged forward a step, so close his chest brushed against mine as his eyes lit with that gaze I knew he'd saved for his most ferocious opponents. Pinned on me, it was enough to have me shaking in my Birkenstock sandals. And yet still, he didn't reach for me.

"Keep lying to yourself. You've gotten awfully good at it, but don't think I'm going away. Or that I'll back down. We both might have grown, Eden, but I'm still that same man who will fight for what I want. And win at any costs."

"And what is it you want? To drudge up the past for no reason? We've grown, moved on. You have Jasper now…and Selma." I fought back a choke as I said her name. Defeat rang in my voice when I spoke again, shaking my head. "There's no point to this."

"You're wrong." He whistled and Bongo jumped out of the lake, rushing toward us. He shoved his head between our legs and shook, springing water everywhere.

"Damn it, Bongo," Cole muttered, while I jumped back.

The cool water and the space settled over me, allowing me to breathe without my head spinning.

"You're wrong about a lot of things, Eden." He bent and grabbed Bongo's collar, tugged him in the direction of the path to his parents' house. "But you'll learn. And while you're replaying this conversation in your head, keeping you up late at night like I know you will, remember this: You've always been mine."

He slapped his thigh and Bongo followed him.

*You've always been mine.*

He was right. Damn him.

I would definitely be replaying *that* particular parting shot later.

Because he couldn't mean….

No way.

I wasn't his. Never had been. And there was no point in trying to be now.

———

Night settled and the air was thick and heavy. Perfectly fitting my mood, after Marley fell asleep watching *Jeopardy!* and I was able to wake her to get her to bed, I opened a bottle of wine and headed out to the front porch.

Avoiding the backyard and the temptation that would come with the path, I settled into one of the four white wooden rocking chairs. They were as sparkling white as they'd been seven years ago, and I had no doubt who had maintained them along with most of the rest of the property.

The Buchanan men had always spent their weekends helping Marley.

Cole had been right earlier. His last words rang in my ears all day, so much I burned the grilled chicken on the grill, tossed it out and Marley and I had ordered pizza instead.

Not that she complained. She loved an extra meat and extra cheese pizza with cheese stuffed crust. I hadn't had the energy to tell her it wasn't on her diet.

Knowing Marley, she tossed out the option assuming today of all days would be one where I wouldn't correct her or shovel Brussels sprouts in her direction.

I'd eaten them all instead.

*You've always been mine.*

The sentence reverberated in my head like a bass drum, on repeat, like a mosquito you couldn't swat away when you were trying to sleep.

Outside wasn't any better, with nothing but country songs coming from my playlist on my phone, but everything made me think of Cole. The music, the thickness in the air, this house…this place.

I sipped my wine and was turning on my Kindle only to straighten when a shadowed figure appeared at the end of Marley's steep gravel drive. I marginally relaxed as I recognized Kate Buchanan's petite stature. Compared to Cole and Dave, she was tiny, but her presence was no less unsettling as she made her way up the drive, pebbles kicked beneath her feet. When her face finally showed beneath the floodlights of the house, she tossed me a small wave and matching smile.

She hadn't changed a single bit. Not a single new wrinkle, or gray hair on her head had grown in the years since I'd seen her. I still stood from my chair uneasily.

"Mrs. Buchanan," I said, and she laughed, the pretty, playful laugh she always had.

"Stop that. I've been Mama B to you since I met you and I'm no different now."

Something warm fizzled in my fingertips, making me itch to touch her. Hug her, but I stood my ground as she came closer. *Mama B.* I'd missed her.

"How's she doing?" she asked, gesturing toward the house with a nod.

"The same. Nurse is coming next week."

Kate's kind, barely there smile, diminished. "And how are you?"

"Wondering what in the world I'm doing here."

I could be honest with her. I'd always been able to, but the truth of it surprised me, even if she didn't seem shocked by it.

Kate made her way up the wooden steps of the front porch. I expected her to take a seat, but she pointed at the bucket where I'd stashed my wine in ice before coming outside. No sense in making trips inside when I didn't plan on leaving the porch until it was empty.

"Mind if I join you for a glass?"

My eyebrows rose in surprise. I couldn't think of a time when I saw Mama B have a drink. On holidays, if she was feeling fancy, she threw together a Shirley Temple.

"Things change," she said with a shrug. "And some people loosen up over the years."

I chuckled and pushed off the rocker. "Have a seat and I'll go grab a glass."

"Thank you, dear."

A feeling of warmth rushed over me at her words. Mama B had always been kind, but there was a bite to her. She had no problems letting loose when necessary. Fortunately, I'd never been the one in her path.

She settled into the rocking chair next to me like she planned to stay all night and as I went inside to grab her glass, I settled in as well.

She'd leave when she was good and ready, and she'd say what she felt like she needed to.

I was getting used to it.

After grabbing one of Marley's crystal goblets, a pale purple color that was much nicer than the simple wineglass I'd used for myself but figured Kate would appreciate, I headed back outside to find her rocking slowly in her chair, head tipped back, eyes closed.

"Not sleeping, just resting my eyes."

I retook my chair and poured her a glass. The ice cubes clinked and clanked against the bucket and glass bottle and her smile was soft as she opened her eyes.

"Long day?" she asked.

"Long week. Month."

She took the glass from me, running a finger over her violet goblet and brought it to her lips. I watched, still surprised to see her drinking anything with alcohol.

"No matter how many times Cole and Graham have a beer in our house, always strikes me as funny that you kids are old enough to be drinking." So apparently, we were thinking the same things, at least about alcohol.

I grabbed my own glass, curious to know why she was there, patient enough to wait until she pushed too far. "How's Graham doing?"

"Trying to outshine Cole by breaking as many defensive records as Cole did offense."

"So, nothing's changed between them," I said without thinking but when it came to the Buchanan brothers, they were all competition, all heart.

"A lot has changed," she replied, more serious and quieter in a way that sent ice prickling down my neck. "Not the love between them, but everything else."

"The more things stay the same..." I started the saying everyone knew and trailed off.

"That's about right. I didn't come to talk about my boys though."

"No?" I arched a doubtful brow. "That'd be a first."

"No. Just thought you might need some company. Can't be easy being here with Marley, your past in your face every time you turn around."

"I'd be happy to never talk about my past again to be honest."

"Hmm. That's true, although sometimes you can't learn from it if you don't revisit it from time to time."

"Think I've learned enough lessons."

She pressed her lips together and I waited for the questions, the lessons everyone else was so intent on shoving down my throat, but they didn't come.

"Heard you work with animals now. You like that?"

Huh. So that was a surprise. Still waiting for the bomb to drop, I answered carefully. "I love it. Not at all what I thought I'd do, but I found comfort with them. Peace and simplicity."

"I suppose you earned some time with that. Glad you finally found it. Not many people do."

That prickle at the back of my neck spread to my shoulders, down my arms, and I was prepared for a number of things for her to bring up. Hilary. Marley. Definitely Cole.

"Your ma called me the other day."

Not prepared for that. At all. I choked over a sip of wine and wiped it off my lap. "Excuse me?"

She turned her head so she was facing me. "We kept in touch, you know. Or maybe you didn't."

"No...I, um, well, no I didn't."

"She's a good lady, your mom."

She was. The best. Which was why avoiding talking to her hurt but talking to her hurt worse. "I know that."

"Misses you something fierce. Has for years now."

This had to end. I'd already been hit with a one-two punch about Cole earlier. I didn't need my parents brought into this. Not today of all days.

*You were always mine.*

"I don't want to talk about it. Or them."

She stared out toward her own house through the trees, not even visible in the dark.

"They love you, you know. Still do. Always. A parent's love, well it never ends, just grows deeper." She kept talking like she didn't hear me, although Mama B could hear gossip going on in town from all the way out here if she was so inclined. "Although can I tell you something that you can love even more than your own kids? Grand-kids. A whole different way, but man, every time I see Jasper, I think my heart might explode with happiness."

Her smile told her truth. It was brilliant, bright enough to light the entire porch if the electricity went out.

I thought back to the boy I saw on the streets the day I rolled into town. The boy I saw at the game, sitting next to his mom with Kate smiling on from behind them.

"He's cute. Seems sweet." Looked like his dad and made my heart hurt because there was a time I wanted that to be me.

*You've always been mine.*

The words slammed into my chest making me suck in a breath. Why…why did he have to say that?

And why did Mama B need to come over and rub my nose in what Cole had that I never would and say it directly into my face with a sweet smile on hers.

"He is. Jasper's the best thing that happened to this family in a long while, especially Cole. He was hurting, too you know, after all that happened. And I dare say he wasn't quite right again, had lost his purpose and his focus until that boy was put in his arms. Means the world to him. Absolutely everything."

Damn her and her sweetness. Every word she spoke hit me like a barb to the chest.

"And that Selma, you know her. Been trying to lock him down ever since. Probably shouldn't tell you that, gossip and all…" she trailed off, glanced toward the street with her glass at her lips while she took a leisure pull, acting like she hadn't just thrown a bomb the size of Texas into my lap.

*Been trying to lock him down…*

They weren't together. She'd let me believe that. Heck, the photos of them led everyone to believe that.

And that hug at the game…

Been trying to lock him down ever since….

"I'm sure she's a good mom."

"Good as anyone that selfish can be, but can't blame her fully for that, knowing who she comes from. But Jasper's the best thing to happen to us, always will be. And I suppose you're right, she's not so bad. Picks him up and spends the day with him when she's not working at the hospital. Has him while Cole's working and training. Traveling most of the time. She wasn't what I wanted for him, either of them, but they make do."

I snorted, surprising myself. There was no love lost between Kate and Dave and Selma's parents, Irv and Teresa. I'm sure knowledge of the feud of theirs had spread from Nashville to New England due to the fierceness of it. "Y'all haven't made up yet, I take it."

"There's a greater chance of a meteor landing in Marysville." She finished her drink and stood, pushing off the rocker with the grace of a gazelle, but that was Mama B.

Although I was learning she was also sweet when she was manipulating people, like she'd just done to me.

"I should go home. Need that beauty rest and it increases the older you get."

She was fifty if that and looked ten years younger, probably because the only time she drank was when she was trying to get close to people to tell them everything they didn't want to hear.

I didn't let on that I knew what she'd done. She was too sweet to admit it.

Tricky was Mama B. I shouldn't have underestimated her visit.

"Have a good night, Mama B."

"You too, darlin'." She leaned over and brushed a kiss onto the top of my head before brushing her hand down my hair. "Good to see you. Always has been. Always will be."

Pretty sure she skipped down the steep drive, pleased as all could be with herself.

Leaving me alone—thinking of everything she'd said—and everything she hadn't said along with Cole's words still ringing in my ear.

*You've always been mine.*

Well…shit.

Now what did I do with all of that?

# CHAPTER 14
## COLE

Crazy the things that changed once you had a kid. Back in college, my roommates gave me shit all the time for burning toast, even though the toasters had that little dial on them. I once burned a pot of noodles so bad we had to throw out the pot. No amount of football players scrubbing the hell out of the thing was getting them off the stainless steel. Nope, that ramen was cemented to the sides for as long as the earth spun. Probably still were, even in a landfill.

But once Jasper came into my life and I started solo parenting, it became a necessity. While I didn't mind the occasional morning of cereal and milk, I also remembered waking up to the full breakfasts my mom made. Biscuits, eggs, bacon, and toast made to perfection. The whole set up, every morning.

I might have been a young, single dad, struggling to make everything work between football and family and school, but I was damn motivated to make sure Jasper never felt like he'd ever lacked for anything—including mealtimes. So, I learned, and after a boatload of badly burned dinners and breakfasts, and a shit ton of takeout I couldn't keep eating if I wanted to stay in shape for football, I finally found my groove in the kitchen.

I was flipping pancakes, the seats at the kitchen table already set, complete with placemats and syrup out, three different flavors because Jasper was adventurous with his food toppings and frying sausage when he sleepily ambled down the stairs, straight to me in his pajama shorts and a T-shirt with *Paw Patrol* characters stamped all over them.

As he always did first thing in the morning, he came directly to me, rested his head at my hip and wrapped his arms around my thigh. I made sure he was out of the way of any grease spittle and ran my hand down the top of his head to his back.

"Morning, bud."

"Ga-mornin'. Where's Bongo?"

"Sleeping in the living room. Want to watch some shows while I finish up breakfast?"

"Good here." He held me tighter and I took a break from cooking to pick him up, settle him on my hip. At five, he was young enough I could still easily do it, and since he liked it, I did it as much as I could.

There'd come a day, and probably soon, where he'd be calling me *bruh* and handing me a fist to pound instead of wanting hugs and sleepy morning wake-up snuggles. I'd take this for as long as I could get it.

"You sleep good?" I kissed his temple and flipped another pancake.

On top of learning how to cook, I had to learn how to do it with one arm while holding Jasper, so I alternated between the sausage and pancakes easily.

"All right."

Hmmm. Usually he had a lot to say about his day with his mom, but he'd been quiet last night, too.

Hell, maybe they'd gone to the pool, and he was worn out. Or getting nervous about school starting or something. I'd give him the day to see if he snapped back to his normal self by tonight and if not, then I'd hunt down the problem.

I finished up the pancakes and sausage, setting him on the floor with a pat to his backside to get him moving toward the table. "Orange juice or milk to drink?"

"Chocolate milk?" His grin almost had me.

"Nice try. I think there's enough sugar in the breakfast already, don't you?" I pointed to the syrup bottles and his eyes lit up.

"Yummmm." His hand went to his belly, and he rubbed it in circles before climbing into his chair.

Chocolate milk forgotten, I poured him a glass of plain old regular milk. While he started drowning his pancakes in both blueberry and regular syrup, I fried eggs for me.

I was just getting done, flipped off the burner when the doorbell rang.

The clock on the microwave above my stove top told me it was early. I glanced at Jasper, to find his shoulders straightened, pulled back together and his fork hovering before his mouth.

The hell? "Jas?"

"Huh?"

"You okay?"

He shoved his fork into his mouth. "Uh-huh."

The doorbell rang again and this time, woke up Bongo who barked. From the living room, his collar jangled and rattled as he shook his entire body and bounced toward the door.

"That's probably your mom," I told Jasper. "Keep eating, I'll get it."

She had to have gotten off work early, but he wasn't anywhere ready to head out quite yet. The thought of Selma coming early just to spend time with us had my chest tightening before I reached for the front door handle.

I'd learned the other day and started keeping the door locked so she didn't walk through my home like she had the right.

Which meant now, every morning, I opened the door and was welcomed with the sight of her pinched lips, irritation tightening her features.

"He's still eating breakfast," I said through the storm door. "It's gonna be another fifteen minutes before I can get him outside. That okay?"

Selma huffed, hair still perfectly in place and scrubs with no wrinkle in sight even after her shift. "What am I supposed to do, Cole? Wait in my car? Come on—" She reached for the door handle, but I grabbed it from the other side.

"Don't," I scolded her harshly but softly, careful of my tone. "I've told you already, I don't want you just walking into my house. It's not cool. And if you haven't noticed, Jasper hasn't run to the door excited to see you and I'm trying to figure out why he just froze when you showed up, so until I know why that is, you can wait on the stoop, or in your car, but you're early and I've got fifteen, now thirteen more minutes with him alone and I'm taking them."

"Why are you being so difficult?"

"Same thing I could ask you." I closed the door, locked it. She could stew on the front porch for all I cared, angrily tapping her heel to the pavement for the rest of the time I had with him.

No one cut short my time with my son, unless it was my choice, even his mom, who had some super bug up her ass lately and I wasn't going to tolerate it. Or let it affect me.

With a heavy, quiet sigh, I blew out a breath and shook out the tension in my arms. Freaking Selma.

She could go from a decent friend to a brutal enemy in the space of a day and it sucked it was always on her terms.

"Eat up, bud," I said, and ruffled Jasper's hair as I sat down with my eggs.

"Mommy's here?"

"Yep. She's waiting outside for us. Had a call to make." A lie, but one he needed. He glanced down at his plate, lip twisted as if he just realized his pancakes were swimming in sugar and no longer edible.

He stabbed a soaked chunk of pancake and chewed it. Leave it to my kid to suck up everything put in front of him. "She was grumpy yesterday."

"Yeah? Happens sometimes, you know?"

"She yelled at me." His little chin quivered. Typically I'd try to have Selma's back. We'd always agreed, no bad-mouthing each other in front of him. And everyone lost their temper, Lord knows I was guilty of it a time or two.

"She say anything?" I prodded. Because so help me...if she was trash talking...

He shook his head, but his chin was still wobbling.

I didn't push. I wasn't always the winner of the Best Parent of the Year Award and despite my personal frustrations with Selma, I'd trust she was still trying her best to keep her personal feelings toward me away from our kid.

But I'd be keeping a close eye on him, that was for sure.

Ten minutes later, he was done eating breakfast and I'd sent him upstairs to grab his shoes. "Make sure you use the spinny brush on your teeth today, okay?"

No way a manual toothbrush would do the job after the syrup he drank off his plate. Normally I'd help him, but I wanted him occupied.

"Okay Daddy."

I hurried down the stairs, feet pounding and echoing against the wood floors and pushed Bongo away from the front door. "Not yet, Bongo. Wait."

Selma was resting on the front bumper of her Armada when I opened the front door. She glanced up from her phone screen as I opened it and pushed off to come toward me.

"Don't start," I said as she opened her mouth and jumped down the few stairs of my front porch to the driveway. "It's been less than the fifteen minutes I said and you're still getting him earlier than normal."

"I had a long night, and I don't need this from you." She was fire and brimstone and not nearly in the same way Eden could be. Selma's fire was straight from the pits.

"If you've had a long night, maybe Jasper should spend the day with one of our parents so you can rest."

I said it casually, tried to at least, must have failed because her lips pushed out and her eyes narrowed. "Now who's trying to keep the kid away?"

Lord help me from toxic women. "Not doing anything of the sort. If you need your rest or are stressed, I'm trying to help you out. Jasper said you were grumpy yesterday."

"I thought we weren't going to ask about what happened at each other's houses."

"I didn't." Damn, she made my blood boil. Always the victim. *Please.* "But you showed up and he started to cry, so maybe drop the innocent act, Selma. You got a problem with me, you got a problem with anyone or anything, that never gets taken out on Jasper so maybe think about that today. He froze as soon as you rang that door-bell. He started crying as soon as I got back inside."

"Well maybe if you'd let his mom *in*, he wouldn't have been mad."

"Frankly, from the way he behaved, that had shit to do with me not letting you inside, it was all you and however you treated him yesterday. Get your head on straight, Selma. I'm not attacking you. I'm thinking of our kid. Are you?"

I was surprised flames didn't shoot from her mouth, but the front door slammed shut and Jasper was there, Bongo dancing around him.

"Come here, bud." I held out my arm and he ran right to me, hugging my waist again.

Bongo barked from his perch on the front porch.

"Have fun with your mom today, okay?" I bent down and kissed the top of his head. "Love you, kiddo."

"Love you, Daddy."

I glanced up at Selma, and while she'd been pissed as a kicked hornet's nest a minute ago, she smiled easily down at Jasper. "Come on, Jasper. Let's go see what Nana T is doing this morning. Maybe you can help her bake something?"

"Cookies?"

I chuckled, and still grinning, told Selma, "Be warned, he had pancakes for breakfast."

"And a bowl of syrup?" she asked him.

His nose scrunched up in a way that mirrored hers when she was pouting. Fortunately, Jasper's look was cute. "You eat pancakes off a plate."

"Silly me," she teased back.

I hugged Jasper one more time and he let go.

*This* was when we worked well together. At least she was doing it now, which meant I sent him off with his mom feeling better.

Hopefully yesterday was just an off day.

It happened.

At least, I hoped so.

———

I washed the dishes when I went back inside, cleaned up the living room and tossed in a load of laundry before taking Bongo out back for his morning playtime where we were throwing the ball around the backyard. I'd drop a tennis ball into the holder and fling it as far as I could. The ball was back in the trees, and Bongo tossed leaves every which way as he shoved his nose under them, hunting for the ball. He charged at me, ball halfway out of his mouth, fur flying out behind him, and I crouched down so he could bring it to me. At the last second, he weaved, almost making me fall from the surprise. Coming from the front of the house, I heard the purr of a car's engine.

"What the hell?" I muttered, as Bongo took off toward the house. "Bongo!"

Damn it.

I ran after him, barefooted, and prayed I didn't step in any of his dog piles in the yard. The engine noise was too quiet for a delivery truck, but it was rare I had visitors.

Maybe Selma forgot something for Jasper?

I made it to the front corner of the house and spied a silver, 4-Runner parked on the driveway. Bongo's tail was visible from the driver's side, in front of it.

I shoved my fingers into my mouth and whistled. At the piercing sound, he ran back to me, smiling, at least as much as dogs could smile. But our visitor had clearly made him happy.

He barked at me, jumped on his back feet, and ran back to our visitor, who was just standing from the other side of her SUV.

*Eden.*

Her blonde hair was piled on top of her head, and she had the bottom corner of her lip tucked in between her teeth.

"Is Marley okay?" I ignored the rapid kick to my heart at the sight of her looking slightly rumpled in an oversized, wrinkly blue T-shirt and that lip between her teeth. There was only one reason she'd be here. Why would she seek me out.

"She's good. Really good this morning actually. I…um…well… your mom came and talked to me last night."

I stopped in the driveway. Bongo ran and barked between the two of us like he wanted us to play. Eden held up the ball he must have brought her as a welcome present and with a questioning look toward me, she chucked it to the other side of the house.

Bongo took off, giving us about three seconds of quiet.

"What'd you say?"

"Your mom. I was on Marley's front porch last night and she stopped by to talk."

"Okay…" Knowing my mom, it could go one of two ways. Knowing how we left things at the lake yesterday, I could only imagine. "And you came to tell me that?"

She shrugged, looking adorable and lost and so damn sexy in that shirt that swallowed her body—at least her upper half because she still hadn't walked around the front of her vehicle so I could see all of her.

*Please. Please let her be wearing shorts beneath that shirt that would make it look like she had nothing on at all.*

Or maybe not. Probably not what I should be wishing for.

She stepped, then, like she knew the trail of my thoughts and I didn't know whether to curse or thank God as I took in her legs. Long, tanned, and trimmed, they disappeared beneath the hem of that shirt that hung to her mid-thighs.

Not a pair of shorts in sight, but I imagined them perfectly. Tiny, tight little booty shorts, the kind girls wore to work out or for yoga were most likely hidden beneath them. Or frayed cutoff denim shorts, the kind that would only be visible if she was sitting in my truck, bare feet pressed to my dash like I'd so often wanted her all those years ago.

I blinked, shook the runaway train of thoughts away.

She'd sought me out. And I couldn't fathom the reason for it.

# CHAPTER 15
## EDEN

Standing in Cole's driveway, his beautiful, newer home that was large enough for a family but not overly huge for a man whose last contract renegotiation netted him thirty-six million dollars over the course of four years—and yeah, I knew that—it was a miracle my knees weren't knocking together, and I was managing to stay on my feet.

At the sight of him appearing from the back of his house, I almost fainted. Skintight gray T-shirt. White athletic shorts. Bare feet that were hidden in the long grass, but the tan of his arms and the muscle in his arms, the curve of his chest and even his legs were a sight to behold.

Something I'd imagined for years. Dreamed of.

*You were always mine.*

Those four damn words.

They'd kept me up last night. Not even the wine I drank had an effect on me being able to forget them and neither did my sleep. No instead, I was tortured by those words, a dream of Cole hovering over me, that dark hair flopping over his brows as he leaned down above me, that sandalwood scent of his surrounding me while he brushed his thumb over my cheek and bent down, brushing his lips over my cheekbone.

Damn him and his sexy looks and his good guy attitude.

If only he could be a gigantic asshole with a string of red flags in his wake, it would have made it so much easier to avoid him, to not show up here and seek him out.

This might have been the worst decision I'd made since showing up in Marysville—or the best step forward I'd made in seven years.

"Can we talk?" I finally asked.

Cole had gone quiet, clearly waiting for me. He watched me with the same intensity I imagined he stared down opponents across the line of scrimmage.

He waved his arm out, gesturing toward his house, but I wasn't ready for that.

Not to see where he lived exactly, or *how* he lived. If he'd made his house a home for him and Jasper and Bongo or if it was a barren space looking more bachelor pad than family home. No…the inside would wait, but he followed me up the steps to his porch where he had three walnut-stained rocking chairs, so very much like Marley's with a different finish. At the edge of the porch was a water table, filled with boats and a couple Hot Wheels cars. Water that needed to be changed and cups that probably needed a good washing.

"Is Jasper here? I should have asked—"

"Selma picked him up a while ago. You want to come in? Have some coffee?"

"No." Instead I slipped into the farthest rocking chair and gripped the armrests to keep me seated and not launching myself back into my car to flee.

He chuckled, a low gravelly sound that was amused, and I couldn't look at him. Not with the morning sun beating down on my face, already making sweat prickle at the back of my neck. It was going to be *hot* today, and the humidity already made my skin sticky.

Especially not when I probably looked like I was being a coward, but in truth, this was the most courageous I'd been in seven years.

It was terrifying.

I'd either surprised the hell out of Cole, showing up here, or he was as nervous as I was because for the first time since I'd been back, he wasn't the one starting the conversation.

Although, I had shown up at his own home out of the blue—not too unlike what he'd done to me at Marley's—so really, he had this surprise visit coming to him.

"I always thought you and Selma were together," I finally said, and it wasn't how I wanted to start. Wasn't what I wanted to say, but I could be honest with myself.

It was at the top of my list of things I was curious about.

"Always?"

"What?"

"You said always. You've *always* thought Selma and I were together."

Well, that just gave away a lot. Too much. Heat ignited on my cheeks, and I turned back to the sun, hoping he'd think I was flushed from the heat of it instead of embarrassment.

But Cole didn't miss much, never had when it came to me.

"You followed me," he finally said, in a low rumble. "All those years I spent looking for you, wondering where you were, and you were following me?"

There was a tinge of anger to his tone. Like I'd betrayed him by remaining hidden from social media.

I couldn't bring myself to admit it.

Next to me, his rocking chair groaned. "Fucking hell, Eden. Why are you here? And I don't mean Marley. I mean here. My house. My space. To throw one fucking night with Selma in my face?" He scrubbed his hands down his face and groaned. "I don't fucking get you. Not one single bit."

I'd started wrong. I knew I had. I'd come to apologize for being so damn difficult whenever he wanted to talk. I wanted to ask him how he'd moved on. I wanted to ask him how in the hell he was doing so good with his own life when mine was still such a mess.

I'd come to ask him for help. To learn his secrets to getting over the guilt that still buried me every single day. All I'd had to do was sit my ass down in the chair and genuinely ask, *How did you do it?*

Instead, I was still stupidly fixated on the wrong thing. Selma and his son and none of it had anything to do with *us*. "One night?"

He shoved from his chair, the thing rocked wildly from the brute force he used to push out of it and then slammed his fingers to the railing. He gripped it so hard the wood creaked beneath his hands, and he spun, swiping a hand over his mouth.

"That's what you want to know? With all the shit, you want to know about *that*?"

"You have a son, Cole. He's kind of important."

"Damn straight he is." He leaned toward me, his chest heaving and the ferocity in his expression chilled me to my toes. "Jasper's *it*. The one thing. The only thing that pulled me out of that shit. You think, what? I decided to go to Vandy for the *fun* of it? I gave up my full ride to walk on at a lesser school like I wasn't taking a huge ass risk to make it to where I am now? You think I did that for fun? Fuck you, Eden. God fucking damn it!"

He shouted and shoved off the railing, the wooden front porch trembled from the weight of his heavy steps back and forth, the path he wore in the wood scaring me and Cole had only ever scared me in the best ways.

"I'm sorry," I said and stood even though I wasn't sure I could stand. "I'm sorry. But I wanted to know, because I thought—"

"You thought, what? Hilary fucking died and I couldn't have you, so I just said, 'oh well, I'll take this one'?"

"Of course not." My hair flipped out of the holder as I shook my head. We were so severely off the track and like everything else, it was my fault. "I just...I was a wreck, okay? I could barely get out of bed. For *months*, Cole. I ruined everything—my own life. Yours. Hilary's—"

I choked out her name and I still felt like such a low life every time I said it.

"It was a fucking accident!"

"That we caused! *We're* to blame for that, Cole. And you...you just went to school, yeah, a different one, but you just kept on...and so yeah, I followed you. Yeah, I wanted to know what you were doing, *how* you were doing, because I was so fucking destroyed my parents eventually had to drag my ass out of bed one day, forced me to do something because I was refusing to do anything and there you were...throwing passes, making touchdowns...living your life."

"I wasn't fucking living. I was surviving." A low growl rumbled from deep in his chest and he spun, putting his back to me. My hands burned with the desire to go to him, settle my palm between his shoulder blades until he relaxed.

He wouldn't want that from me.

Not now.

"I need a damn minute," he finally said, and glared at me, freezing me to my spot. "You move a single goddamn inch before I get back out here, and I'll hunt you down. You're not leaving until we're finished with this shit."

He prowled toward his front door, and I jumped at the force of his slam.

"Well. Crap," I muttered and took the time to close my eyes, use all those relaxation breathing techniques the therapist my parents forced on me tried to teach me.

They'd helped initially with panic attacks in large crowds but did little standing on Cole's front porch, wanting to kick my own butt for how I handled this and more of Cole's words sliding through me.

*I was surviving.*

Was it possible I'd gotten all of this so screwed up and wrong in my head this entire time?

———

Minutes passed and the step counter on my Apple phone increased to an obscene amount due to the pacing back and forth on his porch before his front door opened. Bongo, long since tired of my frantic back and forth walking, grew tired and collapsed onto the porch. I was on the far side of the porch when I heard the creek of the door, followed by the hinge squeaking on the storm door. Cole came out, hair wildly scrubbed and sticking in every which direction, holding two white coffee mugs.

"This is for you." He set down my mug on the railing and stepped back, leaving twenty feet of space between us but it might as well have been the distance from there to Florida.

My feet hesitated but moved toward the mug and when I had it cupped in my hands, I rested my hip against the railing.

"I'm really sorry. About this. I didn't come for a fight."

He had his mug lifted, and as he blew on the steam billowing from the rim, his eyes barely lifted to meet mine. Dark pools of *nothing* looked back at me. No anger. No frustration and absolutely no life in his eyes before he closed them and took a sip.

"Jasper saved me. Truly."

"I don't need to know about you and Selma."

"There *is* no me and Selma outside of us parenting the child we had. And you're right, it isn't any of your business, but maybe I want to tell you."

I licked my lips and shrugged. He didn't owe it to me, but at least some of my questions would be answered.

He sighed heavily, gestured for the chairs and I took a seat in the far one. This time, he didn't sit next to me, but the one furthest. He turned it and the scrape of wood on wood echoed.

His features were so strong, so tense, but he was still the most beautiful man I'd ever seen in my life. Not what I should be thinking about, so I stared into my mug, pretending my coffee was fascinating.

"It was spring break my sophomore year, and I was a wreck. You think I moved on so easily, you don't know anything. You didn't see me, Eden, and I'm not gonna sit here and scream at you, but damn, that shit pisses me off. You know how much I cared about Hilary."

At the mention of her name, everything in me tightened. My chest was in a vise, slowly squeezing the breath out of me. He *had* cared about her.

"God. That was all supposed to go so differently, you know?" He wasn't looking at me, and I couldn't nod my agreement. The times we'd spent together alone, neither of us wanting to hurt her, finding it harder to stay away. The countdown had been on, and we'd only had four more weeks to go before he left. Maybe it made us cruel to plan any of it.

At my silence, he made a sound that was neither amused nor sad and leaned forward. Forearms to his knees, he cupped his mug and stared at it as if he was reliving the memories in the reflection of the coffee.

"I had still planned on going to Tennessee. Had my bags packed, everything was ready. I'd assured the coach there I'd be good to go, and the night before I left, I couldn't do it. Couldn't sleep. Couldn't eat. I was pacing my room and it was the middle of the night when I stormed into my parents' room and told them I wasn't going.

Hilary…God, she'd barely been buried. Her mom had come over so many times, asking what happened. Her brother—he'd kicked my ass."

Nate was two years younger. Had always seemed so much younger and while he hadn't been scrawny when I saw him at the brewery, he was back then, not yet grown into the width of his shoulders and hadn't put weight on his long limbs. He was different now, but back then? I imagined his punches to Cole would have been harmless.

"He did?"

"Showed up one day, absolutely destroyed, screamed it was all my fault and before my parents could calm him down took a swing at me." He huffed and pointed to the corner of his eye. "Got a scar from him. Small, but it's a reminder and I stood there and let him. He didn't do much damage so I guess I can't say he kicked my ass, but he broke his knuckles on my face, split open my lip. Gave me a few bruises on my ribs. Trust me, I took that. Knew I deserved it, too."

Apologies burned on my tongue and stayed there.

"Want to know why I took that from him?"

I didn't. I absolutely did not want to know whatever he was going to say next, not with the way his head tilted in my direction. Sunlight hit him, making that tiny scar I couldn't see before visible. Just a small, crescent moon that held my gaze captive while Cole said, "Because I deserved it, and it wasn't even because of Hilary, it was because I stood there, him screaming at me, devastated at the loss of his sister at my hand and all I kept thinking about was that if you were here, it wouldn't hurt so damn much."

My eyes burned and tears fell before I could hide them, before I could seal up the cage my heart had been wrapped in.

"Trust me, I deserved that beating. So yeah, I didn't go to Tennessee. Everyone thinks I got in at Vanderbilt because I was so fucking destroyed over Hilary, but the truth of it is, she and I were over. I already knew that. I loved her, you know that, too and yeah, I felt like an absolute dick for how that ended…but I was the only one who knew I'd already moved on. I saw my future with the girl I truly loved in Tennessee and you just…fucking disappeared. Bailed on me."

I earned every lash of pain from what we did to Hilary. "I fucked up—"

"We did."

That huff again. God, I wanted to know what that sound meant. He shook his head and pushed it against the back of his chair. Head against the back, eyes closed. Shaking his head, he frowned.

"That's where you're still wrong, Eden. You were the good one. The one who wanted to wait. The one who wanted to do right by her and not hurt your friend. I was the selfish asshole who took what wasn't mine to have when it wasn't mine to have it. I made that decision, that step. I talked you into it and trust me, I still remember that night so damn clearly. Wake up thinking about it, work out thinking about it. Everyone thinks I'm the fucking town hero, the guy with the tragic backstory, but I'm not the hero. Never was. I forced you into that kiss that night, selfish as fuck, taking whatever I wanted and not willing to listen to you. Trust me, if we're comparing who's to blame, Hilary's death is at my hands. Not yours. Not when you tried to talk me out of it, and I was too fucking selfish to think any different."

# CHAPTER 16
## COLE

*od*, that killed to say. So many damn years I pushed that down, and sitting here, next to that girl I saw myself with all those years ago at Tennessee, waiting until we could be together, waiting until I had everything I wanted, and I'd just laid that truth in her lap, I couldn't find any regret for spewing it all to her.

She *had* to know. Had to know that even if she didn't believe it enough then, didn't trust in it, that was exactly how I saw our future headed. *She* was why I couldn't make myself go to Tennessee.

I hadn't just taken a life, I'd lost *everything* that meant anything to me outside of football and there was no way I could step foot onto that campus, do my job as a player, and not spend every single second wishing I had Eden with me.

That wasn't what happened though, and I'd had to come to terms with it. Those terms simply didn't happen until Jasper.

Next to me, Eden was silent. She had no rebuttal, no argument as to why it was really her fault, why she was to blame, and I couldn't see how she'd still think that after everything I said.

And my story wasn't even done yet.

"I was a wreck those first couple of years, Eden. Barely passing classes, doing the bare minimum because all I had was football, and I'd finally started my sophomore year. Everyone looked at me and thought I had everything and kept talking about how strong I was after everything I went through. Trust me, every damn time that feel-good hometown boy hero bullshit comes on the air it makes me want to puke. I'm so…so fucking over that crap, but back then it was worse. I'd helped lead Vanderbilt to their first winning season in seven years. We had a bowl game. And I had *nothing*. Nothing good anyway. Selma called one night, crying."

At the mention of Selma, her breath hitched, and I couldn't bring myself to open my eyes. That night had been a mistake from the beginning. One broken man, a crying, manipulative girl. I should have seen it all earlier but the drinks and the guilt and my own selfishness to want to *forget* Eden opened the door to me making decisions I normally wouldn't have.

"She was upset. Said she was missing Hilary and wanted to talk to someone who knew her like she did. Said she felt like everyone was moving on and people were forgetting her, and I gotta tell ya, hearing that was like a kick to the balls because no one should ever forget Hilary, you know?"

I peered my eyes open and glanced at her. Eden shook her head and whispered a quiet, "No. She was too good for that."

"Exactly. So, I met up with Selma at a bar near her nursing school. We drank. At first, we talked, shared all the stories about us growing up and it was *good*. It felt good to talk about her and laugh…I needed to remember some of those good times, too."

Eden was silent but watching me closely. She flinched when I mentioned the good times and it made me want to ask why that hurt, but she'd only been here a year. Maybe she felt like all of her good memories with Hilary were tainted and I couldn't blame her for that either.

"I-it was one night. And I'd regret it, one hundred and twenty percent if it didn't give me Jasper. I was at school when she called me a month later and told me she was late. And that…I swear, Eden, the thought of her being pregnant, me becoming a dad, it was the switch I needed to pull my shit together."

"That's good," she said quietly and turned back to the tree-filled front of my property. "It's good you had that."

She made it sound like she still didn't have that, and what a waste.

"Did you ever think of making it work with Selma?"

There was no pain in her voice this time, no accusation. I couldn't fault her for the question.

"No." I shook my head. "That first week, maybe, but never after. To this day, I don't know if she tried to trick me into getting her pregnant so she could have me, and that was why I never would have gone to her. I never would have known the truth or trusted her."

Plus, there was the fact I'd always still loved the woman next to me, even if I couldn't say that about her now—unequivocally—back then, I'd never wanted anyone else even when I couldn't find her.

"Do you think she did? I mean…"

"It doesn't matter. Jasper's worth it, every second, every minute of the day. And for the most part, we co-parent well together."

Outside of our latest argument, anyway.

"She makes it look like you're together. On social media and stuff."

She'd looked that far into me. She would have needed to go to Selma's page to see all of that because I rarely let her tag me in photos she posted of the three of us.

"I let her. I don't care what people think about us together, and it's easier. Maybe it's wrong, maybe it leads her on, I don't know, but I've never been able to find it in me to care."

I let that settle, let her work the truth out in her mind. However long she'd looked into me, however long she'd been so damn close and so far away at the same time, still ticked me off, but there was still more I wanted to know.

More I'd *always* wanted to know about Eden.

"What about you?"

"What about me?" That coffee mug that hadn't been drunk through my story found its way to her mouth. Her grip on it tightened, like she needed the grounding.

I didn't miss the way she cringed as she sipped it in her race to ignore me, that shit was probably cold by now, but no way was she running from this.

"Don't bullshit me, Eden. You know what I'm asking. I don't have the privilege of being able to stalk you online, remember?"

"I didn't stalk you."

I arched a brow as she glanced at me. Not at all the point and she knew it, but avoidance was apparently her new favorite character trait.

She shrugged as I stayed silent. She wasn't getting out of this, not after everything I'd told her. If she needed time, she could ask for it. Of course, I'd give that to her, but allowing Eden to keep running and hiding wouldn't happen.

"I said earlier that I was so upset, I couldn't get out of bed."

"You did."

"Well, it went on for months. I'd pulled my acceptance to Tennessee the day we left town. We were in Florida. My dad was getting ready to start his new job. And I just…couldn't move. I refused to enroll anywhere, not even community college. And then one day my parents said I had to do *something*. So my mom made me shower, and we got in the car and drove. She drove past the community college, past restaurants where I could work. She'd scoped out the entire city and just drove past places and told me she'd stop when I told her to.

"There was a sign for an animal shelter, and I thought of all the lost animals, abandoned, depressed. And I don't know…" She shrugged, stared into her cold coffee like she was debating taking another drink just to avoid this conversation and then peered out into the trees. "I felt their pain, I guess."

"So you went in?"

"That first day I was pretty sure my mom thought I wanted to adopt something, and I'm pretty sure she would have gone along with anything that brought a smile to my face, so we filled out forms, and we got to go to the back to look at the animals. And there was one dog, laying against the metal cage, his whole body pressed to it. I just went and sat by him outside. My mom had gone back out front when I didn't move from my spot and two hours later, that dog and I were just sitting there. Both of us alone, but it broke my heart to leave him. So, I went back, and kept going back and after a couple weeks, they asked if I just wanted to start volunteering."

"Did you adopt the dog?"

"No." She shook her head, and a blank expression slipped over her. "I didn't want to risk loving anyone and losing them, so I never adopted any."

But she'd loved them and lost them all the same. She couldn't fool me even with her stoicism. Eden had always loved deeply. She'd done it with Hilary, and her loyalty to her, me in the quiet ways she was allowed.

She stretched her legs out and rocked in her chair. "Eventually I'd been there long enough, I realized the only time I felt *okay* was when I was with animals. And there were so many who needed help. I couldn't adopt them, couldn't take them into my home, but I could help in other ways."

"So you became a vet tech."

"It was the quickest program I could find that I could finish."

"And your parents? Why don't you talk to them anymore?"

A muscle jumped in her jaw. "I talk to them."

Maybe. But she knew what I meant. They'd been *close*. She adored them. Hell, Angie driving around the city waiting for Eden to make a choice spoke of the love she had for her daughter.

I amended my question. "Why aren't you close with them?"

She shrugged and picked at the hem of her T-shirt. "Don't know why, really. They call all the time, but it hurts to talk to them, and it hurts when I don't, so I just…don't."

"Why?"

"They keep expecting more than I have to give, I guess."

Like what? Their daughter to be *happy*? It burned on my tongue to ask. To push and prod for more, but her skin was paling with every question I lobbied in her direction and soon she'd shut down. Run.

I'd let it go, for now.

Her chair creaked as she rocked. I was finally starting to relax, to settle into her presence without the need to rehash everything when she spoke again.

"You're wrong, you know."

"Very rarely, actually."

She huffed. From the corner of my eye, her lips curled up into the mere hint of a smile. I'd take it.

"That night. It wasn't you."

"Eden—"

It one hundred percent absolutely was.

"I went looking for you. Was talking to Hilary and Selma and a handful of other girls surrounding the keg that night and all of them were talking about college. Hilary was going on about how she'd miss you, all these clothes she'd already bought to wear to your games, and how you two had made plans to see each other—"

"I hadn't agreed to any of those."

"Didn't matter if you did or not. I'd been drinking. Got so *mad* at that. She had you. She had the boy I couldn't have and wanted so desperately that it didn't matter to me anymore."

Her eyes turned to me and the pale blue in them turned haunted, so eerily blank a shiver rolled down my spine. "You think you made that first move, but I went *searching* for you because I was so damn sick of having to stand there and listen to her talk about how awesome you were when I loved you so much. I *wanted* you. That night. Because screw Hilary and her plans and her dreams. And I didn't give a shit if she caught us or not. If someone saw us and told her." She laughed, but it was so brittle it made my ears hurt. "I might have had a spark of conscience the moment I saw you, but I was just a jealous, seething girl. I was the *other woman*, Cole, and if I had done the right thing all those months earlier, kept my space, never gone back to that damn boulder—or to you—*none* of that would have happened."

Well, obviously. Had we stayed away from each other, none of it would have happened. We'd been kids. Hormonal teenagers who thought consequences were useless, imaginary things parents talked about and assumed would never happen to us. It wasn't that I hadn't cared about Hilary or didn't still grieve her occasionally. I still thought of her. I remembered her. There were times, especially still being in this town, I'd drive by a place we went and have a memory that made me smile. Or go home and want to sit in a dark room and miss her. Feel the weight of my own actions.

But I'd healed. And like my dad had said, I'd done it with a village around me.

Eden had no one…or hadn't let herself have anyone.

"You said you wanted to know how I moved on. How I let it go."

Her cheeks had flushed from her rant, from her own guilt, and she was still breathing heavily when I asked the question. If she'd been waiting for me to continue the argument, which of us was *more* at fault that night, I didn't have that fight in me.

"Yeah," she finally sighed and sank back into her chair.

Clasping my hands together, I leaned forward in my own chair and met her gaze. Gorgeous, light blue eyes blinked as I licked my lips and prepared to tell her the not-so-secret healing tactic. "I apologized to her."

A rapid three blinks fluttered her lashes and her lips parted. "What?"

"That's it." I threw my hands out. "It sounds easy, but it wasn't. I went to the cemetery one day, a couple beers I stole from my dad's garage fridge when Selma had just learned we were having a boy. I thought of how everything was wrong, and I was getting everything I'd wanted but it was all with the wrong people and in the wrong places, and I just...I needed to talk to someone who would let me talk."

It'd been brutally hot. I needed to head back to Vanderbilt for our off-season summer training where our coach made us brutally run suicides up and down a soccer field for weeks before we could get pads on. Trying to figure out how I was going to do football, remain a student, all while I'd be having a son in five months' time had left me more lost than I was before.

"I went to the cemetery, and I plopped my ass down. I didn't say anything for a long time, but I cried. And then I laughed because I remembered Hilary saying if someone was crying, she had to cry too, so they weren't alone and I imagined her crying in heaven, sad for me when she was probably perfectly fine, and I *talked* to her. Told her everything. I told her about kissing you before I took her back, I told her how I treated both of you so horrible. I don't know, I got it all out. Everything I'd carried deep inside for so long and by the end, I told her I was sorry. That it ended with us the way it had, that I hadn't been the kind of my man my parents had raised me to be. That I hadn't been honest with her for so long because I couldn't bear the idea of seeing her hurt."

Tears ran down Eden's cheeks as I talked and tried to fight back the fist in my gut. A tear gathered at her chin and before I could stop myself, I reached out and brushed it away.

That same damn familiar, and old, sizzle of electricity sparked against my thumb as I did, and I brushed it away before I did something more stupid.

"The truth is, Eden, we both screwed up and we screwed up huge. Hilary hadn't deserved any of that from either of us. That night was a mess from beginning to end. But we didn't *kill* Hilary. She got pissed and ran straight into the curve on a road and was hit by a truck. And that sucks. It's horrific and it shouldn't have happened and if we hadn't kissed, she'd probably still be here. That's all true. We played our parts in a horrible, senseless accident because we were too young and naive to consider the ramifications of our actions. I'm sorry for it every day, but my life didn't have to stop because hers did. And it won't. If anything, *trust* me, it's made me a better man. A better person and human in general because now I *do* understand the consequences of treating people poorly."

She nodded, and her throat worked as she swallowed. Her eyes slid toward the trees, and she rolled her lips together.

The silence was peaceful, trees rustling with the breeze, the distant sound of a woodpecker somewhere pecking away at a tree and other birds chirping at each other. Small animals made the leaves crinkle.

Finally, she turned back to me and with a downward twist of her lips and a sad, pathetic little shrug, asked, "So what happens now?"

My resistance, fraying by the minute, snapped. I did the stupid thing. The thing I'd wanted to do for seven years.

Leaning forward, I brushed my thumb over her cheek again, leaned in, and kissed her.

## CHAPTER 17
### EDEN

His lips were on me before I knew what he'd done, and I froze. And then my eyes closed, and I sank into the warm feel of Cole's lips against mine, the brush of his scruff against my cheek. The scent of his sandalwood cologne or whatever he used that made him smell so damn good.

Kissing Cole was instinct. For seven years I'd dreamed of the feel of his body on mine, and since returning to Marysville, this was the first time I'd felt like *home*.

Until a rustling sound came from somewhere and reality crashed back into me.

I shoved back into the chair, yanking my mouth from him and turning away.

God.

He shouldn't have done that.

*We* shouldn't have done that.

The story of us.

"I..."

"I'm not sorry," he whispered, and his voice was gravelly. There was a hitch in it as I felt the weight of his stare on me. I couldn't bear to look. I looked down to the porch, unable to face him. One look at his lips, glistening wet from one and I'd crumble in my resolve that this was a very, very bad horrific idea.

"I need to go."

Except he was still bending over my chair and caging me in and there was no way I could leave until he moved.

And he truly needed to *move* before I did something irreparable like trace him and lean forward, taking his mouth this time and slip my hands behind his neck, lace my fingers together and pull him against me. My fingers burned with the desire to do just that. I curled them into fists to prevent myself. In my peripheral, his hand rose, and I flinched.

He stopped, and I closed my eyes. "Stop."

"All right." He stood, and my chair swayed back and forth as he stepped away and blew out a breath. "I won't apologize for that, though."

Of course he wouldn't. Cole rarely apologized for taking what he wanted…except he had. *Once.*

*I apologized.*

It couldn't have been that simple. Not that Cole had made it sound easy, but he just apologized to a dead girl, and everything was copasetic again?

But no, of course it wasn't, because he'd had Jasper. His son was who brought him back, gave him something to fight for, to accomplish his goals, and I was so damn happy he'd had that.

"I need to go," I repeated because while he'd given me space there wasn't much room to maneuver around him, and it wasn't just that he was large and took up his space, it was fear that if I stepped close, I'd be sucked right back into him.

Dangerous and stupid is what that was.

"I need to get to the field anyway for practice, so I'll let you leave with us not talking about that, but we'll talk again. Soon."

As if I wasn't given a choice in the matter.

As if I could handle the conversation he most likely had in mind. Especially if it involved more of *that.*

"Right," I whispered, and licked my suddenly parched lips.

Cole's gaze fell to my mouth and lingered, before slowly rising. "You going to be able to get back to Marley's okay?"

"Yeah." I hoped. I was still rattled, would spend the rest of the day thinking and replaying every word he spoke to me. Not to mention the *kiss.*

"Good. Come on, Bongo."

He rose from his lounging sleep on the front porch and yawned, licking his mouth as he rose and stretched.

"I didn't tell you this, but I really love your dog." I couldn't help but smile down at him. Bongo must have known I needed the touchstone to stay grounded because he came to me, rubbed his head against my knee so I could bury my hands in his soft fur.

*There.* Exactly what helped settle my still racing heart.

Cole turned and headed down the stairs of his porch, but Bongo stayed at my side, tail gently swaying in the air while he stayed close enough for me to keep petting him.

"You don't have to walk me to my car."

"I know," is all he said without looking back at me, and yet he did it, anyway.

Cole stood by the driver's side until I met up with him, Bongo staying at his side and taking a seat. "We'll talk again."

Of course we would. Cole wouldn't leave this unfinished. Not now that he knew how badly I was still struggling. Not after he'd done what he just did.

I opened the door to my 4-Runner and set a foot on the running board. I pushed up, looked at both the gorgeous man and sweet dog over my door. "See you at BarkTown?"

He chuckled, lips kicking up into a full grin. "Probably, Eden. Probably."

I returned the grin, slid into my seat, and shut the door. Both of them stayed focused on me, only Bongo looked a little cuter with his tongue lolling out of the side of his mouth as I turned the key I'd left in the ignition and did a three-point turn in his large driveway. I'd been so consumed with talking to Cole this morning I hadn't fully taken in the beauty of his large, white, house with black shutters and door and four-garage when I arrived, but as I backed up, my eyes stayed glued to the vision of Cole and Bongo, man, with arms crossed over his chest as I pulled out and Bongo happily sitting next to him, imagining him in that beautiful, newer house and what he'd done to hopefully, turn it into a home for him and his two boys.

Neither man nor beast moved, and as I turned in his driveway before hitting the main road, they disappeared from my view, but I had no doubt they stayed there long after I was gone.

Cole probably wondering what in the hell I was going to do now.

If only I knew myself.

That one kiss made me feel more like any home than I'd had in the last seven years.

———

No way could I return to Marley's like Cole assumed I was headed.

I'd walk into her house, and she'd probably scent Cole on me somehow and not only know exactly where I'd been, but what we'd done. No, I needed time to compose myself even if she'd be wondering where I was.

I'd taken off so quickly after breakfast and hadn't given her any explanation but when I woke up that morning, I could only think of Cole. Needing answers.

I got them all right. Along with a host of new questions and more uncertainty.

He'd kissed me.

*Why* would he do that?

Then there was still Hilary and all he'd said.

*I apologized.*

Right, because it was that simple.

Go to Hilary and apologize but what good were apologies when the person I needed to apologize to couldn't give me forgiveness. Manufacturing it seemed like the easy way out.

Unlike Cole, I'd never had anyone walk into my life giving me some deeper, more meaningful reason to put it behind me. Was that why it stuck to me like an oil spill? Covered and coated every part of me, suffocating me with the weight of it and every breath I took?

After this long, I couldn't just scrape it off, fling it to the side and go about my day like nothing had happened. Like that night hadn't irrevocably changed me forever.

Like that night hadn't ripped out a piece of my soul I could never get back.

I spotted the park up ahead as I drove through town, the same park where only a week ago I'd seen Jasper for the first time, and pulled in. It was empty now, but I had no doubt as the day wore on, it'd be filled with kids his age, boys and girls, running and screaming without a care in their tiny little lives.

Oh the envy I could have for them.

The swings beckoned me, and after grabbing my keys and phone and slipping them both into the hip pockets of my yoga shorts, I trudged through the rubber-looking mulch and plopped down. My back to town, hills in the distance and rooftops of homes peeking out above them, I leisurely pumped my legs, felt the cold steel of the chains in my hands as I started moving. The sun was behind me, heating my back.

I'd need to go to BarkTown after lunch, but other than that, my only agenda was to be there for Marley. In her house where the memories wouldn't cease. Where, if it was quiet enough, I could hear Hilary's laughter from the back patio as she sat on Cole's lap around Marley's fire pit.

God, they'd been so cute together. So adorable my teeth hurt as I got to know them more.

Hilary was tasked with showing me around the school that very first day and at lunch, I'd gone to ask her about the boy I'd met the week before when her large, round eyes had widened even farther, and she'd gotten so giddy. *"Here comes my boyfriend. He's amazing. The best quarterback in the state, but he's also super nice. Just awesome. You have to meet him…"*

I'd turned around and had almost had to pick my jaw up off the floor as Cole strolled into our high school's small cafeteria, plastic tray in one hand, shoving another guy playfully away from him with his free hand.

*Some nice guy,* I'd thought. The guy who had kissed me less than seventy hours earlier smiled at Hilary, so openly and easily, I'd worried about throwing up at his feet.

Because then those eyes of his I got lost in earlier on his front porch had turned to me—and turned to shards of ice. Hard. Pointed.

Accusing me of doing something wrong when I was the innocent one.

...and it'd never stopped me or made me start doing the right thing after.

Seven years later, and I was *still* taking all the wrong steps.

How in the hell did I fix it now?

# CHAPTER 18
## EDEN

"Do you have plans tonight?"

The question came from Sarah, owner of the Waggin' Tails Rescue. She'd stopped into BarkTown to pick up one of the boxer mix puppies to take them for a home visit and was returning Lucy to the doggy daycare, walking toward me and wrapping the pink leash around her hand.

"No. Not really."

I didn't end up coming into BarkTown until after four. After I left the park and went to check on Marley, she and I both fell asleep in the living room for an hour. I'd made her lunch, and packed up leftovers for her for dinner to reheat since I didn't end up getting to the doggy daycare until after four.

"Nora called. She and I are meeting up at McLaughlin's for some dinner. Want to join us?"

"McLaughlin's?"

"Yep. Irish pub, right around the corner from the Buckin' Brews. It just opened last year, and the food is incredible. It's always so busy on the weekends Nora and I usually go during the week."

"Oh." Marley would be fine for dinner and a night out? I wasn't sure if I could go back to the walls of her house with its pasts and stew in the memories of this morning, but my last trip out to town for dinner hadn't gone so well, either. "Um. Maybe for a little while."

"Awesome. I'll see you there, in thirty?"

"I'll meet you there."

Forty minutes later, I was walking up to the pub. I must have had tunnel vision last weekend when I was at the brewery because McLaughlin's was highly recognizable and very Irish in origin with the name in green and white above the dark wood doors. Two Irish flags bookended the name and Celtic music filtered out onto the sidewalk before I was out of my car.

The inside was dark, and while there was a hostess right when I walked in, I excused myself from needing her assistance. Nora was in a booth past the bar and near the back of the narrow restaurant. It was just the back of her head, but considering she was the only woman alone, and most of the other tables were empty, she was easy to spot.

"Hi," I greeted her, and she slid over to make room for me.

"Good to see you. Come on in. Sarah's in the restroom."

"Awesome. This place is cozy."

"Best bangers and mash I've ever had are served here. You'll love it."

What I was loving was how welcoming Nora had been, and I supposed now I could add Sarah to the list.

She joined us and we placed our drink orders, but I was sold on the bangers and mash, so when our drinks arrived, we all ordered three servings of the food Nora swore by.

Soon, conversation drifted to Nora's day at the vet clinic, being called sweetheart by over a half dozen men who brought their animals in and asked if they were looking to hire a male veterinarian to receive the same standard of care they had been.

She rolled her eyes, but none of us were surprised. Some men still had difficulties realizing a penis didn't make them more capable of doing most jobs. "It's just annoying," she said. "And that they ask what qualifications I have or if my grandpa just left it to me because I was family. And really, I'm not even sure who that's more insulting to. Me for treating me like I'm not smart enough to get a decent education or my grandpa, who they're basically saying is dumb enough to give a vet clinic he started and poured his heart and soul into for forty years to someone who has no idea what they're doing."

Sarah and I chuckled, but she had a point.

"How did Lucy's home visit go?"

"It went well, but they always do. I'm not sure if she's the right fit. They strike me more as couch potatoes than owners who know the true rambunctiousness of a boxer."

"That's gotta be hard." So many owners didn't do research into the kinds of dogs who would fit their family and lifestyle long term. They just wanted the cute one, or the popular one, and then a few years in, they decided the dog was too much work. I'd seen it again and again and it was always so sad.

"I know. But the home is safe and clean, and they really seem to be animal people. There's only so much we can do especially with the number of animals we have now. If we get too many more, we'll have to ship some to other rescues and that's always hard because then we lose control of placement."

"I'm sure so many of those placements are a rock and hard place for you," Nora said, equally knowing.

"Enough of that." Sarah flipped her hand in the air and took hold of her drink as the server returned and slid our dinners onto the table. After ensuring her we didn't need anything else, I inhaled the incredible aroma. Potatoes. Green beans. Sausage. It was such a simple, stick to your bones, kind of meal, and yet it smelled delicious. "No more work talk. I need to know what's going on with you and your foray into the dating app world."

Nora snorted. "Please. I've barely checked them in the last week."

"Dating apps?"

"Yep. Nora here decided a couple weeks ago she was going to start downloading them. She needs a man, and I'm happy to encourage all ridiculous ways of finding them."

"She made my prompt be 'do you want an insult or a compliment?' Except what she forgot is that men get *super* touchy when insulted by a female. I've been called a bitch more in the last two weeks than in my entire thirty years."

"Please. That's why you do it. Man can't take a joke and it's an immediate red flag. Right?" Sarah's brows, blonde and perfectly sculpted, arched in my direction.

"I wouldn't do it. I don't really date."

"Why the hell not?" Sarah gasped like I'd personally offended her.

"Ignore her," Nora mumbled around a bite of her potatoes, covering her mouth. "She thinks just because she's happily engaged everyone needs a man in her life, but she forgets that the reason she and AJ work so well is because he lives eight hours away."

"That's not true. I can't wait until we can live in the same town, but that's not possible right now. I'm just saying the fact we only see each other every three to four weeks makes the sex incredibly hot. And *that's* what I want for everyone."

My thoughts immediately drifted to Cole. Hot sex would definitely be his strength and I didn't even need the kiss to know it. Everything about him screamed confidence and control. But *that kiss...*

"Ohhh," Sarah sang, and her finger was pointed at me, spinning in a circle. "Now *that* is a look from a female who knows exactly what I'm talking about."

Awesome. I didn't need my face showing anything. I cleared my throat and tried to force down my runaway thoughts with a sip of my white wine.

Besides, Sarah didn't know me. No way could she read my *faces.* "Nonsense."

She was also wrong. I wasn't sure I'd ever had that kind of hot sex.

"Leave her alone, Sarah. Not everyone is as sexually free as you."

"Shame," she muttered and dug into her green beans. After she chewed, she thankfully refocused on Nora. "So, the dating apps. Don't think I didn't see you change the subject on me."

"They're pointless. At this point, I really do think I'm going to be the woman who ends up alone with ten cats except in my case I'll also come with four dogs, two birds, and a ferret."

"Ew on the ferret." Sarah cringed.

"Too far?"

"Yes. And you're lying. If you have ten cats, you'll obviously have at least that many dogs."

"Of course." Nora laughed. "My bad."

She lifted her hands in surrender and I took a moment to enjoy their friendship. It'd been a long time since I'd sat and ate dinner, surrounded with drinks and smiles and good food and enjoyed myself.

Too long, probably.

Since it was obvious Nora and Sarah had become close friends in the few months since Nora moved to town, I settled into my dinner, laughing along with them, but in the background. There wasn't much I could contribute even as they tried to include me. I hadn't made a lot of friends in Florida, in school or afterward. My choice. I couldn't even say I would have been a good friend to anyone had the invitation and opportunity been there.

For too long I'd been focused solely on myself, my grief and my past.

Maybe it *was* time to start putting that behind me. Because this? Dinner with friends and teasing and laughter—I was starting to think I desperately needed that again.

It was after our dinner plates were cleared and we all ordered another round when Sarah gently cleared her throat in a way people did when they were trying to get someone's attention.

"Yes?" I asked, and while she'd been laughing and vibrant with Nora, her features had softened.

I buckled up and waited for her question.

"I don't mean to pry—"

"So don't," Nora cut in.

Sarah ignored her. "But well, that thing with you and Nate last week. And after you left, there was talk. You said you used to live here, but isn't Nate younger?"

I should have known the question would come at some point. I'd hoped Nora's disdain with gossip would help, but I wasn't that lucky.

I glanced at the table. Too bad I didn't have any more food I could shovel into my mouth.

"I lived here for a year, my senior year. I was friends with Nate's older sister. Hilary?" Her name got stuck in my throat, but I forced it out. Jagged cuts in my throat remained behind.

"Oh." Sarah's lips formed a perfect circle. "I'm sorry. I didn't realize…"

"Why just that one year?" Nora asked. "I mean, that must have been hard moving to this town in your last year of high school and everything."

"My dad is, or was, an economics professor. He got passed over for the department lead chair at the university where he worked, and well, there were other things going on at that university and he wanted to do something new. Nashville College had a short-term, one-year opening while they looked for a full-time professor and since he didn't know where he wanted to end up, he took the job down here. He was eventually hired at a university in Pensacola, so they moved there after graduation."

"And you went with them?"

I'd planned on following them and going to Florida State or Miami, had even been accepted once my dad got the job down there. But then Cole happened, and my acceptance for Tennessee came...

"Yeah. After Hilary..." I clutched my glass so painfully it was a wonder it didn't shatter in my hand.

"So that means you know Cole. Cole Buchanan?"

Sarah asked, and her eyes lit in that way I imagined most women did when he was around.

"I did. Well, do. We were all, well we were close that year."

"What's he like? I mean, there's always talk about him, and I've been introduced to him before and everything, but even when he's around town and hanging out, it's not like anyone approaches him or anything. But still...he's *amazing* at football."

Nora pushed up, reached across the table and gently pressed her fingers to the bottom of Sarah's jaw, snapping it closed. "You're drooling in public."

I chuckled. "Cole's...he's Cole. He's just this guy. I don't know. I mean, we were all friends, and Cole was always great. At football. At school. At being a good friend."

The lie burned the jagged pieces in my throat, and I flinched, taking a sip of my wine. I'd *never* talked about him and in less than twelve hours I'd not only been kissed by him, but now was trying to explain who he was. To me?

To me, he was the guy I could never have and never should have wanted.

He was unattainable. And absolutely perfect.

"I'm sorry," Sarah said, more of a broken whisper. "I shouldn't have asked, but I'm always curious and I don't always think before I ask such questions."

I went to tell her it was okay, I didn't mind, but movement caught my eye nearing my table and then I prayed for the ground to swallow me whole.

"It's amazing you're even bold enough to show your face in town."

Next to me, Nora made a choking sound.

Across the table, Sarah's jaw once again unhinged. She paled as Selma scanned the company with me at the table, almost fearful of what Selma would do to us.

I was determined, for Cole's sake, and Jasper's even if I'd never met him, to do better. Be the bigger person. Selma had always been horrid to me.

"Good evening, Selma. Care to join us for dinner?"

"Like hell I'd ever associate with someone like you, and to hear you talking about Cole like you have the right to? You haven't changed a bit, have you?"

She was wrong. I was a completely different person these days, and more recently even, someone better.

"I think you're the one who still thinks you're the queen bee, Selma, but this isn't high school." I sighed, tired of her, her threats and the hold she thought she had on this town. Her parents might have been a staple, their diner owned in her father's family as far back as his great, great grandparents who helped found the town, but this was Marysville. A mere pinprick in the size of the world. And she didn't own that.

"Go away, Selma."

She turned, stood tall and spine made of steel toward the new voice, and I sucked in a breath.

Nate stood behind her, dark hair a shaggy mess and flopping to the side, and his green eyes, so similar to his sister's, narrowed on her old best friend. He held a white plastic bag stuffed full of Styrofoam to-go containers inside.

"Nate," she said with a saccharin-sweet smile.

"Don't give me that manipulative bullshit." He rolled his eyes at her. "Leave them alone and go back to your table or leave all together. Preferably Marysville."

Ohhhh. My eyes widened at that in surprise. Nate didn't *like* Selma? When did that happen?

"You have no idea what you're talking about." She flicked her hair over her shoulder and speared me with a glare that would have once had me fleeing the table, doing whatever I could to settle her down, but I was rooted to my wooden seat, more surprised with Nate taking a stand than anything.

"I know the owners, and I know if Palmer sees you here, berating his customers he's going to kick you out again. So what's it gonna be? You leave on your own or I have him make you?"

She huffed and stepped back. "I used to like you more before you started thinking you were hot shit, Nate."

He twisted in the narrow aisle so she could stomp past him.

I would have applauded had he not spun and faced me. I prepared for the onslaught of his attitude he'd directed at Selma, considering our history.

He lowered his voice and glanced at the three of us, Nora and Sarah still frozen in shock, before he returned his gaze to me. This time kinder. "You should let Cole know what just happened, unless you want me to do it, but either way, he's gonna hear and you don't want him to hear it from her."

Yesterday, I could have just told him Cole wouldn't have cared, not one bit what Selma said to me and meant it every word. But that was yesterday.

Too bad I didn't have his number, but I knew who would.

"I will."

Nate left and as soon as he was gone, Sarah grinned at me from across the table. "I feel like you left out pieces of that *you knew Cole* story, and I have to tell you, this town needs a bit of excitement every once in a while, so I'm damn glad you're here to provide it."

"Yay me," I grumbled.

Nora chuckled and clinked her glass against mine. "Drink up. Something tells me you need it."

Wasn't that the truth.

# CHAPTER 19
## COLE

"**L**et's goooo!" Davis threw his arms up in the air as he stormed into the locker room. He swung his helmet in the air before dropping it and doing some stupid little dance.

"Happy?" I asked, laughing at him. Three years younger and the kid was usually wise but days like today showed that playful excitement most rookies held. Not a bad thing at all. Even only being in the league five years their excitement and attitude often spurred on the most veteran players who'd lost the shine and awe of reaching their dreams after fifty-some games.

"Damn, skippy. You see that run I made? Broke Carr's ankles on that last play." He slapped my shoulder and across the room, Charles Carr, one of our tackles, threw a towel at him.

"The fuck you did."

"I'm telling ya, man, only takes once and soon you'll be eating turf every time we line up."

"Yeah?" Carr stood, groaning as he pushed off his thighs to get off the bench. The man was taller than me by several inches and probably had one hundred pounds on me. The largest guy on our roster, he wasn't a man I'd want to face off against. Ever.

Davis bounced all the balls off his feet, shaking out his arms like he was prepping for a boxing match. "Hell yeah, I do. Try it, right now."

"Ohhh...Hall is throwing down."

"Hell yeah, baby."

Chairs and benches were pushed to the side, cleats kicked and in seconds, the inner circle of our locker room had become an area just for them.

"I got twenty on Hall!" someone to my right shouted.

"Hundred on Carr!" someone else shouted.

As captain and quarterback, I shook my head. Idiots, all of them, but this was too good to not join in on. I stepped onto the bench and threw my arms straight out to my sides. "All right. No punches. No tripping. Keep it clean and let's see what you fools got."

Butler, usually not one to join in on this stupid shit, walked between them and scraped his cleats against the carpet. It left a line in the carpet pile, and he waved him both in.

"On hike, let's see what you got."

He shoved Hall playfully, but Davis managed to stay on his toes. Carr lined up across, dropped down and growled. Made sense. The man was as big as a grizzly.

The entire team bounced and in unison, counted down. Hut one…hut two…

On hike, they threw off, Hall juked to the right. Carr followed. Hall duked left, and right as he went to break and get around Carr, Carr reached him, went low.

I flinched. If that man actually tackled him, injuries could be had. But nope.

"Let's gooo!" Hall screamed, as Carr wrapped his arms around his knees, but he didn't lay Hall out, he stood, throwing him over his shoulder in a fireman's carry.

"That's what you get, kid!" Butler shouted as Carr stalked off around the corner toward the lockers.

We heard a pitiful, feminine scream from the showers and Carr returned.

"What the hell'd you do to him?"

"Figured a soak in the ice bath would help him out."

"Nice." I fist pumped Carr and turned to my locker. Instinct had me reaching for my phone. It was usually the very first thing I did even before slipping out of my cleats. I was always on, always waiting to get a call about Jasper or Selma needing something.

Fortunately, there was only one missed call from a number I didn't recognize. My voice mail icon told me they'd left a message, but whatever.

Coach came in with the rest of the staff and clapped his hands. As soon as he got everyone's attention, he shoved his hands to his hips, started pacing in the open circle we created for Carr and Hall. "Good job today. You men are looking like a good team. A good damn team and I wanted to tell you I'm proud of the work you not only put in during the off-season, but every second since you've been here. I've told you before, and I'll tell you again, I have nothing but love for all of you. We fall as a team, we rise as a team, and there's nothing that makes me prouder than seeing you grow, focus, strive for perfection every time we step out onto that field."

"Yes, sir!" Cheers went up which he silenced quickly, with a motion of his hands to bring down the noise. Coach was the best man I'd ever met outside my dad. Softer than some pro coaches, he rarely lost his cool. Didn't mean he didn't shout at you every once in a while, but he didn't lose his mind like some others. He believed positivity bred optimism and strength and excitement for the next task— or game.

"We got a second home game in a few days and then none until the second week of the season. Stadium will be packed, the crowd will be electric. You go out and play every second of all sixty of them like you've been doing at practice, and I have no doubt we'll give those fans what they love and bleed and pay for. You got me?"

"Yes, Coach!" I led the charge and pumped my fist in the air. We all crowded together around him, and as he calmed us down again, he scanned the room.

"Where in the hell is Hall?"

A muffled, chattering, "Here! Go Steel!" echoed from the ice bath in the other room.

"I don't want to know," Coach mumbled as we hid our laughter. "No hazing the rookie, guys."

"He likes it," Carr replied, shrugging. "Makes him feel loved."

He wasn't wrong for a second. Hall was always up for shenanigans.

———

I'd managed to throw my full focus into the day's practice, but as soon as I pulled my truck into my driveway, this morning's memories flashed through my mind so real I wouldn't have been surprised if Eden had been sitting in that rocking chair, tears rolling down her cheeks and then pushing me away, unable to look at me after I kissed her.

Broken. She'd looked so broken and beautiful, and my heart had only pounded for her since I hadn't been able to help myself. Made me an asshole, probably, that I didn't even stop to think how she'd react to it, or hell—if she even *wanted* it. But as soon as my lips pressed hers and she melted into me…*heaven.*

Absolutely heaven. I'd had to go back inside, take another shower and take care of the fire she'd ignited before I could even think of focusing on work.

Now that I was home, my thoughts raced. What in the hell did we do *now*? Would she run after my idiotic display of desire for her?

"Daddy, are we going inside?"

I jerked, surprised by the sound of Jasper's voice. Shit, there was no time to wonder about Eden now. Not with Jasper around.

"Yeah, sorry, buddy. Thinking of today's practice." I grinned back at him over my shoulder. I picked him up from the diner, but he hadn't eaten yet. Tonight was one of the nights during the week Selma set aside for girl time so Jasper helped his grandma do baking in the kitchen and she got him nice and sugared up for me.

I turned off the truck and hopped out, and then opened Jasper's door while he unbuckled himself from his booster seat. He wiggled out of the shoulder straps and flung his arms around my shoulders. I set him on the ground and once he was on his feet, he took off toward the door.

"I'll let Bongo out and I'll play with him, okay!"

The neighbors, four acres away probably heard him screaming but I didn't care. "Keep an eye on him, though!"

"I will!"

He had the code to our front door lock tapped and the door opened before I'd grabbed my gear out of the back of the truck and reached the porch. Bongo's excited whines came from the back door, and I cringed at the flour from the diner Jasper must have tracked through the hallway on his way to let the dog out.

"I'll start dinner. Want to help with burgers tonight?"

"Sure! With cheese and fries?"

"You got it," I called out.

The back door slammed shut and the house turned quiet again, and while thoughts of Eden lingered and tried to push to the forefront, I held them back by a wing and prayer.

My phone buzzed in my pocket and I pulled it out, frowning when that same unknown number from earlier lit up my screen, this time with a text alert.

The Face ID signed me in, and I pulled up the message, only to have that same fire from earlier returned in full force.

*It's Eden. I called earlier. Figured you probably deleted unknown numbers. Or maybe you're busy. Can we talk?*

Damn. One stupid text message from her and my blood was sizzling. She could be calling to tell me to leave her alone, or she was leaving. Maybe it was Marley. It could be anything. And was I ready to hear what she had to say?

I set down the phone and grabbed the ground beef from the fridge I'd set out last night. The phone stayed right next to me, tempting me, but if I didn't get Jasper fed that sugar high of his would turn him hangry and grumpy like a light switch.

That didn't mean I took my eyes off my phone, trying to interpret what she wanted, needed, from me. As soon as the patties were made, I grabbed potatoes from the pantry. Scrubbed them, washed them, and then sliced them into fries. Once I had them doused with oil and garlic salt and pepper, just the way Jasper liked them, I then laid them out on a baking sheet while the oven preheated.

Jasper was still outside, and Bongo was still in the yard based on the barking I heard from the backyard and yeah, I should have gone right out back, turned on the grill.

But as soon as my hands were washed, curiosity and impatience got the best of me. Picking up my phone, I went right to my voice mail, and as soon as Eden's soft, worried voice came through, my chest squeezed tight.

*"Hi Cole. It's me, well…it's Eden. I got your number from Marley, and I hope that's okay, and if it's not, feel free to block me, but you should know, well, at least Nate said you'd want to know, so I wanted to call. Because I was out with some, well, friends, I guess, maybe that's what they are? Anyway, there was an argument, altercation…I don't really know what to call it, but it was with Selma."*

I ended the message before I broke my phone and tossed it to the counter. It rattled across the butcher block island, and I slammed my hand over it before it fell onto the other side.

What in the hell had Selma done now? If it involved Eden, it couldn't have been good. Not if she was calling me, but I could imagine what Selma had to say to her given our morning argument.

**I've got Jasper. Will call when he goes to bed tonight.**

I stared at the screen, willed her to respond immediately. Three gray dots appeared. Disappeared. Re-appeared. The cycle continued for several minutes until they disappeared for good.

I was staring at the phone when the door opened, and Bongo rushed in. Nails clicking on the floor and his tail thumping against the wall, I braced myself for impact right before his snout collided with my thighs.

"Hey, boy." I scratched his fur and gave him a good rub down. "You have a good day? Have fun playing with Jas?"

Bongo woofed, tongue lolling out of his mouth.

"Hey Jasper, I need to turn the grill on, will you please feed Bongo and give him some fresh water?"

"Yup!"

The dinner rush got crazy after that, me reminding Jasper to wash his hands, go back and do it again after he used the bathroom then go back again and turn off the bathroom light. He slipped and slid all over the wood floor, on his socked feet, spreading the flour he'd tracked in earlier in a way I'd be mopping the floor after he went to bed. By the time burgers were done, fries were crispy, and we were getting ready to eat, my phone chimed with a new text.

I glanced down with Jasper's milk cup in my hand and had to fight down a laugh.

***Okay.***

That was it. Thirty-five minutes and she'd finally found her nerve to text me back.

At least she didn't ghost me, but Eden, and whatever drama Selma was starting would have to wait.

———

I couldn't get Jasper to bed until eight, later than usual, and that'd come back to bite me in the morning, but whatever. The clock had ticked by at an unnaturally slow speed the entire evening, and once I knew Jas was settled in bed, I made sure I took Bongo outside so he wouldn't go nuts while I was on the phone, and then I turned on music through Alexa, so it was softly playing through the house system. All done so I wouldn't be distracted with whatever it was Eden had to say, even though I already knew I wouldn't like a word of it.

"Hello?"

To my surprise, and utter delight, she actually answered. She was quiet, and her soft tone drifted through the phone full of hesitation and nerves, that one word shaking.

"Hey, it's Cole. How's your night?" I kicked my feet up on the ottoman in front of me.

"It's good. Quiet."

"Marley taken care of?"

"Yeah."

There was a pause that didn't sound great. "What is it?"

"Oh, it's nothing. She's fine, just had an incident in the bathtub earlier I had to help her with. It's hard, you know? Seeing her like this. Failing. She was always so strong."

She sniffed, and I wished I was there, comforting her through it. There to help more with Marley. Yeah, I'd helped over the summer and done her yard work, repainted her front porch and went and bought her a new fridge. I did all the heavy lifting, along with Dad, that she'd allow, but there was always more to do.

"What happened?"

"She slipped. I always give her privacy, because she says she can handle herself, but I know she gets dizzy, and getting out of that old tub is tricky enough. So, anyway, I don't know. She's fine, really, but we talked about getting her a stool to sit on, and some other things. And then right as we were done with the conversation, she mentioned needing a bath." Another heavy sigh. "More things to add to the list to ask the nurse about, I guess. But that's not why you called."

"I'm always here to talk about Marley and help if you need it." Wasn't exactly true considering after next week I'd be traveling for three weekends straight. There would be times I couldn't be there. But if Marley's memory was starting to decline like that, I'd figure out a way to make the time.

"Right. So…earlier tonight."

"Please," I groaned. "Tell me Selma wasn't a complete bitch."

"On a scale of one to ten…"

I chuckled. I'd always tolerated Selma because Hilary loved her, but Hilary could love a porcupine and ignore the quills it could shoot right into her face at any given moment.

This was the first joke Eden had attempted around me and way back when Eden was full of wit and sass and a humor that would leave us busting at the seams.

"She was a nine?"

"Maybe an eight-point seven, but it ended quick. Nate stepped in, which…was surprising?"

Not really, but a lot had changed over the years. "Trust me, there's no love lost between the two of them. Where were you when this happened?"

And who was she *with*? Because she'd mentioned friends, and as far as I knew, she didn't have any here.

"McLaughlin's. I um, well, I ran into the new veterinarian last week. Nora?"

"Dr. Kessick, right? I know her. Take Bongo to her."

"Oh. Of course, well, I ran into her and since I wanted to do some work with animals, she introduced me to the woman who owns the Waggin' Tails, the dog rescue? That's why I've been at BarkTown, they're short on foster homes for dogs, so BarkTown has been letting them board dogs there. I volunteered to go in and help them out, take care of the rescues during the day so they can focus on their own business."

"That's nice of you, Eden."

"Being around animals helps me," she said and stopped so abruptly I wouldn't be surprised if she didn't mean to speak it out loud.

Too late now, but we'd get to that.

"So you went to dinner…."

"With Nora and Sarah. Selma showed up. She was, well, mean, but whatever, didn't say much except surprised I'd show my face in town again. Then Nate showed up, told her to leave or the owner—"

"Palmer."

"Right, or Nate would have Palmer kick her out again. Anyway, she left, but Nate said you'd want to know…so here I am."

There she was. Skittish on the phone, even with me, and rambling over a story that didn't sound like much, but given Selma's recent attitude toward me, I was glad to know.

"It's probably nothing, same old crap, right?" She tried to laugh it off, but I wasn't in a laughing mood.

"Selma…shit, there's so much more I need to tell you about her. And I don't want to do it over the phone."

As I said it, my phone buzzed with an incoming call. Glancing at the screen, I let loose a low growl seeing Selma's name. There was *no* reason for her to call me, except to rant about Eden, or do more threatening with Jasper and it'd been enough hours since dinner. She was probably a few glasses of wine in and on a rampage.

"Oh. We can wait then. I should probably go—"

"Don't. Come over here. I can't leave with Jasper here but come here."

She inhaled a sharp breath. Surprise, probably, but that sound went right to my groin, making me think of other raspy little sounds she could make.

Not tonight though. Talk.

We still needed to talk.

"I can't. Marley—"

"I'll call Ma. Just come, Eden. Please?"

# CHAPTER 20
## EDEN

For the second time that day, I pulled into a driveway I'd insisted I'd avoid with every fiber in my being once I agreed to help Marley. But there I was, his floodlights braced at the corners of the garage illuminating my way up the drive and the porch lights on, welcoming me.

And it wasn't just the porch lights, Cole himself was outside, standing on the top step and leaning against the dark stained post as I turned off my engine and climbed out of the 4-Runner.

"Hey. Your mom get to Marley's?"

He told me to get in my car and come here, Mama B would let herself in when she could get there.

"Was just sitting down to cross stitch while Dad was watching baseball. She's good. Happy to head over."

Based on the conversation we had last night, that didn't surprise me.

"Thanks for coming," he said, and went to open his door. He gestured for me to go first, but I paused at the threshold.

"Will I wake Jasper up? Or will Bongo?"

"Bongo's kenneled in my room upstairs with the bathroom fan on, just in case."

Oh. He'd thought of everything, but I still hesitated. Because Jasper was here…and what if…

No. He was asleep.

"Jasper's asleep, Eden. I swear it. You're good to go in."

Of course he knew what I was thinking. Probably stamped all over my face, but it didn't need to be. Cole could always read me like a well-loved book.

We entered and I moved to the side, off to a formal dining room to the right while he followed me in. Across the front entrance from me were closed French doors, all the wood I could see that same, dark walnut stain that'd been on his porch and chairs. The home was dark, but clean, at least the few rooms I saw, and the floors shined like they'd just been mopped.

I slipped out of my Birkenstock sandals and followed Cole through the house.

"Want anything to drink?"

"I'm good." I was too mesmerized by the house, and at least one question I'd had was answered.

He'd made this a home. Family photos, professional ones, of him and Jasper at every stage of Jasper's life hung on the wall by the stairs. Pictures with his mom and dad, in many of them, and there were some candids but still most likely shot with a professional camera of him throwing Jasper in the air while he was in his football uniform, sweat drenching his hair to his temples but the grin on his face made my heart thump double time.

He'd obviously just won a game and was celebrating on the field with his son.

"My first start with the Steel," he murmured, and I hadn't realized he'd stopped when I did, or maybe came back when he realized I wasn't following him. "Wasn't a home game, but since we knew I was starting, Dad brought Jasper to the game in Raleigh."

"You're a good dad." It was out before I realized I said it and when I turned, faced Cole, he was giving me a look I couldn't decipher.

Amused? Thankful?

"Because I held my son after I won a game and was happy about it?"

"No." I shifted on my feet. "I can just tell. These pictures…your house." From where I stood, I could see the kitchen off to my right and the family room beyond. All of it was done in the same warm, dark wood, but there were pops of brightness in the cream-colored, massive couch that could probably fit four linemen and the white marble countertops. Everywhere I could see were photos, with mature but simple and relaxing decor.

A small stack of envelopes at the edge of the kitchen island and a set of keys and probably Cole's wallet next to it.

Other than that, everything else seemed to be in place, cleaned up, and the entire vibe of his home felt comforting and relaxing. Even with the shine of the floor.

"Everything is so clean."

He laughed and nodded his head toward the kitchen. "Come on, and trust me, that takes work. I'm not the same high school kid who used to throw his crap all over the house and expect Mom to clean up after me. I'm already dreading the day when Jasper turns into that kid." He reached into the fridge and pulled out two bottles of water. "I was still that same messy, irresponsible kid when I was in college, but after Jasper, well, everything changed. I didn't want him to lack for anything, so I worked hard to give him the kind of life I had, a clean home, good food. Love."

He lingered on that one that left my toes curling into the wood floor beneath my feet.

"Right," I mumbled.

"And as far as everything being clean, Jasper sometimes goes to the diner and works with Teresa in the kitchen. He must have stomped through flour there today because he came home and tracked it all through the house before he took off his shoes, then skated across the floor for half the night, smearing it everywhere. It's not always this clean."

His lips lifted at the corner, that hint of a smile appearing beneath his scruff.

"Right," I whispered.

"And maybe, I cleaned up everything else before you got here because I wanted to impress you."

Oh. *Ohhh.* "I'm not sure what you want me to say to that."

"Don't have to say a thing." He pointed a finger at my face. "That blush says enough."

"Shut up." I rolled my eyes and grabbed the water bottle. He didn't take his eyes off me while I opened it and took a swallow and once I was done, he chuckled again.

"Come sit with me. And I'll give you the full Selma saga."

"Sounds thrilling."

"If you enjoy horror movies, sure." He shrugged.

I laughed. Probably shouldn't have, given she *was* the mother of his son, but it was Selma.

She'd always reminded me of the Wicked Witch.

———

He led me toward the living room, and I'd been right about the couch. It was a massive sectional, soft, cream microfiber material that had chaise lounges on both ends. In the middle, was a matching ottoman that closed off the entire space between the lounges making the couch turn into what could be a bed that could easily sleep four adults.

I attempted to *ignore* that thought, especially while he splayed out on the chaise lounge far from me, bare feet kicked up and crossed at the ankles, the muscles of his legs and lower thighs on display beneath his athletic shorts and simple white T-shirt. He'd showered again, probably after practice, and his dark hair was neatly cut, swept to the side and his beard and scruff was perfection.

Cole had started growing facial hair before I knew him and while he hadn't had a lot back then, those two times we'd kissed, the scrape of the hair at his upper lip had always sent a delightful little shiver through me as it scraped across my lips.

I cleared my throat and tore my gaze off him before my face could tell him what I was thinking.

He took a sip of his water, easily held the neck of it in between two fingers and tossed his other arm over the back of the couch. He was staring at his gas fireplace, currently turned off, and the blank television screen in front of him, but I once again found my eyes glued to him as he started speaking.

"I've suspected, and am probably right, although it doesn't really matter and doesn't mean anything, that Selma knew exactly what she was doing the night she called me."

"You already implied this morning she wanted to seduce you."

"Yeah. But I don't mean just that. A girl who'd claimed to be on birth control since she was fourteen for her period cramps, who took it religiously as far as I knew back then, and then all of a sudden that *one night* and she ends up pregnant?" He twisted his neck and met my eyes.

"It happens, Cole." As much as I didn't want to admit it, that happened to girls all the time.

"Yeah, sure it does. But when it happens, when it's a complete shock and surprise, do most girls start talking about getting married five minutes after they shove a pregnancy stick in the guy's face?"

"Um." He had me there. I mean, I doubted that's what *I* would do. "Maybe she was scared."

"Or maybe, considering it wasn't the first time she'd tried to hang out with me since we went away to school, but I'd only seen her a few times over the summer after our freshman year, the crying act she gave was all just that. An act and she planned it. Like I said, I can't prove it, but Selma's always had a way to get what she wanted, and I think a couple years had gone by…Hilary's parents had moved…she saw the success and attention I was getting at Vanderbilt, and she took her shot."

It'd sound arrogant and cocky of him, but the only person who didn't think Selma would take a shot at Cole if Hilary wasn't around was Hilary herself. Ironic, and hypocritical coming from me, but it didn't make it less true.

I tucked my feet up to my backside and twisted so I was resting against the back of the couch, facing Cole. "What'd you do? Or say? I mean…did you consider it?"

"Not for a second, and I think the fact I laughed in her face and told her no way in hell we were getting married really set her off. I mean, she got *pissed*. Screamed at me that I'd done this to her, ruined her, like she was some noble living in the eighteen hundreds. I promised her I'd be there, that I'd help take care of our child, but I swore up and down I'd never marry her."

"How'd she take that?"

"I was worried for a while she'd end the pregnancy just to spite me, to be honest, and that would have been her choice and all, but she knew I wanted that baby." He closed his eyes, and I imagined him reliving those moments, that time, and he swiped his hand down his face.

"The day she shoved that test in my face, right after I asked her if it was really her test and I swore she almost slapped me, that was when I finally started getting my act together. I had something *bigger* than me to fight for. I didn't even need Jasper to be born yet, and already I was figuring out the kind of Dad I wanted to be."

He was a great one. Probably. I hadn't quite seen him in action, but the home and the photos couldn't be faked, and besides, he was a Buchanan. They were good people.

"I'm glad you have him."

He huffed and grinned at me like I was silly. "Me too. Not the way I wanted to start a family by any means, but he and I do all right."

"What's he like?"

"The best. Loud and active and full of questions. Never shuts up when we're alone in the car and loves dinosaurs and trucks and dogs and anything he can throw or catch."

"Like his dad and uncle?"

"We'll see. I'm not like some other dads who push their kids to be a pro athlete or think they will be because they understand the rules of tee ball. In fact, I think a lot of us guys on the team are the opposite. We know the costs, the work and commitment, the sacrifice. It's a hard road to make it where we are, and you can't push someone who doesn't want it or is on the fence about it. Jasper will be his own man, whether sports is in his future or not."

My eyes stung, and for no damn good reason except I'd been right earlier. "See? I told you you're a good dad."

His smile turned soft, more meaningful in a way my nipples pebbled beneath my bra and thank the good Lord as Marley would say I remembered to throw one on before heading this way.

"Back to Selma," he said, and that smile evaporated along with the lightness in the room and the mess going on inside my body.

Selma. Right.

On cue, his phone lit up and her name appeared. Without taking his eyes off me, Cole reached down and silenced his phone. "She apparently has a lot to say about your run-in with her earlier, too. This is the sixth time she's called."

"Don't you need to take it? Jasper—"

"Is upstairs, tucked into the lower bed of his bunk bed, and probably holding the stuffed giraffe Graham gave him before he went back to school last fall. Jasper's fine, which means anything Selma needs to talk to me about can wait."

"Right," I muttered.

"And this is what you need to know about Selma. Over the last few years, every once in a while, and more often recently, say, in the last few weeks, she'll get it in her head that if she simply tries a little bit harder, switches up her tactics, I'll finally commit to her. When Jasper fell down on his bike one day and she'd turned away and missed it, she told me if we'd been living together, it wouldn't have happened. When I didn't catch his little hand when he was three, and he touched a still hot stove after I cooked dinner and he got burned— minor burns, mind you—she said the same thing. She's tried to worm her way into the family pictures I occasionally have taken and sometimes invites herself to our family dinners Mom always makes after home games for us. Trust me, I've seen all her plays and so I know for one, her phone calls tonight are all because she's pissed she saw you, more mad you're in town, and she knows what that means for her. Which is insane, because she never had a shot to begin with."

There was a lot to unpack there, mostly a reminder that Selma's ego knew no bounds, and how vindictive and manipulative she could be. But there were other things. Like... "If she's never had a chance with you, what does me being in town have to do with anything?"

He laughed, that silly little *you're cute* laugh, but it was true. This didn't mean anything. So, we didn't hate each other. So, we could talk. Perhaps it'd help me move on once I finally left Marysville...

"Because she knows, as well as you do, that you're the only woman I've ever wanted in that way. The only woman I've ever loved."

# CHAPTER 21
## EDEN

"You can't mean that," I whispered. The shock of his words caused the blood to rush from my head and I shook my head.

There was no way he could mean what he said.

Cole slid his feet to the floor where he planted them and sat in the corner of the couch, making sure he was looking directly into my eyes. "I absolutely mean it. One hundred percent, and it doesn't matter to me if you don't feel the same now, or maybe won't admit it. That's not what this is, but I'm preparing you now, that while you're here, and while I have the time again, we're going to get to know each other again. We're going to learn about each other all over again, and then once you're ready, I'm going to explore every single inch of you I never got to do before."

"Cole—"

His name was a rasp on my parched lips. The things he said.

The things he made me *imagine*.

He scooted closer, like he was afraid I'd flee but the joke was on him. I was frozen to that couch cushion.

"We can't," I whispered as he moved even closer and then he was there.

In front of me.

Surrounding me with his scent and that heat of his that just sucked the air straight from my lungs, leaving me breathless.

"You're scared." He lifted his hand. My gaze focused on that palm of his moving closer, the calluses at his palms and the strength in those thick fingers and hand as he brushed it over my cheek. "And I get that, too, and more, I get why. But I've wanted you back in front of me for seven long years, Eden, so I've lost restraint to go slow like you might need."

I was shaking my head, and his thumb brushed over my cheek, close to the corner of my mouth and *oh* how much I wanted to dart my tongue out, steal a taste of him.

"Cole," I whispered again, because he'd turned me speechless.

"I know, Eden. I get it." He leaned closer and the cushion beneath me shifted from his weight. His head tilted, those dark-blue eyes of his showed a storm brewing right before he brushed his lips over mine.

There was no freezing this time. Not like this morning.

There was only the heated thrill of anticipation and excitement whipping through me at that first taste of him, and just like this morning, it took a moment to sink into it, for my eyes to flutter close and for me to *respond*.

And *oh*, he was so delicious. He tasted of mint and crisp, cold water, and his kiss was firm as he moved his lips over mine. His tongue swiped at mine, teasing me for entrance before retreating, repeating that little game until I was fighting to squirm in my seat, but my hands found their way to his shoulders, where I held on, possibly tugged him closer and a loose growl slipped through his parted lips right as I opened for him.

And then Cole devoured me, sent my body overheating and my core throbbing with just a kiss and a gentle tantalizing brush of his thumb at my cheek. He didn't move closer, didn't push the weight of him against me. I wasn't quite sure if that was a blessing or a curse because I was pretty sure if I did feel the weight of him, I might shatter.

This was so wrong, so not the time. We'd barely stopped sniping at each other, and I was still an internal wreck and there was Marley to consider, Jasper and Selma and his career and oh but dear God.

"Stop overthinking," he murmured, and screw him for being able to read my thoughts with his eyes closed.

"Shut up," I whispered right back and this time it was me pressing my mouth to his, me taking the kiss and discovering the taste of him. It was me, whimpering my excitement and pleasure into his mouth while he slipped an arm around me and braced my lower back with his palm.

His phone rang, and then the harsh chime of a bell ringing in the distance had him yanking back and cursing.

He swiped the back of his hand across his mouth and my eyes were barely opening before he was standing, glaring at the front door and then me, and then his phone.

"See? Fucking Selma is a goddamn piece of work."

*Oh no.*

I clambered off the sofa and thank goodness I was still wearing the same oversized T-shirt I'd had on this morning, my most comfortable shirt I threw back on after I got back from McLaughlin's earlier. My shorts barely peeked out from beneath the hem, and as I jumped from the couch, I tugged them down.

Cole's hand curled over my shoulder. "She's going to know you're here from your car, but please, *stay here.*"

I was already shaking my head, along with my knees. "I should go. She's going to be pissed and she's going to think—"

"I don't give a fuck what she thinks right now. She knows better than to pull this. Just please, wait here."

I couldn't leave him. Not to deal with this alone when it was all my fault in the first place. Had I just stayed at Marley's—

No. I shook my head. I was allowed to have a life, as small or simple as it was. Selma couldn't dictate that.

"I'll stay here."

"Good girl." He winked, kissed my cheek, and as he stalked toward the front door, my stomach fluttered.

*Good girl?*

Why in the hell did that feel so good?

The click of the door unlocking echoed followed by Cole's rumbling voice. "What are you doing here?"

"Let me in." Selma's voice was harsh and high-pitched, not nearly as angry as earlier but something else.

Panicked.

"Go home, Selma. You don't show up at my house and do this."

"I tried calling. You didn't answer. I got worried."

"Bullshit," Cole laughed, but it was cold and brutal. "You got your head all twisted up over seeing Eden in town and now you're throwing a fit. The fact you even *came* to my house is disgusting."

"Why? Did I interrupt something? That's what's disgusting. You fucking that waste of space with our child in the house."

"Don't." My spine straightened at his tone, evil and so low I so desperately wanted to see the look on Selma's face. I was scared from here. How was she holding up?

"Who I *fuck* or don't, isn't any of your goddamn business, either. We co-parent, Selma, and I'm so goddamn sick of your bullshit. Every time, every goddamn time you don't get your way, you pull this insane shit with me. And it's getting fucking old. Jasper might still be young, but someday he's going to see how you are, how you treat people, and I know my boy. He's not going to like it."

"Threats again?" She whipped back.

My brows furrowed. Threats?

But there was something else in the way she spoke. Something I barely caught.

But leave it to Cole. "You're slurring your words. Are you fucking drunk right now?"

She mumbled something I couldn't hear and as desperate as I was to watch this, I stayed right where I was, out of sight from the front door and Selma's wrath. Cole was doing his best to stay quiet and I had no doubt that was for Jasper's sake, but there was a sudden, quick slam that made me jump and then he was in the living room, swiping his phone off the couch.

"Be back. You stay here. I swear to God…driving fucking drunk all the way here to see me. This is such bullshit."

"What are you doing?"

He grabbed his phone off the table where he'd thrown it when the bell rang. "Calling the cops because Selma fucking drove here drunk, and I want that shit on the record. She pulled some bullshit early this week about me not being a good role model for Jasper and fuck her for that. I want this shit at least noted that she's here, drunk and causing a disturbance so I can start a paper trail for any shit she does in case she tries to take me to court for Jasper."

He didn't give me a chance to reply.

Not like I had anything to say.

The front door slammed again, and this time, I moved. I ducked into the living room to see if I could see him.

They were both on the porch at the far end. Cole was on his phone. Selma's mouth was moving, and her hands flailing in the air.

She turned, stomped down the front steps and as she did, Cole hurried after her. He still had his phone at his ear and with his other hand, he snagged the keys straight from hers. Turning, he chucked them into the dark.

"I fucking hate you!" Selma shouted and even from inside, her voice was shrill, loud enough to wake…

The floor upstairs creaked, and I spun as Jasper appeared at the top of stairs.

Oh shit. Oh shit, oh shit, oh shit.

This was *not* good.

"Who are you?"

His words were slurred from sleep, his hair in complete disarray and dressed in shorts and T-shirt, skintight pajama set, snuggling the giraffe Cole mentioned earlier, tears flooded my eyes. No boy should have to see this. Or have a strange woman in his house.

With every second that passed, I wanted to run to him. Squeeze him.

"My name is Eden. I'm a friend of your dad's."

"Why you here?"

"We were talking. I stopped by to say hi."

"You come wiff my mom?"

"No kiddo. I didn't come with your mom."

There was another scream from outside and Jasper took a seat at the top of the stairs. "She's loud."

"Sometimes mommies get that way. And people."

"She's loud a lot."

My heart thumped almost out of my chest. Jasper's tired little eyes stared at the front door, head resting against the banister. I had *no* clue what to do except sweep him into my arms and promise him no one would shout around his precious little self ever again.

I couldn't do that, but maybe I could help.

"Hey, Jasper?"

"You know me?"

"Yeah." I smiled. "Your dad talks about you a lot. He loves you tons."

"I know. He tells me all the time." His little face scrunched up in the cutest way.

"Do you like books?"

He nodded.

"Do you think maybe you could show me your room and I could read to you?"

It'd get him away from the noise still happening on the front porch, and Selma's occasional shrieks.

Slowly, he stood and stepped down the hall. I followed quickly and met up with him as he walked into a room where there was a bunk bed on one wall, the bottom bed larger than the top. The room was decorated in all manner of bookshelves with toys tucked into every cubby. And books. So many books.

"Which ones are your favorite?"

He pointed to the table next to his bed.

*If you give a Moose a Muffin* and *Chicken Soup with Rice* were laid out on top, likely already read to him once tonight. I grinned at his bed, the lack of headspace between the bunks and tried to imagine Cole tucked into bed with Jasper, reading him bedtime books.

I quickly banished the thought for fear of my ovaries exploding and sat on the edge of the bed while Jasper climbed in.

"You gotta put your feet here." He pointed to the end of his bed and then to the pile of pillows at the top. "And put your back here."

"Do I?"

"Daddy does."

Well, if Daddy did it...

He didn't seem to have much hesitation in letting me get close to him, so I did as I was told, and he snuggled right up to my side. As I grabbed the books and settled them in my lap, my other hand went to the top of his head and brushed down his hair.

"Wanna talk about why you woke up?"

"Loud noise. Scawed me. Where's Bongo?"

"Your dad said he's sleeping in his room. Want me to get him?"

I hesitated to ask. Bongo would probably wake up and be excited and not wanting to sleep.

Jasper shook his head. "He snores loud. Keeps me up."

His dad probably did, too.

"Okay then. Which book first?"

# CHAPTER 22
## COLE

could not believe the absolute shitshow this night turned into. Selma was losing her mind, pacing back and forth on my porch. She'd already kicked a rocking chair and thrown some of the toys from the water table at me.

I tried to ignore it all, more focused on keeping her from getting in her car than anything. Which was why I threw her keys into the woods.

She'd never find them. Hell, they were probably lost forever but if I'd put them anywhere else, like in my pockets, I didn't doubt she'd dive for them. No way her hands were getting anywhere near me.

"For the thousandth time, let this go, Selma."

God, I was exhausted. Seven years. This wasn't the first or fifth or twentieth I'd explained things to her.

"It's because she's here. She's back. I know it. Fucking Eden. If she'd stayed away. She never should have shown up here."

If Eden hadn't shown up here seven years ago, maybe, but I was still convinced I would have found her at some point in our lives. "God, you must drive yourself insane with these batshit theories, Selma. Kyleigh feed you this bullshit or something?"

If anyone loved drama more than Selma, it was Kyleigh. They'd met at nursing school and Kyleigh lived in the same neighborhood as Selma. Those two within walking distance to each other was trouble in itself. I still figured Selma told Kyleigh she ran into Eden that first day she came back to town and Kyleigh was the one who spread it through town, so Ma ended up hearing about it at Frank's.

"Don't bring Kyleigh into this."

"Don't bring Eden into this. She has nothing to do with why I don't want you. I didn't want you when we were twelve, when we were fourteen, when I was with Hilary or when I was twenty. I don't get how you don't fucking understand that." I tapped my index finger to my temple.

"If you'd give me a chance."

"Dear God, woman. I don't *want* to give you a chance. Give it up!" My hands slammed to my hips and thank the Lord, Mother, and Joseph because lights turned at the end of my drive and slowly crept up the hill.

"I still can't believe you did this."

"You drove drunk, threatened to force your way into my home and take our son from me while he slept." Although I had no doubt he was awake now. Jasper wasn't a light sleeper but no way had he slept through the doorbell and me slamming the front door. I couldn't go check on him *or* Eden until this was handled. "You're damn right I'm having this documented."

"You're a fucking asshole."

From the woman who wanted to sleep with me, marry me, and lock me down.

I didn't reply, just inhaled a calming breath as Grayson Hodges, the county Sherriff, slid out of his cruiser and headed toward us. I assumed they would have sent a deputy, but this was better.

"How's the night, Cole?"

"Been better, Gray." We shook hands while Selma scowled at both of us.

It'd be a shame if she never pulled that stick out of her ass. She wasn't bad to look at, just bad everywhere else.

"Selma." Grayson nodded in her direction. "Let's say we get you home."

I would have preferred if he breathalyzed her, but she crossed her arms over her stomach and swayed, a clear enough sign she was toasted.

Grayson's eyes narrowed. "You drive here after drinking?"

"Had a couple at dinner hours ago."

It was nearing nine. She would have gone to dinner around five. That left a lot of hours to sober up which meant she'd probably done what I suspected. Went to Kyleigh's and got all riled up.

"I can test you, can't charge you for driving under the influence since there's no proof, but I need to check before I let you get behind the wheel."

"I want a lawyer."

Goddamn. She never did anything easy. "I can let you call one down at the station. So what's it going to be? I test you and if you're good, you head home, or I take you."

Selma glared at me. "My dad can come get me."

The hell he would. Irv spoiled her like crazy and he'd be piping mad to know I'd called the cops on her—but he'd be more than mad if she really was driving drunk. The man had sobered up nearly thirty years ago and hated alcohol.

"Sure." I shrugged. Playing along. "I'll call your dad, tell him you're drunk, drove here, tried to take Jasper home with you while you're behind the wheel and drunk—"

"Shut up."

Her dad hated me, but he'd hate that more.

"What's it going to be, Selma?" Grayson's tone showed his impatience.

"Fine." She glared at me again and stomped toward the stairs. "You can take me. Officer."

She spit out the word and stomped all the way to his cruiser.

"What's her problem tonight?" Grayson asked.

We weren't close friends, and he'd been older than me in school, but it was his youngest sister who worked at BarkTown, and he'd had a brother in my grade. "She's still pissed I won't marry her."

"Damn. Would love to know your secret to drive the ladies crazy like this."

"Really?"

"Well no." He chuckled and shook his head. "Not like that, no way."

Figured. "So what now?"

"Now, I get her home. I could take her to the station and let her dry out, but you can always come in tomorrow and give a statement if you want. You pressing charges?"

"For what?"

"Disturbing the peace, driving impaired. Threats to kidnap your son."

Tempting. "No. But I will come in and give a statement so it's in writing. Want my security footage?"

"Not if you're not pressing charges, but I'd download it somewhere safe if I were you in case anything else happens."

"Right. Thanks again for coming out."

"It's the job. Take care and good luck on Sunday."

"Thanks, Grayson."

He was already walking toward the cruiser and lifted a hand in the air. He opened the front passenger door for Selma. She slumped into it, still scowling at him and when he wasn't looking, gave me the finger. I shook my head at her, a little disappointed he didn't throw her into the back seat like a criminal.

I stayed on the porch until the car was gone, until my racing heart had settled and until I figured I could talk to Eden without raising my voice to wake up Jasper.

It took a while, but I found the calmness inside of me eventually.

———

The main floor was silent and without checking it was obvious Eden wasn't still down there. No way would she stand back and hide once I told her I was calling the cops, but at least she'd stayed out of sight.

In the state Selma was in, she could have dived headfirst through the dining room windows had she caught a glimpse of Eden.

That left only a few other places where she could be, and I had my suspicions, so after throwing back a quick glass of water to smooth the frazzled nerves after that confrontation I'd deal with *later*, I headed up the stairs. My legs ached, proof of the workout earlier and the day and my ribs ached from a particularly difficult hit I took against our defense. Not quite a tackle, but he'd gotten his feet tangled up with our left guard and down I went.

Outside my bathroom's fan humming quietly, the upstairs was as quiet as downstairs which meant she could only be in one place. Of course, the fact that Jasper's door was wide open would have pointed me there anyway.

This definitely wasn't how I wanted them to meet, but at least she'd been there tonight to help him. It was better than Jasper either sitting inside, terrified of what was going on or coming downstairs and watching everything explode.

I would have had to physically hold Selma back from taking him from me and that wasn't a trauma I wanted on my kid.

Damn Selma and her need for attention and ridiculous notions she refused to drop.

Pushing open Jasper's door, the most beautiful sight awaited me, and I leaned against the doorframe to take it in. Light from the backyard flooded through his cracked blinds and his nightlight illuminated his bedroom so I could see both of them clearly. Eden, legs kicked up on his bed, back against the pile of pillows where I read Jasper his books at bedtime. Two books from his nightstand, his current favorites, were closed and on her lap. Her head was tilted back, and her eyes were closed, but she wasn't asleep. A soft, gentle smile curled the corners of her mouth up and her fingers were running through Jasper's hair.

His head rested against her stomach, and he had an arm draped over her lap. His favorite stuffed giraffe and blue baby blanket he still slept with were tucked between his stomach and Eden's hip.

Beautiful.

A piercing pain pinched my chest as I took in the sight and all the years I didn't have with her slammed into me.

*This* is what we should have had. What I'd always wanted for us.

I cleared my throat, careful not to be too loud to wake up Jasper again and Eden's eyes peered open.

Her smile vanished and she whispered, "Hey."

"He's asleep, you know."

"I didn't want to move until I knew things were okay."

They weren't. I wasn't sure how to make them so, either. I'd figure it out, though, because no way in hell was my son going to be with a woman, ever, who would think it was a good idea to throw him in the car after who knows how many drinks and scream like she'd done to me earlier.

I walked toward her, holding out my hand for her to take as I moved closer. "Selma's gone, so it's as good as it's going to get for the night."

"Oh."

I helped her slide out of the bed, lifting Jasper's arm slowly as she did. The bed barely moved before she was on her feet, and I moved Jerry the Giraffe and his snuggie under his arm.

Jasper moved, curled up his leg toward his chest and brought Jerry closer to him until it was tucked beneath his chin.

He made no other movement and once I was certain he'd stay that way, I guided Eden out of his room and closed the door behind us.

"Want to tell me what happened?"

"Not really, but also yeah." I wrapped my hand in hers. Like everything else with Eden, her hand, so much softer and smaller than mine, fit into mine perfectly and I skipped past the stairs to the other side of the house.

"Cole—"

"Shhh. I need this. Five minutes with you, talking, in my bed to relax and get rid of the night. I won't even kiss you if you don't want it."

Kind of a lie, I'd probably try.

"All right."

I left the door to my room open in case Jasper woke up and slipped out of my slides before I slid onto the bed, on top of the covers, and pulled Eden down with me.

She landed with a soft bounce and rolled to her hip, resting her hand on my stomach.

Like it was the most natural thing to touch me.

Like she'd done it a thousand times.

My hand settled over hers, and between the worried but patient look in her eyes and the feel of her hand on my body, beneath my own hand, I told her everything that happened outside.

By the time I finished, she'd flipped her hand, tangled her fingers with mine, squeezing me tight. I scrubbed a hand down my face and sighed. "Now I just have to figure out what to tell Jasper tomorrow, about why his mom's car is still out front if it's not gone by then and go to the station to file a report. Such a damn mess."

"Well, I think for Jasper, just tell him his mom wasn't feeling well. He doesn't need to know specifics and he didn't see anything."

"You sure about that?"

"I was in the living room—"

"Peeking through the blinds?"

"Guilty." She shrugged, and it was so damn cute I chuckled despite the tension still coiled tight in me. None of this was funny.

"I heard his door open, and I went to the bottom of the stairs as he reached the top of them. He sat down and asked me who I was and why his mom was mad. I suggested I read him a book and we went to his room. He was only out of his room for a minute or two, and he never came downstairs."

"Good." At least that was a relief. "I'm glad you were here. It wasn't how I wanted you two to officially meet or anything, but if you hadn't been…"

"He'll be okay, you know. Lots of kids see their parents fight every once in a while."

"Maybe. But if she keeps this up…"

"Am I really her trigger for all of this?" I hadn't specifically told her she was, but Eden wasn't dumb.

I lifted my free hand and brushed it down her cheek, curling it around to the back of her neck. Her skin was smooth, warm, and as her hair shifted, I caught a faint scent of something minty.

"I think you're her final trigger." I had to be honest. With Eden, I refused to be anything else this time. She was here, in my bed, and that kiss we shared earlier would have brought us up here with far fewer clothes on than we had now if we hadn't been interrupted.

Someday I'd have her here.

Eden blew out a breath that made her shoulders fall. "I don't get it. Why? I mean, how hasn't she caught on that you don't want her?"

"I have no idea. I've always been clear with her on that and she's only making everything harder than it has to be. You want to know something else?"

"Not really."

Funny was Eden.

I let go of her hand and pushed up so I was sitting with my back to my headboard. Eden followed, sitting up and facing me, her knees bumped against my legs as she crossed them like she was getting ready for children's story time at the library complete with her hands in her lap.

"I think she planned it."

"You already said the pregnancy—"

"Not that. The night Hilary died, I think she was the one who dragged Hilary through the house looking for us."

"What?"

"She wasn't stupid, I think she always knew how we felt about each other. And that night, when I couldn't find you, I'd found Hilary and Selma in the kitchen at Brandon's house. I was searching for you, but I tried not to make it obvious and made some crack about where the third musketeer was. Hilary said she had no idea, that you'd been around inside and out, but Selma had given me this look…like she knew what I was doing…I tried to hang out there, but I was antsy, wanted to find out and when I told them I'd see them in a bit, Hilary had gone in for a kiss. I dodged it, and Selma smiled, but it was that kind of smile, you know."

"Where she looked like she swallowed a handful of lemon slices?"

"Something like that."

"Okay, so she did. She grabbed Hilary and took her to find us, or you, but that doesn't mean she knew what she'd find, or that we'd be doing anything."

"Yeah, but think of Selma *hoping* for something like, something that would break Hilary's heart, break us up, and then I'd be free for her before I left for school."

Eden pressed her hands down her cheeks and groaned. "She didn't know that. What would happen."

"Neither had we, you know. So why do you hold yourself fully responsible?"

I hadn't wanted to go there, but she was so willing to absolve me of blame, and now she was willing to do the same for Selma.

"I don't know." She pushed her lips to the side, rolled them together. "Because I still feel bad. Because she'd be here if I hadn't come to town. If I'd been able to stop what we were feeling."

"Don't you think that says something, though? That neither of us could despite how hard we tried? I could have hurt Hilary that first day back at school as soon as I saw you. I took her back *after* we kissed, because I figured it was just a thing, you know."

She flinched, and I hadn't meant to hurt her, but Hilary had been trying to get me back, begging me, reminding me of everything I promised her and all the ways we'd spend our senior year. It wasn't guilt that drove me to kiss Eden before I took Hilary back, it was desire and curiosity and me wondering if I even loved Hilary. And after that kiss, I'd known I didn't, that'd I'd already moved on from my high school girlfriend but breaking her heart and dating someone else seemed so cruel.

"I didn't mean it like that."

"I know." Eden nodded and reached out, brushed her hand over my stomach where my shirt had ridden up. Her touch was soft, tentative, and at the first brush of her warm flesh against mine, my stomach tightened. "I should go though."

"Probably."

"Your mom is probably getting tired."

"Yeah." Or she was asleep already, her cross stitch in her lap and her mouth slightly opened like she always fell asleep in the evening.

Eden chewed on the corner of her bottom lip and glanced up at me. "Do you think, well, can I have a kiss before I go?"

Absolutely she could.

# CHAPTER 23
## EDEN

A devilish gleam curled Cole's lips, and he didn't waste time accepting my request.

His hand slipped to the back of my neck, his other went to my waist and with a quick pull of my body, moving me like I was no heavier than a football, he had me settled on his lap, my legs bent and straddling his.

"Come here." A firm press of his palm at the back of my neck sent a flash of excitement sliding down my spine and then his scruff was scraping my cheek as his mouth brushed along my jaw. "You never have to ask for this, after all the years I've waited for you to be right here."

His words were a balm to my heart, soothing me, but at the same time, forced a panicked ball of emotions into my stomach. He was so certain. So sure.

After all this time and now barely knowing each other.

My feet itched to run even as I moved in closer, twisted my neck until our lips brushed together.

A sated sigh fell from my parted lips as Cole took over, gently at first, discovering the taste and feel of me, until whatever control he had snapped and then his mouth pressed to mine, his tongue dove in.

He kissed me like he'd been dying for this. Like we hadn't spent seven years apart and like he knew exactly what I needed to get out of my mind, to silence the doubt and fears quickly fleeing to the dark recesses of my brain.

My hands slid up his chest and as they burst over his chest, a beautiful, low groan fell from him and he cupped the back of my neck harder, slid me closer to him until my breasts were pressed to him and the beautiful, thick hardness against my core couldn't be disguised or hidden.

Cole Buchanan had been the only man of my dreams and fantasies and nightmares for as long as I could remember and the reality of him having me here, like this, his passion for me thrumming through every tense and pressured touch of his hands on me proved he wasn't only a god in football.

He'd be the master in bed as well.

A shiver rolled through me and a mewl tore my throat as he rocked me against his hard length, large and obvious against my center.

"Cole," I rasped against him, and I didn't know what I was asking.

For him to finish me off like this. For him to take *everything* or for him to slow, allow me to regain my bearings.

He tore his mouth off mine and shoved his lips to my ear. "Think of this later, how hard I am for you, and how much I want you, and how good this feels for you when you start conjuring up your escape plans."

My body was so electrified from the lust he'd stroked so quickly it took me a moment to realize he was no longer kissing me but running his hands slowly up and down my back, and when I finally registered his words, I frowned. "What?"

He smirked. The devil. "You heard me."

"You're just…stopping?"

Was he kidding? His dick, still hard, pulsed against me, proving his need and desire.

"For tonight." His smirk fell and he leaned in and brushed his lips to my cheek. "I don't want to move too fast, and it's not for me, I don't want you getting scared on me."

Well. "Too late for that," I huffed.

Cole's grin lit up the room with his white teeth and amused smile. His hands went to my hips, and he slowly moved me off him, groaning in pain as he adjusted himself.

Which I watched, because who wouldn't. I'd been right, too. That bulge was massive, and I swallowed, already salivating for when I could see it. Feel him.

"I should go," I muttered, and yanked my gaze off his hand to his face.

"Running already?"

Yes. Yes, I was, but I wasn't going to *let him* know that.

"You've given me a desire to finish the workout you started."

I climbed off the bed as he laughed and lunged for me, but I was faster somehow, surprisingly.

"Good." He took my hand in his and yanked me to his chest. My hands came up and slammed against his chest as he smiled down at me. "Think of me while you do that as well because I can guarantee as soon as you leave and I jump in the shower, it's going to be your sexy little body I'm thinking of when I shoot all over the shower walls."

The visual shouldn't have been sexy, but my lips parted, imagining.

Cole in the shower, all that wet, warm water running down his body and over every peak and valley of his muscles, his calloused hand working…

"I've only been back in town for less than two weeks," I whispered, my fears already tapping at the corner I shoved them into when he kissed me.

"And in two more weeks, it'll be a month, and we'll have spent more time getting to relearn each other."

He was so certain.

"I should go," I said again.

"I'll walk you out."

He held my hand down his stairs, back to the kitchen where I grabbed my purse and keys I'd dropped earlier, and he held my hand while I slipped on my sandals, and he opened the door and walked me to my car.

"Don't overthink this, Eden," he said when he'd opened my door for me. "And don't hide when I call you tomorrow, okay?"

I wouldn't make promises I couldn't keep. "I'll try."

He chuckled, and a hint of a smile broke free. "Good."

Like this morning, tonight ended nearly the same way.

With Cole disappearing from my rearview mirror as I drove away.

It should have made me feel good, but all I could remember was the first time that'd happened…

And it'd taken me seven years to find my way back to him.

What would happen if we destroyed each other again this time?

———

"You're quiet today."

I jumped at Sarah's voice, where I was huddled in a corner of the indoor playroom, letting puppies climb all over me.

"What?"

She laughed and pointed to Lucy, the boxer mix who was going to her new home today. "She's eating your shoelace."

"Oh." I tugged it out of her mouth and brought her into my lap. Her paws immediately went to my face, and she gave me a giant slurp with her tongue up my cheek.

Sarah laughed. "Ready to say goodbye to her?"

I hugged Lucy to me and pushed out my bottom lip. "Not really."

She rolled her eyes, but instead of taking her from me like she needed to, she plopped down next to me. Three of the pit mixes lunged for her and while she tried to give them all attention, asked, "Did you talk to Cole the other night?"

Like every time I thought of two nights ago, my cheeks burned, and I shoved Lucy back into my face, so Sarah didn't see. "I did."

He'd also called me last night like he promised, but it was late, I'd already had two glasses of wine, and I was getting ready for bed. I could have easily picked up the phone, but I let it go to voice mail. Partly for fear of us crashing and burning, mostly because I was worried if I talked to him, I'd do something stupid, like tell him to come to Marley's, sneak in like he was a teenager all over again.

I did, however, do exactly what he said that night I got him and thought of him very vividly while I slipped my hands beneath my sleep shorts and finished what he started.

I also did it again this morning, moments after I saw his **Good morning, Eden. Hope you dreamed of me last night because I had a fantastic dream about you**…text.

I snapped him a selfie of me, barely awake, head on my pillow, hair a complete bird's nest of a disaster in response.

"What'd he say about Selma?"

"What?"

She bumped into my shoulder. "Are you always so spacey?"

"Never. Sorry, things on my mind."

Her teasing smile wiped clean away. "Marley?"

"No." It was probably the first time since I'd been back she hadn't been. "Life. The past. The future."

"Oh, so nothing heavy."

"Not at all." I laughed.

"I asked about Selma. What'd Cole have to say about that?"

"He's dealing with it. Like Nate said, he was glad I told him."

I wished for a friend who I could vent to, let loose about everything that happened the other night, everything Selma did and driving drunk to Cole's and wanting Jasper to leave with her, but gossip would spread soon enough after Cole went to the police department if it hadn't started already and none of it would come from me.

Selma hating me was bad enough. I didn't need to add fuel to the fire.

"That must have been one hell of a phone call. You okay with it? I mean, I know what you said the other night, about Hilary and everything, but I hope you're not still blaming yourself. I know that sounds trite, but sometimes shitty things happen to really good people."

"Yeah." I stretched out my legs and rolled my shoulders.

Easy to say. Harder to live it.

"All right." Sarah clapped her hands together and wiggled her fingers. "I need to get Lucy to her new home. The mom said her husband is taking their kids out for an early dinner so Lucy can be there when they get home."

I gave Lucy one last squeeze, accepted one last cheek kiss and handed her over. "Have a good new home, Lucy." I tapped her nose.

Sarah picked her up and frowned down at me. "You going to be okay?"

"I'll be fine."

I always was.

"Okay, but you know, I liked having dinner with you and Nora the other night. If you ever need a friend or anything, feel free to call me."

"Thanks, Sarah."

She kicked her shoe against my foot. "I mean it. It can't be easy being back here, and Nora and I are around if I'm not visiting Jeremiah. Don't hesitate."

It'd been a long time since I'd had a good group of girlfriends. It hadn't been easy for me to be around people for so long, and then it became easier not to try, but while I was in Marysville and with potential drama from Selma growing, having friends might not be a bad thing.

"Maybe next week you and Nora can come to Marley's? She'd love the company, and she goes to bed early so we could sit out back and have a couple drinks?"

"Nora and I will bring McLaughlin's to you two. It's a date."

I gave one last head scrub to Lucy before she left and I promised Sarah I'd call if I needed her before then.

Once she was gone, I looked down at the puppies, most of which were starting to curl into balls and rest in massive doggy piles. I took them back, two or three at a time, depending on their size, and settled them in their kennels. It was almost time to head out, but before I did, I wanted to say hello and goodbye to one of the day's visitors I hadn't yet spent time with.

Almost immediately, Bongo ran right at me and jumped up, his front paws landing on my thighs.

"Hey there, boy." I scrubbed his ears, and he barked.

His paws and undercoat were soaking wet telling me he'd spent plenty of time in one of the play pools and I laughed when he decided to shake his water off him—and all over me.

I was flinging water off my hands when a boy, who had to be at least sixteen, who I'd met but couldn't remember, came over. "Sarah come and take one of the puppies?"

"Yeah. Lucy found her home."

"That's good." He rocked on his heels and the braids he had in his dark hair swayed. "Say, you know Cole, right?"

"Pardon?" My brows jumped on my forehead.

"Yeah. Suzie said it seemed like y'all knew each other last week or something. Am I wrong?"

"No." I laughed off my surprised reaction. "Sorry, it's…I don't get asked that often, but yeah. I know him. Why?"

"Oh, well…" He shifted his weight again, eyes slipping to Bongo, the door to inside. His nerves were palpable. "It's just, well, I'm a fan, and I play, but I don't really know him well and don't want to bother him, so I was just, well wondering if you could get an autograph for me?"

Well, now *that* was not what I was expecting, from anyone in Marysville. "He's a really nice guy, you know. He'd love to talk to you himself, especially if you play."

"Yeah, well, I'm not as great as he was, or is, and I'm better with dogs than people, I guess."

Now that, I understood more than he could know, and I chuckled. "Me too. What's your name?"

A grin split his face, showing off a full set of white teeth behind his tan lips. "Jacoby, but everyone calls me Jake."

"All right, Jake. I'll see what I can do."

"Thanks, Eden. Thanks a lot." He bounded off to the far corner of the fenced-in play yard.

I smiled down at Bongo. "Your dad probably gets this a lot, huh?"

He nuzzled my thigh as a voice came through the speaker.

"Bongo's family is here for him. Can someone please bring him out?"

"Will do," I called to Suzie and since Bongo was happily sniffing the scent of puppies all over me, I grabbed his collar.

I might have avoided Cole last night, but maybe this would show him I was doing what I promised—and trying.

———

He grinned easily this time when I handed over Bongo's leash. "He's been playing like crazy. Should rest well for you later."

"Good. How'd your day go? Any dog attacks?"

"Nope." I shrugged. "But something exciting happened."

I let that linger, and Cole's curiosity was instant.

"What is it?"

"You have a fan. Out back."

He leaned back so he could see through the large window that showed the play yard. There were four workers back there and he glanced back at me. "Who?"

"The boy. His name's Jacoby, goes by Jake."

"Huh." He scratched his jaw. "A fan, huh? What'd he say?"

"He asked if I knew you, and then asked if I could get your autograph."

"Why doesn't he ask me himself? Not that it bothers me he went to you, as long as it doesn't bother you."

"No." I chuckled and glanced at Suzie. She was tapping on her computer's keyboard, but I had no doubt she was listening to every word we said. "It surprised me though, wasn't expecting it."

"Took a while for me to get used to, but yeah, I'll get him something for sure. I've got gear in my office at home."

"He said he plays, but I don't know what position or anything, if that gives you an idea of what to give him. He was embarrassed, or nervous, I guess. Said he's better with dogs than people."

A knowing gleam hit his blue eyes. "Something you have in common?"

"Exactly. And thanks again, it's nice of you to do this so willingly."

He shrugged. "I'm a nice guy, and also, don't make plans for Sunday."

He had a game, and I knew that, but he couldn't mean…

"Cole, I'm not sure—"

"Not the game." He smiled knowingly. Softly. "I can't do much about those seats or anything right now, and that'd make everyone uncomfortable. No, Mom always insists on a family dinner after home games. I want you and Marley to come over. Have it with us. She's always done it before."

She didn't mention a thing about it last Sunday. I would have happily taken her over there or had Mama B come and get her. She'd done that for me, probably knowing how uncomfortable it'd make me and never made a single noise about it. Or she'd forgotten…

"Are you sure?"

"I want you to meet Jasper, more than just when he's half-asleep and scared. Come over, Sunday, Eden. Bring Marley. It'll be fun…." Bongo shoved his nose against me and sniffed wildly. "I'll even let you play catch with Bongo."

"Sold." I laughed.

"Ah. You just want me for my dog."

"It's a cute dog."

He leaned in and whispered, "Sunday."

A quick peek told me Suzie was trying *real* hard not to pay attention to us and I stiffened as his breath skated across my cheek. "Still thinking of the other night too and making plans for the next time I have you like that. Know now, that'll involve a lot less clothes, for both of us."

*Oh*…well…my eyes fluttered closed, and an image flashed, bright and hot and vivid in behind my lids. Of Cole…shirtless.

"Bye, Eden," he said, and this time his voice was louder. When I opened my eyes, he'd taken two steps back and was fighting back a laugh.

Jerk.

"Bye, Cole," I said grumpily and bent down and smiled at Bongo. "Bye. See you soon, good boy."

Cole left and I stared after them.

"Eden?"

"Yeah, Suzie?"

She wiped her index finger against the corner of her mouth. "You've got drool…"

"What?"

The girl laughed and shook her head. "Just kidding."

"You're grounded."

"You're not my mom, so you can't do that, and the owners love me so you can't even fire me."

"Yeah, yeah." I pushed through the doors and headed to the back.

It was time to go home and find some way to cool down. I suspected BarkTown employees wouldn't like seeing their volunteers fling themselves into one of the dog pools.

# CHAPTER 24
## COLE

t was the fourth quarter of our game, and we were once again up. The lead wasn't nearly as big as I would have wanted but a win was a win. I was taken out at the end of the first quarter again and was now currently cheering on our backup quarterback with every pass and a few great runs of his own. But now that the game was winding down, for the one-hundredth time, I scoped out where Selma and Jasper's seats were in the stands. Like every other time, I did it, smiled.

Thankfully, she didn't come to the game and so my parents were sitting on either side of Jasper, their seats behind them empty. My heart ached not seeing Marley there, cheering me on, knowing the likelihood of her ever sitting in another one of those again was slim. Somehow, some way, this season I'd make it happen—and fill Selma's seat with Eden, too while I was at it.

Selma, fortunately, hadn't called at all this week. The morning after her drunken insanity on my front porch, I'd woken up to find her car already gone. By the time I got to the police station, one of the officers on duty said they'd seen Kyleigh picking her up and driving her my way.

Didn't thrill me that she and Kyleigh were on my property while I was sleeping, but the car was gone, which meant when Jasper woke up, I'd had less to explain to him.

He didn't ask me about Eden, so I didn't mention that topic, but it had reminded me of how badly I wanted them to get to know each other.

After Jasper was born, I promised myself that if I ever did find a woman I wanted to date, she and I would be serious, months of dating, before I'd bring her around my son, and despite the risk of Eden leaving in the dark of night—or after Christmas—whichever came first, I didn't want to hold back.

Eden had to know I was in this for the long haul, and we could be discreet around Jasper. He'd see her around town or with Marley eventually anyway.

After a quick talk with Jasper explaining sometimes moms and dads fight but we both loved him very much, I'd sent Selma a text saying she could pick him up from my parents. I loaded both him and Bongo into the truck and took them over there, giving her plenty of time.

Mom had called me later and said Selma showed up around ten, tired, but sweet as pie to everyone.

We hadn't talked since outside the text I sent her saying I'd be picking up Jasper at the diner and taking him to my parents or hers in the morning and she'd responded with a *Fine. Whatever* response.

If she thought her rudeness bothered me, she was wrong. The less I spoke to her right now, the better.

I was hopeful that night woke her up and she was trying to put her bullshit ideas to bed once and for all, but the past being the perfect indicator of future predictions meant it was more likely she was licking her wounds and forging her next plan of attack.

No way would Selma back down with Eden still being in town, which was why I also had a note to call a family attorney to talk about how I could protect myself and custody with Jasper since we'd never put anything official on paper or filed with the courts.

But most importantly, I was counting the clock, not until the game ended in two minutes and thirteen seconds while we had a lead of ten, but until I could walk into my parents' house and plant a kiss on Eden's cheek that would be sure to turn her cheek the color of a fire engine.

As soon as the clock ticked down, and the final score of twenty-eight to eighteen lit up the scoreboard, Davis Hall threw his arm around my shoulders and yanked me around.

"Undefeated, QB! How's that feel?"

I chuckled and shoved him off me. "It's game two."

Every win felt damn good, though.

"I'll say it after every game we stay that way. With your arm and my speed, I'll be saying it a lot."

Together, we walked toward the center of the field and shook hands with players and coaches before heading off to the locker room.

"Damn, I love this game," Hall said, swinging his helmet. "Best damn game to play."

There was always something about rookie's attitudes, even in preseason. They were infectious with their excitement and optimism. Davis was getting a ton of attention since he'd been one of the top five running backs in the country at Clemson. They were a fierce rival with my brother's team, and I knew Davis well since Graham's job was often to take Hall out the last couple years. The kid was loud and fun, but he was also as down-to-earth, levelheaded as they came.

A good kid with a good head on his shoulders, he wasn't one of the fools who hit the NFL, spent their millions in signing bonuses and crap that really didn't matter in life and swung his fame around like a badge of honor.

"What are you doing after this?" I asked him.

"Coming to Mama B's for dinner." He smirked. "Where else would I be on a Sunday night?"

He didn't need the invite. He'd stayed with me for two weeks before training camp while he waited to close on his condo in the city. It wasn't super common, but it happened, and I was more than willing to take him in. Since then, Ma always made sure he knew he was always welcome. He's originally from Nebraska and his parents were at last week's game to see him get his first preseason start, but they weren't planning on coming back to see him again until our regular season first home game.

"Jasper will be thrilled." I stopped him before we hit the locker room. "Remember that woman I talked about last week? Eden?"

"Yeah." He scratched his cheek like he was thinking, trying to remember.

"She'll be there too, so be cool, okay?"

"You betcha." Blue eyes gleamed with mischief.

I shook my head. "Seriously dude. Marley too, so don't make a fool out of yourself, all right?"

He placed his hand to his chest. "Moi?"

I slapped his shoulder and almost shoved him into Bronsky, my left guard, who pushed him farther away. "Exactly."

Hall laughed. A good head on his shoulders, slightly immature—he reminded me a lot of my own brother, and when Graham couldn't be there, Hall was second best.

I should probably tell him that sometime.

———

I loved the house I'd had built and the home I created with Jasper, but there was nothing better than stepping foot into my childhood home, a place I'd always been loved and accepted for exactly who I was and not what I was good at. A tightened little stress ball deep in my chest I usually carried with me, all the responsibilities I had as a young dad and professional athlete released like a valve as soon as I stepped inside, and the soft, minimal floral scent of Ma's perfume mixed with the tangy spice of whatever Italian dish she was cooking up invaded my senses.

Jasper's feet pounded on their worn wood floor straight to me.

"Daddy!"

I crouched down, picked him up, and threw him in the air before hugging him tight. "Have fun today?"

"You didn't play a lot."

"Nope. Usually don't in preseason." Jasper had never missed a home game of mine his entire life except for when he was two and had the flu around Thanksgiving, but every once in a while, like now, it hit me how little he remembered from year to year.

"Are you not good? Because Tim at school doesn't get picked on any teams ever because he can't catch a ball."

Leave it to a five-year-old to keep me humble.

"I'm good, kiddo." I set him on his feet and ruffled his mop of dark hair, so close to mine but in dire need of a cut. "I'm great actually, but I need to rest to make sure I don't get hurt before the real season begins."

"Oh. Right." He grabbed my hand. "Come on. Grandma's already given me a cookie *and* she let me have cotton candy at the game today even though she said I needed to make sure I brush my teeth really good tonight."

"Well."

"Huh?"

"You'll need to brush your teeth well tonight, not good."

His little brows puckered together, and I let it go. He didn't always need an in-depth grammar lesson. Behind us, the door opened, and Davis stepped in with a smile, a bouquet of roses, and a bottle of white wine bundled in his arm.

I took in the gifts and groaned. "You're such a suck-up."

He shrugged, shameless. "Got to become the favorite son somehow."

"You're not her son."

A yellow and white checkered towel slapped my bicep. "Nonsense. You're all my kids, always will be."

"Hi Mama B," Davis crooned and reached down to give my mom a hug, as he did, the idiot winked at me and mouthed *favorite*. When she pulled back, Davis handed her the flowers and wine. "Here you go. Thought someone as beautiful as you should have these beautiful flowers."

My mom smiled and laughed. "I can see a suck-up coming from a mile away you know."

"I have no idea what you're talking 'bout."

"Sure you don't. But thank you. They're beautiful."

"Just as beautiful as you, Ma," I chimed in, because screw him. If *anyone* was going to be Ma's favorite, it would be her eldest *blood*-born child.

Davis made kissy noises and kicked off his shoes and shrugged out of his suit coat. We'd come straight from the game, and I followed him. "Want to borrow some shorts or anything?"

I had an entire wardrobe upstairs for this very reason. Also, because when Jasper was a baby, his spit up could shoot halfway across the room. Doctors called it acid reflux. I called it disgusting and a pain in my ass and clothing so I either kept a change of clothes in my car, or more at my parents' house in my own childhood bedroom. It was a guest room now, and no longer held my high school trophies or pictures of friends and maybe a poster of Taylor Swift above my bed—but we didn't speak about that.

"I'm good. Thanks." I headed upstairs and left Davis to help himself. After throwing on a T-shirt and changing into a pair of pale blue linen shorts, I was rushing back downstairs when the front door opened again.

The creak of the hinges was all it took for a ball of anticipation to knot itself together in my stomach before Marley stepped in, followed slowly by Eden.

Her hair was down today, curled, and fell halfway down her back, pulled back at the sides in a tiny clip. Wisps hung loose in front of her ear, and she had her head bent, watching her step and keeping an eye on Marley so I had the unhindered joy of being able to take all of her beauty in. Her deeply tanned skin, probably from years of living in Florida exposed at the shoulders, arms, and chest by a flowy pink tank top with ruffles at the V-neck. Her shorts were white, ironed, and so short I bit my tongue so I didn't groan in appreciation.

When Eden forgot to look so miserable from all the pain our teenage, irresponsible actions caused, she was devastatingly beautiful.

As she stepped inside, my mom came around the corner from the kitchen, and Marley glanced up and grinned at me.

"Nice throw in that second possession to Butler."

"Don't forget about that touchdown run by me!" Hall shouted from somewhere deep in the house, probably sitting and having a beer with Dad, dissecting today's game and the upcoming ones.

Marley grinned at me, and behind her, a stunned Eden had a soft pink rising to her cheeks. "Thanks, Marley. Missed you today."

I skipped the last couple steps and jumped to the bottom, bending down to give her a hug. "Always with you, kid. Right here." She tapped where my heart was, and a painful squeeze hit the same area.

Someday, and soon, that'd be the only place she *was*, and it wasn't fair.

"Right."

"Would you like to help with the salad, Marley?" Ma asked. "Eden, lovely to have you, make yourself at home. Oh, Davis brought me some wine, would you like a glass?"

"Maybe with dinner, thanks Mama B."

"Our home is yours, just like always."

Ma escorted Marley into the kitchen leaving Eden and me alone in the entryway.

"Davis?" she asked, and ran her finger through her hair, head tilted to the side.

"Davis Hall, one of our rookie running backs. He comes and has dinner with me sometimes."

"Oh." Worry drew a line between her brows. I wanted to smooth away with a kiss or something more delightful.

"And Jasper?"

"He's here. Probably sitting on Hall's lap or running with Bongo outside. Nervous?"

She gave me a shaky grin. "Terrified."

"Don't be." I took her hand in mine and guided her closer, aware of her nerves, but for now, there was privacy. "Come here. Everything will be fine."

"Selma—"

"Isn't here and isn't a problem today." I put pressure on her hand, still pulling her until I could curl both of our hands to my lower back. "It's a family dinner. Enjoy yourself, okay?"

"I'm trying."

"I know." She was. I was worried that first day after Selma's incident when she didn't text me that she was running, even away from me in her mind if she wasn't halfway back to Florida, but she'd made an effort since, and I knew it was difficult for her.

"You're safe here, though," I whispered, and brushed my lips over her cheek. "No enemies in this house, got it."

"Right," she huffed but pressed closer to me, turning her head just enough my lips found the corner of her mouth and movement caught my attention from the hall.

"Well, hello." Davis grinned. "Who do we have here?"

# CHAPTER 25
## EDEN

Davis Hall was nothing like I'd expected under the padded uniform and helmet. For some reason, I expected all football players to be this burly, muscular, scowling, and broad-shouldered kind of guy like Cole.

Davis was the exact opposite with a face that probably had him getting ID'd constantly, or even having his true ID called a fake, a smile that made me think of little children who got caught sneaking cookies after bedtime, and while he was clearly muscular, his frame was leaner than I anticipated.

"Hi," I said, and he wasted no time hurrying down the hall toward me and pulling me into a hug that lifted me off my feet.

"Bruh," Cole rumbled.

"Chill. I'm making a new best friend."

I laughed, unable to stop myself and was quickly set back on my feet and yanked to Cole's side. "I'm Davis. Not to meet you…"

"Eden." I held out a hand and he laughed, slapping it out of the way.

"Handshakes are for acquaintances. You and I are going to be best friends."

"We are?"

"You are?"

I grinned up at Cole who was wearing that scowl I'd assumed all football players wore on the field.

"Yep." Davis nodded resolutely.

Cole shoved him into the living room off the entryway and guided me toward the kitchen. "Don't listen to him. Pretty sure he got a concussion last week."

"Not true!" Davis called and lumbered after us. "So, Eden. You've known Cole a long time, right?"

"Um. Yeah?"

He brushed the palms of his hands together. "Tell me all his deepest, darkest secrets."

Cole and I both froze. Our deepest darkest secret? He'd hit too close to home with that request.

"Um…I'm not sure…"

"Oh come on," Davis pleaded and his large, pale green puppy dog eyes and his hair that flopped over them almost made me laugh, and would have, had it been a different topic. "He has to have *some* skeleton in his closet."

"Leave it alone, Hall."

Davis shook off Cole, but he'd touched on a word. I didn't have to tell him the *darkest* secret, but I could give him the most embarrassing.

"All right. Hey Mama B?"

"Yes, dear?" A flush of happiness flooded through me. It'd been a long time since I'd been called that.

"You clean out Cole's bedroom?"

"All but the closet. Why?"

Bingo. "No reason!" I called back and Cole caught on because he stepped into my path.

"Don't even think about it."

"Oh…all the good things are kept in the closet!" Hall took off, running around Cole and me, and thundered up the stairs.

"You're going to pay for this," Cole warned before turning and taking off after him.

"Wrong room!" I shouted, laughter bubbling from me in a free way it hadn't in *years*.

I chased after them and caught up to them, but it wasn't hard. Cole had Davis pinned against the hallway wall, Davis smirking, Cole looking murderous. "These are real pretty family pictures you have here. Almost forgot how goofy you were before the braces,"

Davis taunted, lifting the arm he could to point at a picture of Cole when he was thirteen. He hadn't yet hit a growth spurt, and Davis was right. In the picture, Cole's teeth were a bit too large for his mouth.

"This way," I called, and ran around both of them to Cole's old bedroom. I'd only spent time in here when it was him and Hilary, sometimes Selma too and other football-playing friends of his, but I still remembered the first time I stepped into his room, saw the posters all over his walls and busted out laughing.

"Don't, Eden."

"Cole, Cole, Cole. What kind of friend would I be to my new bestie if I didn't spill your secrets?"

"I'm gonna get you back for this." He said it as a threat, but there was humor in his tone that halted me.

He'd stopped at the doorway to his room that had been changed and updated over the years with a smile on his face, simply watching me.

He was going to let me do this. Happily.

It hit me.

I was being silly. *Free.* I was acting just like I had all those years ago and he was loving it.

"Come on," Davis groaned. "Show me. Show me."

I winked at Cole, letting him know I understood.

I was loving this too.

I flung open his closet door and froze. There were clothes hung neatly, boxes piled beneath a row of T-shirts and next to a shelf of shorts and pants. Figured he'd have clothes here, I guessed, but the lingering scent of his cologne assaulted me, forcing me to take a deep inhale before I was nudged to the side.

"What are we searching for?" Davis asked and his chin hit my shoulder, looking into the closet. "His old porn magazines?"

"No, you perv."

I shoved him off and moved a pile of boxes while he muttered, "People gotta stop shoving me around all the time."

"Be tougher," Cole quipped back with that same laughter in his voice.

It made me smile while I shoved a heavy box out of the way and found what I was finally looking for.

"Yes!"

The posters were rolled up, but still together.

I didn't know whether to give Cole crap for having them in high school, or the fact his mom didn't throw them away when she clearly took the time to pack up his things.

"Posters?" Davis arched his brows disapprovingly. *"This* is his big secret?"

"You haven't seen them unrolled yet."

I took them to the bed and undid the band. Keeping the back of the last one facing Davis, I unrolled them, already laughing when the one in front appeared.

"Cole's not just a music fan, Davis. He's a *female* pop music fan."

"Noooo." He drew the word out like the scandal it was.

"What happens in this room stays in this room," Cole said, still at his perch in the doorway. I figured he was enjoying this, watching me be silly, and there was little heat in his threat.

Davis glanced back at him and barked out a laugh. "The hell it does. Show me. Show me!" He clapped his hands together, and I tossed down the first poster.

Flattening it on the bed, Davis started laughing. "Okay. The female pop music thing is funny, but this woman's iconic."

"True," I said. It was, after all, Beyoncé. "But this one?"

I tossed another one down and then another. Davis excused himself to the bathroom threatening to pee his pants as posters of Katy Perry appeared, then Carrie Underwood who was still in her country days, but she worked the boots Cole used to like so much— and we were near Nashville.

"Not done yet!" I called out to Davis.

"I'm coming!"

"He better not be after seeing all these posters," Cole mumbled and moved back to let Davis back into the room.

"Gross." I could barely get the word out through my laugh.

"Okay." He wiggled his fingers toward his chest. "Hit me."

"There's this beauty." I tossed down a poster of Adele, and Davis lost his smile. "I mean, damn. You know. Those curves. That class. Can't say I haven't imagined her taking a ride on—"

"Don't finish that," Cole cut in.

"Right. My bad. Forgot my company."

With the final two posters, I took one in each hand and slowly turned them around. Davis's eyes went wide, and he took in one, then another, back to the first one again and he spun around.

"Oh Cole! I didn't know you were a Swiftie!"

"Shut up, idiot."

"I'm all about that bass, 'bout that bass, no treble." He smacked his hip and turned, blowing a kiss back to Meghan Trainor. "This is awesome. Truly, Eden. I can work with this information, for sure." He spun back to face Cole. "What will you give me to be quiet about this?"

"I'll let you stay alive."

"Huh. I was thinking of something more—"

"Kids!" Cole's mom shouted. "Dinner!"

Davis took off, running down the hall screaming, "We are never getting back together!"

I pushed at my ear to drown out the sound. The kid had absolutely no singing ability whatsoever.

"No running in my house," Mama B called back.

As Davis shouted out an apology, Cole pushed off the doorway and stalked toward me. "You enjoyed that, didn't you?"

"A bit."

I was still laughing when he reached me, slid his hands to the sides of my neck, and grinned down at me. "You're never more beautiful than when you're letting loose like this."

And then he kissed me, dove his tongue inside my mouth and made me forget all the reasons why I hadn't laughed in so long until I saw him again, until his mom yelled for us again and Cole pulled back.

"Ready to go have dinner with the family and spend some time with Jasper?"

Not at all, but I was no longer terrified, and somehow, everything felt a little bit easier.

Jasper inhaled a deep breath. "And then, Miss Eden, my preschool teacher said that we don't get naps in big kid school and I'm not sure I really like that because I don't like naps, but sometimes it's nice to lay in a dark room and stuff and I don't think I want to do kindergarten next week if I don't get to rest at all, I mean, sometimes my body needs it."

Across from me, Cole chuckled.

Apparently Jasper was used to new people, or maybe it was because I read him books, but he wasn't thrown in the least when Cole and I sat down at the kitchen table. Dave and Kate took their spots at the ends, Cole and Jasper sat on one side, leaving Davis, Marley, and me across from them.

As soon as Dave said the meal's blessing, Jasper launched in about school, and told me about Bongo and the trip they took this summer to Cancun.

"But you still get recess. And you can make new friends."

"I guess." He moved around roasted broccoli and carrots Cole had forced him to scoop up even though Jasper said they smelled funny.

I wasn't sure he'd eaten much of anything with all the talking he'd done, and he'd done enough of it to keep everyone focused on him.

Worked for me. The less Davis pried for more *deep dark* secrets the better.

I turned to Kate, who was happily smiling at everyone. "I know I asked the other day, but how's Graham doing back at school?"

"He's good, dear. Back at school. Breaking hearts—"

"And records," Dave cut in. "Their first game isn't until the end of the month, though, so we'll see how he does this year, but he's happy. Working hard. Same as both my kids."

It was surprising Dave and Kate had somehow raised two boys with professional-caliber athleticism. From what I remembered, Dave hadn't played much football, maybe in high school, but he definitely hadn't gone further than that. He was from a neighboring town where his dad had been a history teacher for his entire career and Dave went to college to do the same before realizing a finance degree, working in business would give him a better life for his family. No sports at all, and yet somehow, there was Cole and Graham.

"He graduates in the spring, doesn't he?" I didn't have to do the math. I knew how far apart in age they were by heart.

"He does, graduating with a finance degree like me. Says he needs to know how to invest the millions he's going to bring home."

"He's entering the draft then?"

"He is," Kate chimed in, with all the love of a mom. "Thinks he should go pretty high considering how well he played last year. As long as he stays healthy, he should be fine."

Next to me, Davis cleared his throat. "I'm sorry to break it to you, Mama B, but your son really isn't all that good. I mean, he missed three tackles on me alone the last game I played against him."

"You played against Graham?" I was shocked, but the rest of the table laughed. I gave Dave a wide-eyed look. "And you let him into your home?"

Dave chuckled and shrugged. "Can't be perfect all the time. It was Cole who had a soft spot for the kid."

"Not a kid," Davis mumbled playfully.

"Always a kid when you're in my home," Kate said and patted his hand.

"Thanks, Mom."

If I wasn't mistaken, Cole growled low.

Kate shook her head at the silliness.

"And yes," Davis continued. "I played against Graham. Went to Clemson. He's at Georgia. We met and *beat* them in the championship game."

"Is that weird then? Now playing with his older brother in the NFL?"

He scratched his jaw and pushed his lips to one side. "It's like having your own big brother, kind of?"

Kate placed her hand over her heart. "Aww. That's sweet, Davis."

"It is, thanks, man," Cole said.

Davis nudged my shoulder. "An older brother, who's really, super-duper annoying and probably busts out to Meghan Trainor when he's showering."

A napkin slapped him in the face.

The rest of the table laughed.

All except Jasper. "Daddy?"

"Yes, Jas."

"Why would you shower with a girl, Dad?"

————

"Thanks to you and Davis, I get to have the birds and bees talk with my son tonight so thanks for that. Really."

"It wasn't my fault."

"Best dinner I've had in a while," Marley said, walking in front of us. I wasn't sure if she was trying to get us off the *birds and bees* talk or if she just hadn't heard us.

We stepped up to her front porch, and Cole opened her door, holding it so we could pass him.

"You didn't have to walk us home, you know."

"Maybe I wanted to talk for a minute."

I glanced inside where Marley was fussing with the electric tea kettle I ordered online. This way I didn't have to worry about her using the stove, and she could still have her nightly cup of chamomile tea before bed—one of the few healthy things she enjoyed.

"Talk?"

He pulled the door closed and pushed me against the porch siding. "Yes, talk. With our mouths but without speaking actual words."

"Oh."

He kissed me, smirking as he moved in and tugged my bottom lip in between his with finesse and intention until I gasped, opened for him. One of his hands settled at my hip while he braced himself with his hand on the wall behind me.

With one single, teasing swipe of his tongue against mine, I once again forgot about everything. Marley's sickness, the way she'd stumbled earlier and almost missed catching the back of the couch. There was my mom, whose phone calls had gone silent since I returned but now knew was checking up with Kate. I stopped worrying if Jasper liked me or how badly Selma hated me.

Everything except peace and freedom and excitement melted

away as Cole moved closer, pressed his chest against mine, tilted his head and took the kiss deeper.

His kiss was swift and firm and delicious enough to make me forget all but one thing.

"Wait," I rasped. "Slow down."

His forehead pressed against mine. "Okay. I know. Too much."

"It's not that. I'm scared Marley's going to come out waving Darryl's old shotgun and demand to know your intentions for me."

Cole chuckled and ran his nose along the side of mine as he stood back.

"I doubt Marley would like to know then, that my intentions with you are very, very wicked."

"Shut up." I slapped him. He was so confident. So open, and I admired those qualities almost as much as his work ethic on the field. "You should go. I need to help Marley get to bed."

His humor wiped away to a clean slate. "She okay? Any more falls?"

"A stumble earlier, but she was okay. It's just scary to watch. And sad."

"I know." He cupped my cheek. "I'm glad you came back, you know. Even if it was just for her, I'm glad she has you helping her."

"I *did* come back just for her."

"Okay."

The arrogance. If I was younger, more naive, I'd kick him in the shin.

"Go home, Cole. Get your son."

"I will, but I wanted you to know, our game is away this weekend."

"You play Saturday this weekend, right?"

He nodded. "Saturday night, but we're heading up to New England and it's a night game so we're flying out first thing Friday and returning Sunday." His black, thick brows tugged together.

"Okay. So…?"

"I've never done this."

When he stopped, was I supposed to translate the rest of his thought? "What? Kissed a girl against Marley's house?"

"No. Dated someone. I've never had to date someone and maneuver around my travel and Jasper and everything else."

"Jasper comes first, Cole. Always. Then your job."

"I know…but maybe I want you to be right up there with him and I don't know how to divide my time."

"Hey." Odd how the positions flipped and now he was worried. There were still a lot of things I was terrified about, top of the list—what were we doing? What were we—but this? Not a concern.

"Your focus is on you, your son, and how you provide for that. I can wait, Cole, for when there's time."

"I just, I don't think I'll be able to see you this week, and I'm not happy about it, but once the season starts and I'm on the road so much I have so little time with Jasper."

The stupid ogre. How had he not heard me?

My hands pressed to his cheeks, and I rolled to my toes. I still wasn't anywhere near his eye level with his height, but at least he'd stopped talking.

"Call me or text me. FaceTime me after Jasper's in bed. We don't need to see each other to figure things out. And maybe it's for the best."

His frown told me he disagreed, and he opened his mouth to say something along those lines, but I pressed my thumb to his lips, silencing him.

"Five days ago, I was sure you still hated me. Now we're having dinner at your parents' house, and you let me meet one of your friends. I've met Jasper and you have drama with his mom. We can slow this down, Cole. There's no rush."

"There is if I want you in my bed again, which I do, by the way."

"Then that'll happen when it's supposed to."

He nipped at my thumb and stepped back. "Fine. I need to get Jasper home and in bed. With school starting this week, I'm trying to get him to sleep earlier. But one more kiss before I leave?"

How could I resist?

# CHAPTER 26
## COLE

*t'll be more fun for Jasper if we ride together.*

Like hell it would. Selma wanted to show up at the elementary school on my arm for the pleasure it'd bring her. Besides, we'd already discussed this.

**I'll meet you there with him.**

*It's his first day of school. It's a special day for him.*

I choked on my own growl of frustration. Jasper was finishing up his eggs and bacon, but this was ridiculous and not what any of us needed on his first day of kindergarten.

**I'll meet you at the school.**

*Cole, be reasonable. The parking lot is going to be full. It makes more sense to do it this way.*

By this way, she meant her way, and while my own frustration was growing, I could only imagine how much this was pissing off Selma. There was a time I would have given in for the sake of keeping her happy, allowing her to get the perfect happy family shot for her Instagram.

Not anymore. Besides the fact I was done playing her games, I now cared how people perceived us. I was not going on as the happy family she liked people to believe we were. Not anymore. Not with Eden back in my life.

**Last text you'll get from me: I will see you there.**

Her final reply came seconds later. I took a sip of my coffee and almost spit it out all over my counter when her next reply came. *Is this attitude about the other night? I can't believe you're still mad at me.*

The fucking *nerve.*

If I didn't need my phone, or to have actual contact with her, that reply alone would have had me chucking my phone as far into the trees in my backyard as I possibly could.

Yeah, I was still mad. My bad.

There was no way I was getting into it with Selma this early, and like always, it'd prove futile, so I turned off my phone and set it face-down by my keys and wallet.

She'd been like this all week.

When I woke up Monday and was trying to get Jasper ready by the time he'd need to be once school started, Selma had already been in the driveway, sitting in her car, waiting so she didn't need to pick him up at her parents or the diner even though they were on her way and my house was not.

It was a matter of a few miles and five minutes, but whatever.

She showed up, acted like she hadn't driven drunk, and made a scene, and swept him off for the day.

Considering it was six fifteen in the morning and she was still in her scrubs, dark circles beneath her eyes telling me she'd worked all night, I wasn't all that concerned about another drunk episode, so I let him go, with a kiss and a reminder to call me if he needed anything.

She did the same thing yesterday, and I was trying to be thankful she was at least staying in her car instead of pouting on my porch or banging on my front door.

But dammit. I wanted to walk my kid into kindergarten. I hadn't been able to be at the meet the teacher night last week due to a late night of film watching. I wanted to see the room, see his teacher, get Jasper excited about school, and check to see if he already knew any kids. My parents had always walked us boys in on the first day of school, at least the first couple of years.

Why Selma had to be difficult about everything was mind-boggling. And exhausting.

I really needed to call that lawyer.

———

The classroom was a blur of activity as we entered. Next to me, Selma's pinched expression stayed stamped on her face, only smoothing out when Jasper spoke to her. She'd been like this since she walked up to Jasper and me outside the school, while we took his picture in front of the Marysville Elementary school sign. She'd tapped her foot impatiently when a handful of parents asked for my autograph and sighed heavily when I took Jasper's hand, smiling all while ignoring her plays for attention and took him inside. The classroom he was in was bright with posters about treating others with kindness and the alphabet in various fonts strung along the wall near the ceiling in primary colors. More primary colors were everywhere from the cubbies along one wall, the bins with their names already on them.

"There's your teacher." I bent down close to Jasper and helped him with his backpack and had him hang it up in his cubby area. "Do you want to take me to her so I can meet her?"

"Met her last week. She smells funny."

"Perhaps we don't say that out loud in the classroom, okay?"

"Why? It's true."

"Because it might hurt her feelings and we don't want to do that, do we?"

His nose wrinkled as he thought about it, and he took my hand like he was hanging on for dear life. I couldn't remember a time when I hadn't run into school, excited to see friends. Jasper was usually more adventurous, but while we toured the rooms and found his name on a name card at a round table where five kids would sit, he didn't seem the least bit curious about any of it.

"Hey, you okay?" I asked while we were finally in line to meet Mrs. Griffith. She was older, nearing retirement age, and had been teaching here since I went to school there, so I didn't need to meet her, but it'd been a long time since I'd seen her.

"I don't like school," he mumbled, and his little chin quivered.

"Why not? You liked your last school, remember?"

"It was smaller. And quieter."

Ahhh. So that was his worry. "Want to know something, kiddo?"

"Not really."

I chuckled and pressed my lips together. He was funny, but I didn't want him thinking I was making fun of him. "I get scared sometimes when I step onto football fields and it's really big and noisy."

"You do?"

Not in a while, but that first year, absolutely. "Yeah. It's all new and scary, and sometimes I'm afraid of getting lost, but you know what?"

"What?"

"There are always a ton of people who can help me find my way. There are other players, workers, security guards and my own teammates. We all help each other."

"I don't have teammates."

"No, but you have Mrs. Griffith, and she's been teaching since your mom and I went to school here. She'd never lose you, and I bet she's used to kids being scared, too, so she'll know how to help you."

He kicked his foot against the rug and dug the toe of his new white Nikes into the yellow circle. "Maybe."

"Want to know something else?"

I glanced up and caught Mrs. Griffith's smile as she waited for us, next in line.

"What?"

"Mrs. Griffith has been teaching since before I was born, and I don't think she's lost a child yet. Isn't that right?" I asked her.

"Not once in thirty-two years, and I don't plan to start this year." She smiled warmly down at Jasper. "Do you think you could help me make sure everyone stays safe?"

"Me?" Jasper's eyes almost bugged out of his head and his grip on my hand loosened. On the other side of him, Selma curled her hand around his shoulder. "What can I do?"

"Well, I need a helper and someone who's *really* good at listening and following directions." She tapped her pink-painted nail against her chin. "Do you think you're good at those things?"

"Sometimes. But sometimes Daddy needs to remind me to feed my dog and I don't always brush my teeth like I'm supposed to be doing when they tell me to."

I chuckled. Selma grinned at Mrs. Griffith while she laughed softly. "I think it's okay if you're not perfect all the time, but you can try, right?"

"Sure. I guess."

"Okay then. If you're going to be my helper this week, can you start now? Because there's a little boy over there." She pointed to a blond-haired boy in the corner, sitting in a chair with a book in his lap. "That's Archer, and he and his mommy and daddy moved to town a few weeks ago so he doesn't know anyone. And I know you've been here for a long time. Do you think you could go see if he wants to help you today? The two of you can be line leaders when we go to lunch and recess later."

Jasper was nodding happily, and the worry in his eyes was gone. "I can do that."

He let go of my hand and before he took off, I crouched down. "Can your mom and I have a hug before you go off to make new friends?"

"Sure." He gave me a hug, halfhearted at best, already intent on doing his important job and then hugged Selma.

"Have a good day, sweetie," she said, kissing the top of his head. "Bye."

He was gone, fears forgotten.

"Thanks," Selma told Mrs. Griffith. "He was excited about school until last week and he's been nervous ever since."

"Tends to happen, and if I'm not mistaken, I remember you getting a little teary-eyed your first day, too."

"Oh, I don't think we need to let anyone know that." She said it teasingly, but there was an unkind threat in her words that I didn't care enough to examine.

"And how are you, Cole? Season going well?"

"We're just getting started but hoping for good things."

"And Marley? How's she doing? We miss her at church and fellowship time these days but we're praying for her."

"She's okay. Has some help with her, but I'm sure she'd love some visitors, too."

"Of course, and we should have thought about that sooner. I'll make sure to set something up. She should be with her friends at this time."

"I'm sure she'd love that. You take care, all right?"

"You too, Cole." She nodded at Selma. "You too. I'll make sure Jasper has a great first day."

We thanked her, and I scanned the room but there was no point in saying goodbye to Jasper again. He was sitting on the rug with Archer, and they had a pile of wood blocks in between them.

He was fine. Happy. Which meant I could get to work.

I headed out of the classroom and maneuvered my way through the small building, Selma following me.

As soon as we reached outside and I turned to head to my truck, a cool hand gripped my arm. "Are you going to keep ignoring me?"

People passing us arched their brows. Partly because of who I was, but she wasn't exactly quiet.

I didn't need a scene in front of our kid's school, so carefully, but firmly I yanked my arm out of her hold and spun to face her. "First, you do not ever put your hands on me again. Second, I have nothing to say to you."

"So you are still mad." Her eyes narrowed and it was a shame Selma was so ugly on the inside because she truly was beautiful. It was the insides that seeped through once you got to know her that made her less attractive.

"You drove drunk to my house and wanted to put our son in the car with you. Yeah, Selma, I'm still pissed. Mad you made the scene in the first place and didn't take the fact that I ignored your calls as proof I didn't want to speak with you, but you showed up and demanded crap that isn't yours to demand."

"How do you know? It's not like we have an agreement or anything. I can take Jasper whenever I want, I'm his mother."

Oh, the irony in all of that, and I was done letting her use Jasper as a tool to manipulate me.

I smirked and rocked back on my heels. "Then it's a good thing I already have an appointment with a lawyer, isn't it. Have a good day."

She didn't need to know I hadn't called him yet, but I would be doing that immediately now.

I turned on my heels and hustled across the drop-off line, Selma's footsteps pounding behind me.

"Cole. Wait!"

I stopped outside the door to my truck. "Gotta get to work, Selma, and I think you're right. We don't have all that much to say to one another anymore, so maybe it's best our lawyers speak for us."

"You can't mean that." She shook her head, fear paling her features. "We always said no lawyers. I can't believe you've done this."

"You left me no choice."

"It's because of her, isn't it? Eden."

"Fucking hell, Selma. The only one who thinks any of this is about Eden is *you*. You've been batshit crazy since you heard she was coming back into town because you still can't let go of the ridiculous idea I'm ever going to want you. I don't. End of. But since you're acting irrational lately, you bet your ass I'm going to do what it takes to protect Jasper, even if it means lawyers and taking you to court, because here's the truth that's going to send you into a tailspin if you don't grow the hell up. I love Eden. Always have. Always will, and when it's time for her return to Florida, I'm going to be working my ass off to make sure she doesn't even think of leaving. She's going to be here, Selma, for hopefully the rest of my damn life and you're going to need to get used to that."

"So what? You're seeing a lawyer so you can get custody and Eden can just move on in and become Jasper's new mom? You're trying to take him from me?"

Fucking batshit crazy. How had I never seen the depths of this before?

"No, Selma. The only person who's going to be the cause of losing Jasper, ever, is you and how you treat him and how he sees you treating other people, including me. You are twenty-seven years old, for shit's sake, stop blaming everybody else and start taking some damn responsibility for once in your life."

"Fuck you, Cole. Fuck you!" She screamed the obscenities, regardless of location or company and I was *done*.

I turned my back to her as heads swiveled in our direction and parents frowned at her language and backed out of my truck.

I left Selma stomping her foot on the sidewalk by my truck while inside, fear curled in my gut.

She knew everything about me. The good, the bad, and the horrific. It was possible I just lit a match and gave her all the ammunition to set my world on fire.

# CHAPTER 27
## EDEN

was anxious. I knew it. Marley knew it. Heck, the squirrels sitting happily on the edge of the bird feeder out back and the vultures circling the pines above probably felt it.

It was Jasper's first day of school and when Cole and I spoke on the phone last night, he told me about how Jasper wasn't looking forward to going to school and his worry that Selma was going to cause a scene. I was pacing Marley's living room, wearing down her original wood floors, while she sipped her tea and guessed the prices on *The Price is Right*.

"Can't calm anything down by being this worked up, Eden."

"I know. I know that, but I'm worried, and I want the day to be easy for Jasper and I don't want him to see his parents fight, and…"

My phone buzzed in my hand, and I answered it without looking.

"Hey, how'd it go?" I asked.

"Eden?" That was most definitely, not Cole's voice and it'd been so long since I heard it, emotion swelled.

I collapsed into Marley's couch.

"Are you…are you okay?"

"Hey, Mom."

Marley twisted her head in my direction, lips parted. She muted her television show and closed her mouth while silence turned heavy on the phone line.

"I…well…I've hoped for so long you'd answer when I called, and now I don't know what to say." She laughed, and it was the laugh I remembered, kind and sweet but this time she was also crying.

I started too before I could stop myself. "It's okay. I'm here."

"Finally. It's so good to hear your voice."

I couldn't lie. Wouldn't. "Yours too."

We cried, both of us, and of course it was Mom who gathered her nerves first. "How are you?"

I laughed. How was I?

Better than I'd been in years, but hearing her voice hurt, too. "I don't know," I admitted.

Marley pushed off her couch and walked over to pat my knee. "I'm going to leave you some privacy," she whispered, and before she turned to leave, brushed her thumb against my cheek, wiping away tears.

"How's Dad?" I asked instead of answering.

For five years, I'd ignored their calls. Five years since I'd had any true contact with my mom, and for some reason, now, I couldn't imagine why. Why I let it go so long and get so bad.

My mom laughed again, that crying, desperate kind of laugh when you're trying to stop yourself. "He's good, currently out back building a chicken coop."

"A what?"

My mom said, "Yeah, I guess the country and Missouri is finally getting to us." She talked then about his job at the university in Cape Girardeau. They lived twenty minutes outside of the town on acres of land and he was now the dean of the business school there. No longer doing much teaching, but in charge of the entire business school. I tried to reconcile the dean of a university building a chicken coop and for the life of me, couldn't.

My mom went on to talk about how she'd started gardening. She worked on some fundraising for the school too, but mostly, they were doing what they always had. Dad worked, Mom supported him, and in their free time, Dad followed along with whatever ridiculous new hobby mom started—which in this case, was having a self-sustaining farm.

From the woman who'd never been able to keep a simple house-plant alive.

My cheeks ached while she talked, and I cried more than once hearing the sound of her voice, until it all became too much, and all the emotions I'd bottled up for so many years exploded like a shaken soda can.

"I'm so sorry," I cried. "So sorry I haven't answered you or called or…I'm so sorry for everything."

"Oh darling." My mom's words were a hug, soothing me in ways I'd forgotten I needed, in ways I'd blocked myself from allowing. "It's okay. *You're* okay, and we love you. We always have and we just want you to be happy."

"I think," I sniffed through a sob. "I think I'm maybe finally starting to get there."

"That's good, Eden. I'm so proud of you." She choked down another sob and I could feel the smile in her voice. Her eyes would probably have more fine lines than I remembered, but her smile would be just as happy. Equally sweet.

"Tell me how Marley's doing," she finally said, and so I did. I told her about the nurse coming, about how she's been stumbling more and I told her about our walks, how I'd catch her repeating herself in the span of a few minutes, and through it all, Mom listened and while the phone was quiet on her end, I had no doubt she would remember every word I spoke.

My phone beeped and I glanced at the screen.

Cole's name flashed and I put the phone back to my ear.

I didn't want to say goodbye to her, but I only had a few minutes to talk to Cole, too.

"Hey, um, Mom?"

"Yes, sweetie."

"I'm getting another call. Do you think I could call you later? Maybe FaceTime you and Dad?"

A quick gasp of surprise, followed by, "We'd love that."

"Kay. Tonight?"

"We'll be waiting for you whenever you're ready. Love you, Eden."

I sniffed. "Love you too."

I switched the calls and as soon as I said hello, Cole barked through the line. "What's wrong? Is it Marley?"

"No." I cried again. "It's fine, I'm fine. I just talked to my mom."

"Shit," he cursed and apologized. "Sorry, I didn't mean to say that. I wasn't expecting that, are you okay? I'd come see you, but…"

He had to get to work. I knew. But what I wouldn't give for one of his hugs.

"It's okay." I sniffed again and did that stupid laugh. "How did Jasper do at school?"

"He was okay. Mrs. Griffith put him in charge of helping another kid get settled and he took to it. Was smiling and playing when we left."

"Mrs. Griffith is still there?"

"Yeah. Surprised me, too, when I heard she was going to be his teacher."

Dang. The woman was older than my own parents.

"And Selma?" I asked, although I didn't want to. Nothing good ever came when she was brought up.

"Was great around Jasper, caused a scene in the parking lot when I left. Cussed me out and had people staring at her and thinks since I mentioned I have an appointment with a lawyer that I'm trying to steal Jasper from her so I can replace her with you."

So many things wrong with that, I couldn't begin to pick them apart. Stunned, all I could ask was, "What?"

"Exactly my thoughts, too. Honestly, Eden, I don't know what's gotten into her, and it can't be all because of you. There's something not right with how she's acting, and it's making me twitchy knowing Jasper is going to start spending so much more time there now that I'm traveling."

"Maybe it's a good thing you're bringing lawyers into it, then."

"Probably. Probably should have done it years ago, but we'd been fine."

From what he said, that was a lie. She'd manipulated him for years, he'd just never cared enough to fight her, so he gave in.

"I'm sorry, Cole."

"Me too. I want things to be easy for Jasper, and yeah, I know she's thrown with you being in town, but it doesn't change anything. Not for her, anyway."

That's where he was wrong, but I wasn't going to point it out.

Until I returned to town, I'd bet my last penny in my savings that Selma was willing to play the long game when it came to Cole, perfectly content to sit around and allow the world to think they were together and maybe eventually they would be.

I'd strolled into town and blew her unrealistic fantasies to smithereens and now she knew she had no chance.

That was on her, completely, but that didn't mean she'd go down without a fight for the dream she'd held on to for a decade.

Which meant even if Cole brought lawyers into the mix, things were about to get ugly and a lot harder before they got better.

———

"Talk go okay with your parents?"

Marley stepped out to the back patio where I decided to sit with a glass of wine once we got off the phone. I'd wanted a drink while I was still on the call with my parents but considering I hadn't seen them in so long and the last time I did I wasn't twenty-one, it hadn't felt right.

But boy, was my glass of wine delicious right then.

I stood and helped Marley into the Adirondack chair, so she didn't fall.

"It was okay. Good, I guess, but strange."

"Healing takes time." She patted my hand and then clasped hers gently together in her lap.

Healing. Was that what I was doing? If so, it was making my skin itch and my mind race. There was Cole. My parents. Family dinners and laughing with Kate and Dave. There was Sarah and Nora, who had called to see if I wanted to join them at McLaughlin's again, which I declined.

Healing involved a lot of people I once again had the power to destroy or let down and I wasn't sure it felt all that great.

"Gorgeous night," Marley said. "Got a lovely phone call today from Mrs. Griffith."

"You did?"

"She talked to Cole when he took Jasper in, said he had a great day today, by the way."

I was, I'd been thinking about the boy all day.

"She leads a Bible study at church, and I haven't been there recently. She thought maybe they could begin meeting here so I can continue for a while. Would that be okay?"

"Of course it is. It's your house."

"Yes, but you're living in it, and I don't want to make you uncomfortable."

"Since when?" I teased. All she'd done since I'd been back was make me face uncomfortable truths.

"Ahhh…but pushing and stretching is supposed to be uncomfortable or else you don't grow."

She had a point.

"I'm scared," I admitted.

"Life gets that way sometimes."

I settled my head back into the chair, turning toward her. Marley was resting casually in her chair, head tipped up to the night sky, eyes closed. "Aren't you?"

"Not scared. I have regrets, wishes on things I would have done differently over the years, things I can't go back and say, adventures I can't take, but no fear."

Damn. If only I could say the same.

"Days go by slowly but the years fly, Eden. Never forget that. Someday, you're going to be old like me, and hand to God, I hope you have more to show for it than I do. I hope you have a family, take the greatest adventures of your life. I see you with kids, maybe grandbabies, sitting around and listening to your stories of everything you accomplished and all the things you have left to try. Dogs. All the dogs. Your home will be such a warm welcoming place because you'll have worked hard and suffered much to get there, so you'll enjoy every moment of blissful peace. That's what I want for you, girl."

It was a lovely vision and tears stung my eyes as she spoke it.

She hadn't mentioned his name, but as I closed my eyes and tried to picture it, it was Cole I saw. Carrying a baby close to his chest like he's probably already done, helping a little girl ride a bike, and teaching a boy to hunt. It was Cole I saw, throwing balls across a vast backyard with dogs at his feet and kids using him like a jungle gym.

"It's a pretty dream, Marley."

"And all you have to do is reach out and hold on."

Maybe. Maybe we could have that.

Some day.

# CHAPTER 28
## COLE

wasn't supposed to be there, but thankfully, I not only had the night to myself, but an understanding quarterback coach. When I approached Kollin, asking if I could skip out of the morning practice to meet Marley's nurse, he'd said absolutely yes.

I pulled into Marley's driveway twenty minutes after the appointment was supposed to start. By the time I'd debated whether or not to go—what choice to make—it finally became clear in a breath.

Marley.

Eden.

Family was *always* more important, and I'd miss enough in the upcoming weeks I wouldn't miss this.

An older Toyota Corolla was parked behind Eden's 4-Runner leaving me plenty of room to park next to Eden's SUV in the driveway. I didn't bother knocking on the door, I knew it'd be unlocked and there was no point in interrupting, so I let myself in Marley's front door and three heads turned in my direction from the kitchen table.

"Hey," Eden said. She pushed off her chair and came toward me. "What are you doing here?"

"Wanted to know what was going on."

"I would have told you later."

"Wanted to be here, Eden." My emotions clogged my throat and Eden nodded.

Of course she understood.

"Of course. Come meet Melanie. She's been really sweet, explaining what might be coming for Marley and talking about how much care she really needs."

"Great." I cleared my throat.

Melanie was around our age, possibly a few years older, with long, platinum hair pulled back into a low ponytail. The dark purple scrubs she wore reminded me too much of Selma and my lip curled with distaste before I could hide it.

"Hi there." She stood from her chair and held out her hand with a polite smile and a professional handshake. "I'm Melanie Buckner. Pleased to meet you."

"Cole. Cole Buchanan."

I shook her hand, and she retook her seat.

"I should tell you I know who you are, and I can promise you the utmost privacy with Marley since you're obviously close."

"Football fan?" I guessed, although I wasn't exactly pleased to have her point it out so bluntly.

"Not really." She shook her head. "I lived in Raleigh my entire life, went to nursing school there, and I was once hired to work with Beaux Hale's father-in-law back before he was married to Paige. She's still a very dear friend of mine. If you have concerns about our office, I can guarantee any nurse who's around any of you will not divulge anything private or personal."

Beaux Hale was the quarterback for the Raleigh Rough Riders, one of the Steel's largest rivals primarily because we were in the same division. It didn't matter eight hours separated us, when we played Raleigh, either at home or away, the stadiums were filled fifty-fifty with Steel and Rough Riders fans.

"I know Beaux well." He was a few years older than me, and we not only saw each other twice a year on the field, but we'd done a celebrity golf tournament together last year. "What brought you to Nashville?"

"Change of scenery." She said it with a smile that didn't quite reach her eyes, looking so similar to Eden I took her answer as it was.

A brush-off so she didn't have to give the real reasons and truth be told, her honesty helped settle my nerves. She didn't have to tell us she'd worked with Beaux and Paige. I would have trusted Eden's judgment about the nurse, regardless.

"I get that," Eden muttered, and I chuckled, finally relaxing since I arrived.

After giving Marley a quick kiss on the top of her head and listening to her tell me I didn't have to be here, too, I slid into the chair next to Eden.

"So, now that that's out of the way, what'd I miss?"

Melanie gave another polite smile. "I was explaining to Ms. Bickerstaff and Miss Barclay the services our company provides and what the next few months might look like for you. Would you like me to restart at the beginning? I'm happy that everyone's on the same page."

"No." There were pamphlets and papers on the table, multiple copies of the same things so I took a set for myself, and then one for Ma who was at a Marysville Beautification meeting with the city where she spent time volunteering. "I'm good."

Eden's hand settled on my knee, and she squeezed. I hadn't realized I'd been bouncing my leg until she settled it, so I pulled in a breath, forced myself to get it together.

"So, as I was saying, I know you've mentioned you do some volunteering at the doggy daycare in town, but I'm not sure it's wise to be leaving Marley alone for that many hours a day anymore."

"Okay." Eden drew out the word and glanced at Marley.

She was focused on the nurse with little emotion. "I think I'm doing okay."

"I know. You're doing great, actually, but after speaking with you both today, it's clear there's been changes since your last doctor visit."

Marley huffed. "Minor."

"Marley—" Eden said quietly. "I can cut back the hours, they'd understand."

"Or you can call our service. We have a half dozen nurses who are on call at all times for those who have short-term notice of plans." She faced Marley again. Ultimately, this was all her decision anyway and while she still had more good days than not, Eden would let her decide. "We aren't here to be intrusive or disruptive. Sometimes, clients simply need someone to sit here and read. It gives them reassurance while they're out that their loved one is okay. It doesn't mean they'll take over your life or boss you around."

"Well, thank God for that," Marley said.

"I'd like that," Eden said, so quietly, like she didn't want to hurt Marley's feelings. I couldn't blame her there. None of this was pretty or easy. "It'd make me feel better leaving knowing someone is here when I'm not."

"I told you weeks ago you'll know when to make those calls."

"Thank you," Eden whispered, and her voice was hoarse. She'd had a hell of a night last night and by the time I called her when I got home and Jasper to bed, she'd been too tired to talk. But I knew she hadn't only spoken with her mom for the first time in five years, she'd also seen them on the phone and talked to her dad.

She'd probably stayed up half the night crying.

That would change for tonight, though. I wasn't leaving either of them for longer than I had to.

———

After Melanie left, I spent some time with Eden and Marley. Marley was as chipper and sassy as always, seemingly accepting, or ignoring the fact she'd soon need much more help than Eden could provide. Eden was quiet, and I hated to leave her, but after giving her a kiss at my truck before I headed back to the training facility for a light practice, I'd promised her I'd be back later.

"You don't need to do that," she'd said.

"I know. I want to, and Selma has the night off, so Jasper is with her tonight. I'll come back here when I'm done and bring dinner so make sure you text me what kind of pizza you want."

"Oh." Her blue eyes had turned round. "Okay then."

I'd left, gone to practice and stopped by my house to grab a few things. After a quick trip at BarkTown to grab Bongo, who was surprisingly not soaking wet, I picked up dinner and returned to Marley's.

We were eating the pizza, Marley and I drinking water while Eden sipped on a lemonade and watching Bongo run around the backyard, jumping at every stray leaf that blew in the breeze.

"It surprises me he doesn't take off and run more often for still being so young."

"He's pretty good about staying close, always has been. It's the mischief he gets into when left alone that makes him a full-on puppy."

Marley chuckled. "Sounds like dogs aren't that much different than you and Graham growing up."

"We never tore couch cushions to shreds, but you have a point."

She closed her eyes as she rested her head against the back of the Adirondack chair, and a faint smile curled her lips. "No cushions, but you two made plenty of mess and broke furniture so often you forced your mom to replace the pieces with thrift finds."

"Maybe if she would have bought stuff new it would have held up better."

"Nothing's going to hold up well when two teenage boys decide having a dance party on the kitchen table is a good idea...with friends."

Next to me, Eden laughed. Such a soft, beautiful sound, I forgot to remind Marley that it was Graham and his friends that did that, not mine. It could have been her age or cancer making her memory blurred, but I wasn't about to do a thing to ruin the sweet mood.

"I should get to bed." She yawned. "It's getting late, and you kids deserve some time alone."

"Marley—" Eden started and moved to push out of her chair, but I beat her to it and helped Marley.

"No, no. It's time anyway." I curled her arm around mine and tucked her close to me as she found her footing. "Never forget to remember those silly moments in life, you two. They'll keep you smiling when you don't feel much reason to."

She said it with a smile, but my heart squeezed. She wouldn't have many more nights to either reminisce or share her wisdom with others, so I took it, committed it to memory and helped her inside.

"I can get it from here," she told me once we were past the kitchen.

"You sure?"

Eden had mentioned she'd taken to leaving the bathroom door

open an inch or two so she could hear what was going on, but maybe she was more comfortable with Eden hearing her than me.

Marley patted my hand. "Yup. It's a good night. Feeling strong."

"Okay." I kissed the top of her head. "Good night, then, Marley."

"You too, Cole." She let go and headed toward the bathroom. She turned to me as she stepped through the doorway. "Take care of her."

"Always," I choked out.

I didn't need Marley's blessing for anything, but her giving this to me? I'd treasure it.

She stepped inside the bathroom, closed the door, but like Eden said, she left it cracked so light peered out in the hallway.

I went to her bedroom and flipped on the light so she wouldn't walk into a dark room and headed back to the kitchen where I gave Marley privacy but was close enough in case she fell. While there, I cleaned up the leftover salad Eden had made to go along with the pizza, washed the dishes we'd left on the counter before heading outside, and wiped down the counters. Once I heard Marley's footsteps pad softly to her bedroom and her door click shut, I returned to the backyard, Marley's wisdom once again solidly stamped in my memory.

I'd take care of Eden, emotionally and physically, and I was done moving slow for fear she'd bolt.

If there was a time in Eden's life she needed to know I was in this for the long haul, it was now, with the threat of losing someone she already loved barreling down on us with growing speed.

# CHAPTER 29
## EDEN

ole's lips brushed my jaw, and I clung to him. We were out on our boulder, where he'd brought me after Marley went to bed and we were sure she was asleep. As soon as we got there, he settled me on his lap, facing him. My ankles were hooked together behind him, and his hands were at my lower back.

He'd kissed me immediately, not bothering to move slow or warn me. He'd simply dipped his chin, crashed his lips to mine and we'd been sitting there, his hard length growing beneath us and his hands never once straying from my back for what felt like hours, simply kissing.

As he pulled away, my breathing was raspy and fast, and his pulse at his throat showed the same was going on with him, although I hadn't needed further evidence from the hardness at my sex.

"I'm staying the night with you," he said. "And you're not going to try to talk me out of it."

I could hardly think straight as it was, and the need he'd so passionately stoked inside of me only gave me a moment to hesitate.

"Marley—"

"Will stay asleep downstairs as long as you can be quiet." He smacked my backside and slid forward on the boulder until his feet were planted on the ground. "Come on."

He stood, forcing me to wrap my arms around his neck and hold on as he started walking toward the trail to take us back to her house.

"I can walk, you know."

"I know, but I don't want to let you go."

The weight of his words sent a shiver through me, making me hold on to him tighter. I didn't think he was only talking about *now*, in this moment, and the thought of being able to hold on to Cole for the rest of forever was a possibility I'd never seen coming.

"Cole."

"I know you're scared. But keep holding on and I'll show you why you don't need to be."

Again, not about the walk, and I shouldn't have been so surprised he read me so easily. But I did as he said, held on to him until we were up the steps on Marley's back deck, and he gently set me to my feet.

"Know I said I didn't want you arguing about me staying, but if you're not ready, I can wait."

I'd waited what felt like forever for this moment, so sure it'd never happen I'd given up.

This time, I took Cole's hand in my hand and stepped backward toward Marley's door, tugging him along with me. "I don't want to wait."

---

Nerves hit as we tiptoed through the house and up the stairs.

"I feel like I'm sneaking a boy into my parents' house," I whispered once we reached the second-floor hallway.

"That's because you *are* sneaking a boy into the house. You naughty little thing."

"Shut up." I smacked Cole's hip and hit a wall of hard muscle. He took my hand and squeezed. "Which room?"

"Last one." There were four rooms upstairs, including the primary bedroom but I didn't have the nerve to take what had once been Marley's room even if she'd moved into the downstairs guest bedroom years ago.

She'd claimed then she did it because the stairs were proving too much for her, and she'd moved all of her belongings downstairs, but it hadn't felt right to me to take *her* room when I arrived.

The benefit of choosing the room I did, which I hadn't had to think about yet, is that the room I was in was farthest from hers downstairs.

"It's…flowery," Cole muttered, and I bit down a laugh.

He was right. The walls had been wallpapered over thirty years ago, back when pinks and greens and floral patterns were all their age. There was a quilt on the bed that was most likely equally as old but since she didn't have many visitors or guests who stayed the night, it was practically brand new. Artwork was on the walls, more flowers framed in dark wood with a thin, gold trim, and the curtains were an exact match of the quilt.

Stepping into this room felt like stepping back into my own grandmother's room when I was a young child and still living in Illinois.

I tried to ignore it every time I stepped into the room, but out of all the options, this one was the best. "You should see the other rooms," I told him.

"I feel like my testosterone levels just plummeted." He scanned the room again and shivered. "Did you know that high schools used to paint the walls in the visiting locker room a bright pink color because studies showed men felt less masculine and tough, or aggressive, after being around that color for twenty minutes? It gave the home football teams a competitive edge and it was banned about twenty years ago."

"Well thank you for that interesting and completely non-sexy fact. And how have you never been up here?"

He shrugged. "Don't know. I think Graham and I spent the night here every once in a while when we were kids, but I only have vague memories of it. But I'd know if we were in this room. It'd haunt me forever."

"That explains the bunk beds in the room at the top of the stairs. Would you feel more masculine doing it in there?"

"No, I would not feel better *doing it* in a bunk bed."

"Well, then this is your last option." The only other room upstairs was more of a junk room. Back when Marley sewed and knitted and crocheted, she'd turned that room into her craft room. Now there was a wall of shelving, filled entirely with rolled-up skeins of yarn she probably hadn't touched in years.

"I'll survive," Cole muttered, and then he wrapped his arm around my lower back and yanked me to him.

I fell against his chest with a *thump* and muffled laughter against his shirt before he pressed his thumb to my chin and lifted my face to meet his.

"I've waited a long time for this," he whispered. "Floral bedspread be damned, I want you in my arms and we don't have to do anything you're not ready for."

The flames he'd stoked out on the boulder had diminished somewhat, but all it took was that gentle touch of his hand on me, and the unnecessary reassurance and the embers rekindled, turning me needy and ready for him.

Instead of answering with words, I rose to my toes and pressed my lips to the dip between his collarbones at the base of his throat, the highest point of him I could reach while standing.

A low rumble slipped from him, and he walked me backward until my legs hit the end of the bed and then I was falling, controlled by his arm at my lower back. "I have imagined all the ways I wanted you, all the things I wanted to do to you."

It was a threat. A promise. One I was more than willing to succumb to.

"Prove it."

Cole laughed against my jaw before trailing his lips back to my ear. "I will. Tonight, I'll prove it at least twice."

He was still standing at the edge of the bed, and with one quick move, gripped his T-shirt at the back of his nek and tore it off. He flung it somewhere, but I was focused on the first sight of all that bare skin exposed to me since a pool party we'd both been to shortly before high school graduation.

*Damn.* He'd had the body of a man then, but this… this was otherworldly with the curve of his pecs and the deep groove between his abs. His hair was dark, spread across his chest and following that line, light enough to be sexy as hell. I was gawking at him as he towered over me, it couldn't be helped. I gasped as his hands went to my hips.

With one quick tug, he had my backside settled at the edge of the bed, his finger quickly working the button and zipper of my cut-off denim shorts and then Cole was dropping to his knees in front of me.

"This okay?"

"Yeah." More than. Cole on his knees? Sliding down my shorts? It was heaven. I propped myself up on my elbows and shivered as he leaned in, grazed the skin at my inner knee with his lips before trailing upward.

"You always smell so damn good…like raspberries and sunshine." His large, tanned palms pressed against my knees, spreading me open for him.

A small tremor of fear moved through me. I'd done this before. But it was with a guy from a bar, or a short-term fling and it was generally on the bed under the cover of darkness, not with my blinds open, the moon casting a gentle glow over me, and Cole staring at my sex like it was his most precious treasure.

"Cole," I whispered, and he jerked his gaze to meet mine. "I'm scared."

"I know you are." His fingers brushed along my thigh, up and down, until that fear lessened, and arousal took its place. "You can trust me, though. You know that right?"

Of course, I trusted him. It was *me* I wasn't quite so sure about anymore.

His fingers grazed my sex, the silk of my thong and he groaned, biting down on his lip. "You're soaked. This all for me?"

"Always," I rasped as his fingers found my clit, already pulsing beneath the thin fabric.

"Damn straight." He dipped his head, and kissed me there, pressed his lips over my sex and the friction of the silk, the heat of his mouth had me arching up for more while my head fell back with blissful pleasure.

Oh, dear sweet heaven. He shoved the silk to the side and kissed me again. He ran his tongue through my wetness, around my clit and then my panties were gone, Cole moving back to tug them down. Every scrape of the soft fabric against my skin along with the tenderness of Cole's strong hands further stoked the need for more, and when he pressed his mouth to my core again, he added a finger, drawing out a pleasured moan.

"Oh God."

"You taste better than I expected." It was the last thing he said before Cole stopped his teasing and featherlight touches and he proceeded to drive me wild. First with his mouth. Then his finger. He added a second that had me clutching the bedspread beneath me. He'd propped my feet to the edge of the bed and my heels dug in, totally exposed to him and vulnerable and yet I'd never felt safer.

I panted, bit down on my lip as he continued eating me like a man who'd finally found his favorite dessert after months of denying himself the pleasure of it.

My climax barreled down on me, hot and fast. It burned through me, and I bucked against his mouth and he gripped my hip to keep me still. "Be quiet," he reminded me, "we can't get caught."

And oh dear God. The thought of that, being found like this, so spread out for anyone to see made me go mad with pleasure and when I came, I pressed a hand to his head, gripped his hair. He groaned with satisfaction as the orgasm rolled through me, more powerful due to my need to be silent and when he brought me down, he kissed the inside of my thigh.

"Good girl, Eden."

I would do *anything* for Cole, if he continued speaking to me like that.

"More," I rasped, and I was shuffling further back up the bed. I was still half-dressed and as I removed the tank top I'd worn with a built-in bra, Cole got to his feet.

"God you're fucking gorgeous, Eden. So damn pretty. So perfect." His hands went to his athletic shorts, his excitement evident in the very large bulge beneath them. "I cannot tell you the number of times I've thought of this very moment."

"Cole—"

"I mean it. Every damn word. In my mind, and in my heart, you've been mine since the day we met."

A lump lodged in my throat as he spoke, and then all thought evaporated as he shoved off his shorts and climbed onto the bed. His large, muscled body caged me in, and he bent down and kissed me. "You don't have to agree with me, you don't even have to feel the exact same, but I promise you now, I'm going to love you so damn hard while you're here, returning to Florida is never a thought in your mind or an option."

I couldn't tell him I did feel the same. I couldn't tell him I never wanted to leave either. All of this was happening so quickly, and we had so many things to still work through, but there was no way I could leave again.

I wouldn't survive it a second time.

Instead, I slipped a hand between us and wrapped my hand around his thick, long, and hard length. "Prove it," I whispered, as he groaned into my mouth.

"Damn, you are perfect." I slid my hand up and down his length, loving the feel of him and when he lowered his hips, the tip of him brushed along my clit, eliciting a delightful shiver from me. I was ready to go again, ready for the first promise he'd issued to take care of me at least twice.

"I need you," I admitted and if he heard the depth of that declaration, that it was for more than this night, his body and the promised pleasure he'd provide, he didn't hesitate.

"I need a condom."

"I'm on the pill." I'd never gone without, and I'd surprised him. "Unless, that is… you need that?" He had Jasper after all. He knew the risks of what could come even when you were trying to be safe.

"I'm clean and I trust you. And there's nothing more that I want to feel than *all* of you wrapped around me. You sure?"

I nodded. I was absolutely sure.

A wicked smile curled his lips up right before he slammed his mouth to mine. "Definitely perfect, Eden. At least for me."

His thick head nudged at my center, and Cole grabbed one of my legs, widening me and he pressed against me. The intrusion stole my breath.

"Relax," he whispered against my mouth. "Just relax. I'll go slow, I promise."

Nothing had prepared me for this. His size was large, the strain of his body was evident as he took his time and finally, the head of his cocked pressed inside of me and all the tension I'd held dissipated.

"Perfect," I rasped. "Oh my God you feel incredible."

He huffed against my mouth, grunted something that sounded like *same* as he continued sliding inside of me, an inch at a time, pulling out, pressing in. I felt him *everywhere* inside of me. In my heart. My soul. The most private parts of me were consumed as Cole finally seated himself deep and paused.

He pushed up on his arms, brushed hair off my forehead. "You doing okay?"

"Never better. But you're going to have to move soon." I was already rolling my hips, searching for that delicious friction of my clit against him.

"My pleasure, Eden." And then Cole moved. With his hand at my thigh, he pushed it farther out and as he began rocking his hips, his other went to my clit. Between his fingers, the thick fullness inside of me that pressed against all the exact right parts, it wasn't long before I was clawing at his thigh, his backside, anywhere I could reach to anchor myself against the slow and hard and absolutely perfect onslaught that was everything Cole.

The muscles in his throat strained as he moved and his fingers would leave marks at my thighs, but all I saw was the man who loved me.

The man who would always take care of me.

The man I'd run from who I never wanted to see in my rearview again.

"Cole!" I cried out his name and he slammed his lips to mine to silence me. I groaned against his mouth.

"Come on, Eden." His hips were hard and powerful against me, the slapping of our skin loud enough to wake the town and when I came, I tore my mouth off Cole's and bit down on his shoulder, crying out as pleasure whipped through me with the force of a hurricane, tore me out to sea, beyond, and brought me back with the peace that only came after the most powerful storm.

Cole grunted and thrust his hips against mine. He groaned my name into my ear as his entire body shuddered. I felt him. The heavy pulsing of his release inside of me and I wrapped my hands around his back to hold him against me.

He'd been right earlier.

I was perfect for him.

And Cole, he was even better than that for me.

———

I woke to the first hint of the morning sun peeking in through the sheer blinds, the curtains left open last night, and the warm tickle of Cole's breath at my neck. Stretching my legs, I flinched at the slight sting of pain in between my thighs from last night and I took a moment to revel, enjoy the fact that for once in my life, it truly seemed like everything I'd desperately wanted was not only within reach, but had been handed to me.

Yes, there were obstacles we were going to need to overcome, issues I still needed to find healing with, but Cole had made me a promise the night before, and I was desperate to cling to it.

*Keep holding on.*

"You're thinking so loudly you woke me up," Cole muttered, and his arm tightened over where he'd draped it around me. "What are you worried about?"

"For once." I turned, and the bed shifted as he pushed up so his head was braced in his hand, elbow to the mattress. "I don't think I was actually worried."

A sleepy hint of a smile curled his lips. "Good. As much as I hate to say this, I should probably get going. Selma will get Jasper to school, but I have a morning practice before we fly out later."

*Right.* Because he needed to hop on a plane and head to Tampa Bay.

"Okay." He brushed his lips against mine, a barely there hint of a kiss that still awakened the sore parts of me he took care of many times last night.

"What are you doing this weekend? Anything planned?"

"I'll spend time at BarkTown, might try to take Marley into town, at least get her to church on Sunday. She mentioned missing her friends lately."

"That'd be good for her."

"And I think I'll go see Hilary."

The plan was out before I'd truly considered it, given it much thought, but if I was going to cling to Cole and let go of my fear, this had to be the first step.

His thick, dark brows arched into points. "Yeah?"

"I think I need to."

"You okay going alone? I can go with you on Monday if you can wait."

"Not sure Hilary would enjoy my apology with you there with me."

"She can't actually hear you."

"I know, but it still feels wrong. Like maybe this is something I have to do alone. Face her after all this time."

My vision turned blurry, and Cole curled me against his chest, brushing tears off my cheek as he hugged me. "I get it. But call me if you need me after. I might not be able to answer right away, but I still want to hear you when you're done."

I promised him I would, and we pulled ourselves away from each other. Fortunately for me, Marley must have still been asleep when Cole snuck down the stairs, shoes in hand and a small overnight bag thrown over his shoulder.

"Go before she hears you," I whispered.

Cole laughed and kissed my smile away. "Wouldn't want you to get grounded."

"Exactly." I angled around him and opened Marley's front door. "Text me when you land safely?"

"As soon as I can. And remember what I said."

He'd said too many things to me recently I never wanted to forget, but his worry line digging in between his brows told me what he meant.

"I'll call if I need to," I promised.

"Good. Take care, Eden. Love you."

He kissed me, sealed his mouth to mine before I could react to his words or his declaration. And I was still standing in the doorway, stunned, fingers sealing in his kiss and his love while he climbed into this truck and backed down Marley's steep drive.

# CHAPTER 30
## EDEN

The sun that had woken me up, bringing with it peace and hope turned to gloomy skies and thick, humid air. Fitting, considering it matched the tightness growing deep in my gut with every step closer to Hilary's final resting place.

Whatever had possessed me into thinking this was a good idea was long since gone. Rows of headstones, many crumbling with age, some newer with fresh flowers lined the rows. I forced myself to look away from the ones with the freshest flowers, people who had either been gone years whose loved ones still remembered them frequently, or they could be the opposite—recently gone and I couldn't stop the ball in my throat from growing.

As reality closed in on me, my steps slowed. While the cemetery was quiet, only the rustle of leaves and intermittent singing of birds, I could practically hear the purr of my SUV, promising me comfort if I fled back into the safety and space it could provide.

No.

I wouldn't run from this.

I'd meant what I told Cole. I *was* trying, I just needed to keep walking.

Healing wouldn't come from running—but old habits were hard to break.

Finally, with a deep trembling breath, Hilary's headstone appeared, and with it, the pungent aromas of the roses laid out not only in the provided flower bouquet holder next to it but piled in front.

So many flowers.

So many *fresh* flowers.

Her parents had moved away, but her brother was still here. She'd had so many friends in town from being raised here since birth. Did all of her old friends still come see her so frequently?

I couldn't imagine Selma doing such a kind, selfless thing, but Nate definitely would.

My feet froze as I arrived empty-handed and guilt grew from that. I hadn't even considered bringing her something, something that would have made her smile. That would have made her happy and carefree and would have her infectious laugh making everyone smile.

*Beloved daughter, world's best sister, cherished friend.*

The words were etched into the stone beneath her name and dates and brought a quick smile as I thought of Nate insisting the sister part included.

Tears swarmed my eyes as I moved closer, blocking everything else out around her and all the words I'd planned all morning fled.

"Hey." I kicked at the vibrant green grass, recently mowed, so the scent of grass clippings mixed with the roses. A tuft of grass kicked into the air swarmed and fell with the same heaviness sinking in my stomach.

"I don't know what to say now that I'm here."

This was ridiculous. She couldn't hear me, couldn't absolve me for the part I played in her death. She couldn't wave a magic wand and heal my guilt or hug me and tell me everything was okay, that she was fine and happy wherever she was—if she was anywhere besides buried beneath where I stood.

The thought made my feet itch to move away, but I forced myself to move closer, drop to my knees in the grass and then to my butt.

I picked at the grass, tried to find the words that if she were in front of me, would explain everything but the harder I tried, the more cliché and weak it all sounded.

"I'm sorry," I choked out. "I'm sorry we hurt you and we lied to you. I'm sorry I was a shitty friend to you when you were so kind to me. I didn't mean to hurt you, and I tried so hard to stay away...."

My breath shook and my heart rumbled so hard my pulse thundered in my ears.

Cole and I had been wrong, so very wrong to play the dangerous game we'd played for so long. We'd tried to stay away from each other. We tried to never be alone. We'd done the absolute wrong things with the best intentions when what I should have done from that very first day of school when I realized they were dating, was to stay away from both of them.

If only I'd tried harder, found a different group of friends or been a loner for a year. "If I could go back and make different choices, I would, you know." I picked at the loose blades of grass in front of me and blinked away tears. "We probably wouldn't have ever been friends, but you'd be alive, and I wish I could go back, but I can't, and I'm so sorry for hurting you and for being such a crappy horrible and selfish person when you were never anything but so kind and sweet to me."

She'd spent all of November and December trying to get me a date for January's winter formal, never once affronted when I'd insisted I didn't want to go. And I hadn't because she'd wanted us to double date, me with one of Cole's friends, but there was no way I could have done that. Instead, I'd stayed home, grabbed a blanket and winter coat and I'd taken my phone out to the boulder and had been watching Netflix on my phone when Cole returned from the dance and had the same idea as me.

It wasn't the first time we'd found each other on the boulder, and it hadn't been the last.

*"How was the dance?"*

*"Hilary had fun."*

*"Well, that's what was most important."*

*I hadn't meant it as a slight, or to sound so bitter. "What do you want me to do, Eden?"*

*"Nothing." I grabbed my extra blanket and hopped off the boulder. "You're doing everything you should."*

*"I'm not though, am I? When I'm with her, I think of you, and when I'm with you, I know I'm hurting her."*

*"Then stop hurting her."*

*And yet I'd come to this spot to be close to him, even when I couldn't have him. When he'd made his choice and I was the idiot waiting for him.* "Good night, Cole."

"You're leaving? Just like that?"

"I'm tired." *Of being second. Of understanding why I was. Of being accommodating and still unable to get over this stupid crush that was probably only going to end up crushing me.* "I'm tired of all of it."

"I went home that night, you know," I told Hilary and no one. "Alone and cried, and I was so damn sure I was never going to talk to either of you again. Do you remember that? I avoided you for two weeks, ignored your calls, had my parents tell you I was at work or out on a run when you stopped by to find me. I *tried* Hilary, over and over again to stay away. I'm sorry I wasn't stronger."

Because two weeks in, Hilary finally cornered me on my way out of class where I'd been sneaking out to my car to eat lunch alone instead of with her and Cole. She'd grabbed my arm, said, "No way. I don't know what's going on with you but when life gets hard, you need your friends."

I'd tried to argue about it, had ignored Cole that day and ate my lunch in silence while I'd felt the heavy weight of his gaze on me. She'd grabbed me the next day. And the next. And the fourth until I gave up the fight of trying to stay away.

It wasn't her fault. She had no way of knowing that being around my *friends* was making everything worse.

And then on Valentine's Day, I'd gone to my car and on the windshield was a single red rose that had sent me into tears.

*Someday I'll be able to give you more. And I'm sorry I can't right now.*

Cole hadn't signed the note. I'd crumpled it and thrown it away along with the flower and tossed both into our garbage bins, burying it beneath trash bags already inside and never thanked Cole for the flower. Never told a soul.

We'd played a dangerous game and while it was with good intentions, both of us lost.

Hilary most of all.

I sat there, reliving every moment where Cole and I tried to do right while fighting what we felt. I confessed to all of it, every time I'd knowingly hurt someone with only goodness inside of them, I laid it all out for Hilary. Apologized for every single moment. I owned up to my part, my own selfishness, and by the time I was done, I felt no different.

There was no peace and forgiveness to be had. The clouds darkened, thunder rolled in the distance, and I was so lost in the amount of time I'd spent there I had no idea the thunder had moved closer until the sound of someone clearing their throat behind me made me jump.

"Oh. You."

Nate stood there, khaki shorts and light blue T-shirt with his brewery's logo on his chest. Flowers in one hand, a book in another.

"I think I'm more surprised you're here."

"I had some things to tell her."

He showed me the cover of the book. I didn't see the title, but my lips curled. "You come here to read?"

He shrugged.

Hilary had loved to read. She was always talking about the romance books she loved to read, that first love she always thought was so innocent and beautiful. "Just like Cole and me," she'd say, resting her temple on his shoulder at the lunch table.

"I read to her. Her old books."

"Oh." Surprise had my lips parting and I rolled them together to hide it.

"It's dumb, but she used to read to me before I could, all the time, and she loved it, so now I get books I think she'd like, and I come here to spend time with her. I figure with our parents gone, I'm all she has."

"I'm sorry," I said, and I couldn't stop more damn freaking tears from falling.

"I know you are."

His statement stunned me. No, "You should be," or "good," or "lot of use your sorry does now." Nate didn't scream at me for my role in his sister's death, why he was now reading romance books to her after her death instead of listening to her prattle on about them.

"I don't know what to say to that," I said, realizing I was standing there like an idiot in front of him.

"Cole told me what happened all those years ago, you know. I know what she saw that night, and so I get what happened. But I also know she loved you. If that..." He shook his head, glanced to the distance. "If that truck *hadn't* been there that night, if she'd had another day...if she could have talked to you...eventually she would have forgiven you. She would have moved on, you know? She wouldn't have hated you."

"Why hold all that hate inside you when you don't need to?" It used to be one of her favorite sayings when she heard about people arguing.

He grinned. "Exactly. So, I know that she would have let it go and moved on eventually. I'm not doing her favors by holding on to it for her, and I know you cared about her. It doesn't take a genius to see you still feel like shit whenever you see me, Eden."

"I don't think I deserve her forgiveness or yours."

"We were kids. You're not to blame for her running into the street. You're to blame for hurting her, yes, but it was a bunch of mistakes that ended really bad for her. I've come to peace with that."

And yet, he still came to the cemetery to read to his sister who died seven years ago. How much peace could he really have?

"I come and read to her because it makes *me* happy." Amazing how he read my mind. "Maybe I'm not willing to let go of her, but unless she was reading, she never used to like being alone, so some days I think of her here, alone, even though I know she's not here, and I just want to keep her company. Reading passes the time. Besides," he kicked up a crooked grin. "Some of these romance books have expanded my horizons in some pretty adventurous ways."

I barked out a laugh, unable to help myself. "Yeah?"

"They're like manuals, in the art of getting a woman to fall in love with you and the sex positions aren't so bad either."

"You read them for yourself, now, don't you?"

"I'll never tell."

My laughter subsided and so did Nate's smile.

"I should go."

"You can come back, you know, anytime. And to the brewery. I'm sorry for how I treated you. I was shocked and didn't handle it well."

"I don't think there's ever anything you should apologize to me for."

"Maybe you should think about stopping doing so much of it all the time, too, then. We all make mistakes, Eden, it's how we grow from the after that matters."

"Right." Because I'd done so *well* at that, too.

But I could. I could start.

"Do you think…do you think it'd hurt her?"

"To see you and Cole together? I think it's been seven years and she would have probably been married with a handful of kids by now, loving her own life so I don't really think her opinion matters."

I kicked at the grass, trying to reconcile the dream he had for his sister if she'd lived into the reality.

"You grew up and got smart, Nate."

"It's all these books."

"I should go."

"Stay dry and tell Cole I said hello next time you talk to him. He doesn't come in much during the season to the brewery and I miss his business. Besides, Jasper owes me a game of corn hole someday soon."

"I will."

I couldn't say, as I climbed into my SUV, that I'd gotten the healing and absolution I'd been so desperate for but seeing Nate had helped. Getting everything off my chest made it feel lighter.

Maybe now that I'd taken the first step, the rest would come—as long as I kept trying.

———

"How are you?" Cole's question carried a heavy tone to it, a knowing one.

He'd called me as soon as he arrived back at his hotel after a walk-through practice at Tampa's field and then a team dinner.

"Tired," I admitted. I'd come home and napped after I went to the cemetery. The evening was spent cooking dinner and making chocolate chip cookies from Mama B's recipe. Marley helped, but I kept a close eye on her, needing to step in when she went to grab the one cup scoop instead of the tablespoon, staring at both of them with furrowed brows.

The simplest things, and every few days I saw the struggle.

Melanie warned us about her decline, but it was possible I'd over-looked small things in the last couple of weeks since I hadn't seen her in so long.

Cole had enough on his mind without me needing to bring it up.

"How'd your day go?"

I broke a cookie in half but couldn't bring myself to chew on either piece.

"Nate was there."

"Yeah?"

"Well, he came later, after I cried for so long at her site the grass won't need to be watered for weeks."

It was a lame attempt at a joke, and it fell flat.

"Eden."

"I'm okay. Better, maybe? It was hard, like you said, but I don't know...if Nate doesn't hate us for taking away his sister, and her family doesn't hate you, I guess it's getting harder to keep hating myself."

The silence stretched on through the phone, and I didn't have to wonder what he was thinking. *I told you so*, was probably on the tip of his tongue and I guessed he was trying to find a nicer way to say it.

"I love you," he finally said, and the words rattled inside my chest, sending pleasure straight to my heart. "And I'm really proud of you. I know that wasn't easy."

"Nothing about this month has been easy."

"But you haven't strapped on your running shoes yet, right?"

I chuckled, and glanced to my bare feet, making themselves at home in Marley's home and in Marysville in general.

In the last few weeks, I'd gained women who might be friends, help with closure, and the boy who I'd always loved, loved me back.

"Not yet," I whispered, but there was a smile on my mouth and Cole knew it.

"Good."

"I'm thinking I might not need them?"

A low rumble of approval came through the phone. "Good. That's real good."

Let's hope I could hold on to that thought.

# CHAPTER 31
## COLE

onsidering my last public altercation with Selma, a couple weeks back, I wasn't sure if it was wise or not I was sitting next to Grayson Hodges in a booth at the diner. I'd finally made an appointment with a lawyer, and the Sherriff was legally required to be the one to serve her papers for the custody arrangement my lawyer and I worked on.

I was hoping if we could handle this publicly, and at her parents' diner, it would smooth the road for us to get this taken care of easily and quickly.

At least, with her parents there, she wouldn't shout obscenities.

Irv and Theresa might despise me, but I still doubted they'd heard about Selma's drunken trip to my house and her return trip home in Grayson's cruiser. Small-town gossip spread quick, but most would be cautious enough speaking about the fiasco around them.

And while Grayson was there, he was sitting at the bar, giving Jasper and I privacy.

"Do you want some ice cream for dessert?" I asked Jasper. After I picked him up from school, we'd gone home to play with Bongo. He chased the dog around the yard until both the boy and dog came inside stinking to the heavens. I'd sent Jasper upstairs for a quick bath while I cleaned up the mess he managed to create in an hour after being home from school.

"No."

"You okay?" I tapped his foot with mine beneath the table. He'd been extremely quiet all day. Could have still been his adjustment to school, but he'd been happy and all smiles when I picked him up. He'd also been surrounded by four other boys, including Archer.

"Uh-huh."

"Hey." I reached across the table and took his hand where he'd been coloring on the placemat. "Are you okay? You can tell me if something's bothering you, you know. Anything. Dad's always here."

"Mom won't be." He yanked his hand out of mine.

"What?"

He went back to coloring with his red crayon, except now, the marks were deeper. His hand worked furiously across the paper.

"Jasper…what do you mean by that?"

He flashed me a scowl, something so unlike him, I was still stunned when he said, "Mom said you're finding me a new mommy, and soon she won't be able to see me at all anymore."

That fucking…. A red haze filled my vision as I forced myself to stay calm.

"What's this now?"

Theresa startled me, and I hadn't even realized she'd been headed our way.

She tilted her head in my direction, annoyance on her face. "What'd you just say, Jasper?"

"Nuffin' Grandma."

"Jasper, I'd never let you not see your mom. She's your *mom*. Forever. And she loves you very much." I forced the words out of my mouth through shards of glass. My jaw was clenched so tight it was a wonder I could move it at all.

"Why do you think that then?" Theresa asked.

She'd crouched down at the edge of the table and picked up a green crayon. Finding another picture on the placemat, she started coloring. She never liked me much, but it was Irv who despised me.

"Mommy said Daddy won't let me see her soon. Said he's getting me a new mommy." He glanced at me. "Is it that nice lady who read books to me when mommy scared us?"

Theresa's hand froze on the placemat. "What's this?"

Her voice was startled, quiet.

"Eden is a girl I really like, and yes, I won't lie, I'm hoping she gets to spend a lot of time with both of us when you're ready for that, but like I said, she's not going to take your mom's spot in your life, Jasper." Unless Selma kept being a fucking bitch. Then we'd see.

"Oh." Theresa whistled. "I hadn't realized you were seeing her."

"It's new. And fragile."

Since we were talking about this there was no point in hiding the truth. But there really needed to be a parenting handbook on how to handle children when one parent takes a leap onto the hot mess express out of nowhere.

She kept coloring but stood and scooted onto the bench seat next to Jasper. "How'd your mom scare you, sweetie?"

"Theresa—" I warned, but she'd asked so nicely, I really needed to be taking notes, learning how she was pulling all of this out of him so easily.

"She woke me up one night yelling at Dad. They was outside so I didn't see but I heard 'cuz she was really loud." He pointed to Grayson at the bar. "That police ossifer took her home."

"A police officer," she murmured and lifted her grayish-blue eyes to me. "Well, that seems like quite a long night."

There was accusation in her eyes, like how I dare not tell her about this or wondering if what Jasper said was true, but I stayed silent.

"Yep. And Daddy's friend was there so she read me books and then I fell asleep and wasn't afraid anymore."

"Well." Theresa set down her crayon and ruffled Jasper's head. "I think it's nice to make new friends. You've met them at school, right?"

"Yep. Lots of them."

"Good. Say!" she said with excitement. "How about you head to the back? Maybe Grandpa or Mr. Earl back there will help you bag up some cookies to take to school tomorrow."

"Really?" Jasper's smile stretched across his face. So much for not being in the mood for dessert.

"You bet."

She stood and he took off toward the back and as soon as he was gone, Theresa sat back down.

"Nice diversion tactic there."

"Talk, young man."

I hadn't been a young man in a long time, but Theresa looked fit to be tied with what she heard so I told her what happened, what was going on with Eden, and how she showed up that night after already causing a scene at the restaurant. Then again at school. "She's worrying me, and now this shit with Jasper…I went and saw a lawyer today, which was why I brought Jasper here. I asked her to meet me here before she went into work. Grayson has to serve her papers legally, but I thought if we were together, it'd go better than in private."

"I see." She'd said that a lot along with a few *oh my's* and *oh dear's* mixed in while I'd spoken. "I know we haven't always thought the best of you, Cole. And we didn't make it no secret you and Selma should have tied the knot when you got her pregnant, but I want you to know that I think you're a fine dad. Looking back, I don't blame you for the choices you made back then. I also know we spoiled Selma too much and kept doing it for far too long, but this just isn't right. She's a mom now, and it's time for her to put aside these childish notions she always carried. Irv will come around, too, especially once I tell him what happened."

There had never been a time when Theresa or Irv had come close to praising me. "The custody agreement I worked up with the lawyer I talked to is the same as we've been doing now. I didn't change a thing, I just wanted something formal in case something happens. I also added in child support for Jasper."

Selma worked hard, but she *was* on a nursing salary, and last year after I took Jasper on a summer vacation to Utah and Arizona, she'd made a comment about wishing she could do those things with him. So, I made it so she could. It wasn't much for me and in the end, it'd only give Jasper a fuller life, even if it was also a payoff to get her to shut up.

I figured, though, she didn't really want *me*, she wanted the life I could give her.

This way, we both won—at least, if she was reasonable.

"I'll go get Jasper out of the back so you can get on your way. I think maybe you should take off," Theresa said. "I'll go talk to Irv and we'll have a talk with Selma when she gets here. Will she need her own lawyer?"

She didn't *need* one if she signed it. She could represent herself. "If she wants to make changes, then it'd be safer. For both of us."

"Okay. We'll handle this. Seeing Jasper so upset and worried hurts my old heart and my daughter's better than this, even if she can't see it quite so clearly right now."

"Thank you." My shoulders slumped, relaxed for the first time in what felt like weeks.

She stood and patted the table. "Like I said, you're a fine man and a good dad. You deserve someone who makes you happy, too."

"Thanks, Theresa."

She patted the table, and I handed her the envelope I'd left on the bench next to me, so Jasper didn't ask about it. "Dinner's on us today, I believe."

"That's not necessary."

"I know. Still, we don't need you to keep paying to feed our grandbaby. Seems silly we ever made you pay when I think about it."

It was the largest peace offering she ever gave me. I took the olive branch and nodded and then once she was gone, cleaned up our mess as best I could and tossed a hundred-dollar bill on the table.

Maybe I didn't need to pay for the food, but the server had still done her job and done it well. If Irv or Theresa had a problem with me thanking their employees, I was certain they'd let me know.

———

With the custody papers out of my possession and feeling like Irv and Theresa might actually be on my side—which was really Jasper's side, so I shouldn't have been surprised, as soon as Jasper and I got home, I sent a text asking Eden to come over when he fell asleep.

I needed her. Wanted her. It'd be difficult, especially last minute with the home health nurse system but ten minutes later she assured me she'd be here.

*Melanie has a free night so she'll be here at eight. Everything okay?*
**We'll talk when you get here. Good, though, I think.**

She sent me a smiley face emoji and after Jasper and I played more fetch with Bongo, getting all his energy out after being kenneled again, I sat down next to him in the family room and grabbed Play-Station controls for the both of us.

"Which game are we playing tonight?"

"Why's Mom mad?"

Well, that was a loaded question.

"That's a big question with a really hard answer, kiddo. But, well, you remember how mom and I talk about our friend Hilary every once in a while?"

"The one who died?"

"Yeah. She was really special to both of us, and Eden was her friend, too. There's a lot of history there between all of us and it isn't all really pretty."

"Ugly history? Like wars and stuff?"

He was more on the nose than he realized. "Like I said, it's complicated and I think your mom will stop being mad soon. But until then, all you need to remember is that both your mom and I love you to the moon, with three trips around the sun and out to Mars and back again. Right?"

"Mom says we should all live together, and Eden is stopping that."

Selma needed a lesson on learning how to shut up.

"I don't think your mom and I need to live together to love you as much as we do, but yeah, in a way, kiddo, I like Eden that much that someday, when all three of us are ready—me, you, and Eden living together? I think I might like that. But that never means you won't still see your mom like you do now. You know that, right?"

He shrugged and worried his mouth. The gears grinding in his too-smart brain were as loud as Bongo's snores while he lay across the room on his dog bed.

"I like Eden. She seems nice and she smells good."

Again with the smells. I couldn't disagree.

"Can I see her more if it won't make Mom mad?"

"I think for right now, I'd like to keep our time just me and you since I'm going to start being really busy, but maybe she can keep coming to dinners at Grandma's house. Would that be all right?"

Slowly, I'd introduce them. As much as I wanted to rush things with Eden, it wouldn't be good for anyone and while I didn't need Selma's approval for anything, it'd go smoother if we gave her time to adjust as well—assuming the best of her and that'd eventually happen.

"Yeah, but if mom doesn't come, and if she wants, Eden can come to your games with us, too. That way there isn't an empty seat."

I thought that was a fantastic idea, and personally, the idea of Eden finally in the stands cheering me on was something I'd long since stopped dreaming of since I assumed it'd never happen.

"Maybe some game. We'll just take them one at a time, all right?"

"Sure." He grabbed his controller and until it was time for Jasper to go to bed, we played Mario Kart and Minecraft.

By the time I finished reading him his books and tucked him in, he hadn't mentioned his mom or Eden again, but that didn't mean I wasn't counting down the hours until she got here.

# CHAPTER 32
## EDEN

ole's front door opened and then he appeared in the doorway before I'd reached his porch. His wide shoulders and muscled frame took up the space and a tingle of excitement flickered down my spine.

When he called earlier and told me to come over, I didn't hesitate.

It'd been a week since I'd gotten to spend any real time with him and even though I didn't fully like the idea of sneaking over when Jasper was there, for now, if it was what we had to do to make things work, I'd take it.

The last week had been intense. Marley's forgetfulness was appearing with more frequency, along with her stumbling and balance. Melanie and another nurse, Jody, were alternating days so I could leave the house, so I hadn't been surprised when Melanie didn't have a problem coming over when I called her earlier.

On Sunday, Marley and I hadn't watched the game alone. Nora had texted to see if I wanted to go to Buckin' Brews and watch it with her and Sarah and when I explained I didn't want to leave Marley or have the nurses come on the weekend, they grabbed a couple variety of six-packs from the brewery and two bottles of wine along with a bottle of non-alcoholic cider for Marley and joined us.

We ordered pizza, while I baked spinach and artichoke dip and a crockpot of queso dip.

We watched the game, laughed and cheered as Cole once again

gave his team a fourteen-point lead in the first half of his preseason game before joining the starters to cheer on the rest of the team to victory over Tampa Bay.

I'd even talked to my mom again when she'd texted to ask how Marley was doing.

Mama B brought over lasagna one night for dinner.

I went to volunteer at BarkTown, I took Marley into town for lunch a couple of times, and somehow, in the last week, everything had started to feel like home again, and I was in a constant state of awe at how easily things were going.

At least for me. I'd spent most of the day on pins and needles worrying about Cole and how this day was going to go for him.

"Hey there," I said, excited and nervous to be in his home again. The last time hadn't gone great—at least parts of it.

I took the steps up the porch and as I reached the door, Cole flung out his arm and yanked me inside.

The door closed behind me and then his mouth descended.

"You'll need to be quiet," he said, right before he dove back into the kiss and my back hit the wall. "Oh." The sound of surprise was all I got out before he drove his tongue into my mouth, pressed his body against mine and raised one of my legs, up and over his hip while he ground his fully clothed body against mine.

Fireworks exploded at the first, hard and hot feel of him against me and I tangled my hands in his, tugged him toward me as he devoured me with his mouth and the size and strength of his body.

"Fuck, I've missed you," he murmured, yanking his mouth off mine and peppering kisses on my throat, my jaw, and my exposed collarbone from my tank top with his kisses.

The scruff of his beard scraped against my sensitive flesh, creating shivers of arousal to cascade down my limbs, toward my stomach, to my sex.

It already throbbed for him at that first touch and when Cole brushed his hand up my side, across my stomach and scraped his thumb over one of my nipples, I gasped against his throat.

"You like that," he stated and did it again, pinching it a third time. I rose to my toes and shoved my forehead against his throat.

I was a panting, needy mess of nerves and I'd barely stepped inside.

"We need to move," I whispered. "Somewhere private."

I didn't need to say more. Cole squatted down, grabbed my backside in his hand and once again, was carrying me like I was the weight of a football, through his house and passed the downstairs bathroom.

I ended up in a dark room before he turned on a lamp on a dresser.

"Guest room that's never been used except for when Davis stayed here for a few weeks. Far away from Jasper's room."

"It works." I wiggled in his hold until he set me on my feet and kicked out of my flip-flops, and shoved down the short, terry cloth shorts I usually saved for wearing before bedtime. There'd been no need to get dressed out of my comfy lounge clothes before I came over and I reveled in the surprise, followed by hunger and desperation that tightened Cole's features at my brash display.

I lost sight of him while I tore off my tank top and then I was in this strange room, Cole fully clothed in front of me in shorts and a polo shirt, wearing nothing but my hair clip and a smile.

"You are a fucking delight," he said and tore off his shirt.

The zip of his shorts ripped through the air and then he was only wearing his tight, white boxer briefs that clearly showed the large bulge behind them and his hands were at my waist.

"Cole!" I laughed and clamped my lips together. Right before he tossed me on the bed, following me and caging me in with his size.

"What'd I tell you about being quiet."

"I know." The last thing I wanted was Jasper hearing us.

"Are you going to be a good girl?"

A shiver of delight danced straight to my sex as he hovered over me. There was a threat in his eyes, and I *almost* wanted to know what he'd do if I said no, but instead, I reached for him, slipped my hands to the sides of his neck and tugged him closer until I brushed my lips across his chin.

"You should probably find some way to keep me quiet then."

In all the years I'd had short-term boyfriends and lovers, I'd never dared be so bold.

This was what must have come with trusting the person you made love to, because Cole could tell me to bend over and smack my ass until tears fell from my eyes and I would still crave more. Be desperate for more of him.

He pushed off the bed, went and locked the door. "Just to be on the safe side," he murmured before returning, crossing his arms over his chest at the foot of the bed while he stared down at me. His gaze skated across every inch of my flesh, making my skin prickle and my core grow wetter with the intensity of his perusal.

"Where should I start?"

"Anywhere."

I moved my legs together, but he grabbed my ankles. "Open them. Let me see."

Oh dear *god*. I could climax from his words alone. He settled my feet on the bed, legs bent and spread wide so *all* of me was on display. Thank goodness the lamp only gave off a soft, warm glow. I wasn't sure I could lie still, show him this blatant exam of my body with the harsh, overhead light.

"Cole," I whispered, and my hands curled into the quilt beneath me, somehow understanding he wanted me to stay exactly where I was.

"Should I start here?" His finger brushed against the inside of my knee.

I jumped from the initial teasing touch and then bit down on my tongue as he pushed his finger further up my leg.

"Here?" He circled my inner thigh and drifted up the crease to my hip bone to my leg before heading over toward my belly button.

I shook my head and licked my lips. Killing me. He was going to kill me with his slow, barely there brushes of his flesh against mine. My entire body was an inferno and when he finally, *finally* brushed his finger down my slit, my lower back arched off the bed to get closer.

"Oh," I whimpered, and remembered he wanted me quiet.

He tsked twice and shoved his finger deep inside me with a forceful thrust that left a low groan slipping from my throat.

"Not so good with the quiet game, are you?"

Yet he didn't sound disappointed.

"Never. More, please."

A second finger added a first and then Cole placed a knee on the bed. He worked his fingers inside of me slowly, but with deep thrusts and when he added his thumb to my clit, I almost shot off like a rocket, would have screamed his name except he slammed his mouth to mine and swallowed all the sounds he ripped from me with such incredible precision, I'd wondered if he studied the art of the female orgasm as intensely as he did football.

I came quickly, violently, my body shaking beneath his as my orgasm rolled through, sending shocks of pleasure to the tips of my toes before he kissed my throat, moved his body down mine and sucked a nipple into his mouth. His fingers were still at my sex, and I shivered from the sensitive, well-used sensations, digging fingers into his hair.

He grunted his pleasure as I tugged and pulled on his hair while he worked both of my nipples, tugging them, sucking them, switching between both and then quick teasing flicks with his tongue that left me never knowing what he was going to do next but wanting every single thing he did to me.

Slowly, his fingers slid out of me, and his hands went to my hips. He flipped me over like a rag doll onto my hands and knees. I glanced at him in surprise, but he only bent low beneath me and pressed a kiss to my ass.

"Bite the pillow if you need to," he warned and then he licked his tongue from my clit, the length of my slit.

And oh holy fuh-reaking *cow*. There was no teasing left, no slow build up. Cole ate me from behind like a man who'd fantasized about this and had finally found his gift. My body shuddered and eventually, my arms could no longer hold me up. I collapsed onto the bed, side of my face pressed to the pillow, ass in the air, biting down on my lip while Cole added fingers and brushed his tongue over my clit, working it like he did my nipples.

Another orgasm threatened and whips of pleasure tightened my spine before radiating out and I slammed my eyes closed, my mouth opened in a silent scream I swallowed down while my entire body trembled with the force of it.

And then he was there. Pushing into my center, knees on either side of mine, hands gripping my hips.

"Hand to the headboard to brace yourself, Eden."

I complied without hesitation. He'd already given me more pleasure than I could withstand, I'd do anything for him. As Cole slammed into me, I did what he suggested earlier and bit down on the pillow.

"Did I hurt you?"

I shook my head, managed to squeak out a *more* and he gave it.

Cole pounded into me with a slow, intense but brutally delicious pace I was certain would have the house falling down around us when I finally came again. It did. But I took it, forced myself to be as quiet as possible and then Cole pulled out, flipped me over.

"Want to see your eyes when I come," he said, before sliding back inside. He pressed his mouth to mine, slipped his tongue inside. I wrapped my arms around him, rocked against him, and when we finally came, he grunted his pleasure down my throat while I whimpered into his and he came, shuddering against me while I pulsed around him.

"You're very bossy in bed," I whispered, already replaying what had happened in a way I wanted to commit to my memory forever.

"Did you not like it?"

"I liked it more than I expected to."

"Good." He chuckled against my mouth. "Need to use the bathroom. Want to get dressed or lie in here and talk?"

I wanted to never leave a bed when Cole was around or wear clothes in his vicinity again.

Which wouldn't go great if Jasper saw.

"Clothes," I mumbled, and Cole grabbed mine from the floor.

"Probably the responsible thing, but I'm not happy about it, either."

He tugged on his boxer briefs and used the bathroom. When he was done, we switched. I refixed my hair into its clip, splashed cold water on my face and washed my hands.

When I was done, Cole was in the kitchen, pouring himself a glass of red wine.

"Need a drink after that?" I teased.

"Need something to calm me down before I do it again. Want one?"

I preferred white, especially in the hot summer, but I'd take it. At my nod, he grabbed another wineglass from the cupboard and he brought them both to me.

"Where's Bongo?"

"My bathroom again. It's easier so I don't have to worry about his barking waking Jasper. Come on."

He led me outside where he had a massive patio. The immediate outside had a covered ceiling with a ceiling fan whirring softly. One sectional couch faced a television mounted on the wall. Beyond that there was a larger patio complete with an outdoor fire and grilling station. An outdoor table large enough to seat eight, and a curved couch in front of the fire.

He took me there, and once we were seated, kicked his feet up on the coffee table in front of us.

"Do you want to talk about your meeting today?" I asked.

Cole had his arm draped over the back of the couch and I scooted closer to him so his fingers could trail along my shoulder. He cupped the bowl of his glass between his finger, stem and base hanging down.

"Meeting went fine. I was planning on meeting Selma at the diner so I could talk to her about it with Grayson. Figured if I took Jasper and were at her parents' place, she wouldn't make a scene."

"Let me guess. That didn't happen?"

"She never came. I was talking to Jasper and Theresa walked up, heard him saying something about how his mommy told him I was getting him a new mom and I wasn't going to let her see him anymore."

"What? That's horrible. I mean, besides not being true..."

"It's evil. I know. And nasty. Theresa heard, sat with us while we got the rest out of him and then when she sent him to the back, I told her about her showing up here. Surprised the hell out of me when they seemed to be on my side. Said she and Irv would talk to Selma and get her to let this go."

"Well, that's good." I sipped my wine. Cole was right. It was surprising. Selma's parents tended to be the kind who believed their child could do no wrong. At least they used to be.

"So, it's done?"

"Not until she signs it, but I offered her a shit ton of money for child support so I'm hoping she signs it for that alone."

"You paid her off?"

He grinned down at me. "Wouldn't call it a payoff, and she *should* get something, she just never asked for it. I make a thousand times more than her, and I don't always like thinking of me being the parent who can buy their kid all the expensive things, you know?"

"You haven't heard from Selma yet?"

"Not a peep, although I've been distracted recently."

He kissed me, and the quick brush of his lips sent me tumbling all over again.

Kissing Cole reminded me I was home—or that I'd find my home wherever he was, and I never wanted to stop.

"I hope this helps for you and Jasper."

"He asked if he'd see you again. I hope you don't mind, but with what Selma said, I told him we'd keep our friendly visits to family dinners for a while."

It meant more sneaking over here and hiding, but I understood. "I get it. I told you we can go slow."

"Problem is I don't want that. Not with you. But I do need to be careful with Jasper so for now, it's as slow as I can reasonably speed."

We finished our wine, found *The Last Kingdom* on Netflix and watched two episodes while we made out like teenagers and laughed about it. We spent the next few hours talking about nothing and everything and when I couldn't fight my yawns anymore, Cole once again walked me to the car, kissed me like a gentleman and stayed in my rearview until I pulled onto the street.

We hadn't met under the best circumstances. Certainly, hadn't always done things right and I still held a lot of regrets.

But as I pulled away from Cole's house, for the first time since I'd returned, the pain I'd held on to for so long was nothing more than a whispering breeze in the air.

In its place, was a contentment, for once in my life.

# CHAPTER 33

# COLE

This was it. Our first home game of the season. We won in Texas last week, thirty-five to fourteen, and came home high on our first road win only to get straight to work preparing to host Atlanta.

On either side of me stood Dawson and Davis. Jefferson and the rest of the offense spread out on the five-yard line while we stretched, did quick sprints and loosened our muscles. Half of us had noise-canceling headphones or AirPods in to drown out the noise, but I didn't. I lived this moment.

The stands filling with fans. Men old enough to be my father, or older, with their faces, sometimes their hairy bodies, painted with red and black paint. The weather was gorgeous, the sun was out, and thankfully it wasn't going to be brutally hot. My body was warm, limbs loose, and from their seats at the twenty-yard line, eight rows up behind the home team's bench side sat my parents, with Jasper and Marley in front of them.

Selma's seat was empty, and while she could still show up, I doubted it. I received papers in the mail from some attorney she'd hired asking for double the amount of child support I'd put in my offer. Like I cared. I signed everything and my attorney said it'd be filed with the court within thirty days, making it official.

Since then, the only time I'd heard from Selma was when she sat in her car when she picked Jasper up for school in the morning, or when I knocked on her door to pick him up before she left for her night shift. We hadn't exchanged two words, and while it was nice, I was still waiting for the other shoe to drop.

Unless Theresa and Irv scared the absolute crap out of her with her behavior I told them about, I figured Selma was planning something, biding her time and waiting until I became complacent before striking.

Hell, more than once I'd considered she'd never really wanted me in the first place but the money. If an extra ten grand a month was all it took for us to be decent co-parents, I should have done it sooner.

A whistle blew, and I lifted my hand and waved to Jasper and Marley. She didn't wave back, but Jasper stood and threw both hands wildly in the air and behind him, my parents waved back. I'd run over to them earlier and tossed a ball with Jasper for a few minutes, like I usually did before games, fully aware of the cameras on me while I did so, so I kept it quick, only allowing them a few shots of me throwing the ball with my son.

I hustled off the field with the team toward the locker room, Davis slapping my back as we ran.

"You ready?"

"So damn scared I might piss my pants."

Ah. I remembered that feeling. So full of nerves there was nowhere else for it to go except out your throat or the other end.

"Hey." I clasped his shoulder before we reached the locker room. "You're good."

He grinned beneath his helmet, all cocky swagger, but the worry in his eyes told me he was faking it. Not bad. *Fake it 'til you make it*, right?

But I needed him focused. "You've got this. You've already played five games. You have the lowest dropped pass percentage in the entire fucking league so far. You're fast, and Atlanta might have prepared for you but you're faster. And don't forget—you've got *me*."

"Right. Right." He nodded quickly. Puffed out his cheeks and shook the nerves out of him, shaking his legs and arms to keep them loose. "I know. It's all good. As soon as I'm lined up it'll be fine. Just another game, right?"

It wasn't *just* another game. It was *the* game. Every game was. This was the NFL. Where dreams came true and were crushed in equal measure depending on the player, the luck, and the ferocity of the opposing team.

"Want to know what I thought of that first year when I lined up? And my very first starting game?"

"What?"

"High school."

"Seriously?"

"Yeah." I grinned. "The girls. The stands. The small little fandom. Don't tell me you didn't walk the halls of yours, feeling like a damn king on Monday mornings and Friday afternoons."

"Hell yeah, I did."

"Exactly. We were tough shit, top dogs, whatever you want to call it, but everyone *loved* us, worshipped us. We were the best and we played for the high of the win and a stupid fake gold trophy every season, only dreaming we could someday be exactly where you are now, right?"

"Hell yeah."

"And it was the most fun I'd ever had in my entire damn life. Right?"

"Absolutely."

"Then go out there and line up, remember that fun. Remember that feeling and remember how fucking *calm* you were. The men across from you might be stronger, might be bigger than high school, but we're living our dream, and it's *fun*."

"All right. All right. Yeah. I got you."

He bounced on the balls of his feet, more excitement flowing from him than nerves.

"All right then. Let's go have some damn fun!"

I shouted it and the rest of the guys in the hallway, heading toward the locker room, joined in. "Hell yeah, we are! We're going to kick some ass today, boys!"

———

We weren't kicking ass, but we were winning. Only by three though, and the game was far from over with only forty-five seconds left on the clock, with Atlanta having the ball. They were lining up for a third and long play. If Atlanta got the first down, they'd be in field goal position.

Two more plays decided the fate of the game and while we'd rocked our offense, our defense had struggled against one of their tight ends known for his strength in running. But with twelve yards for them to go due to a sack on the last play and a loss of yards, it was doubtful he'd be the target.

Still, our sideline was tense as our defense took their positions. Atlanta had just called a timeout, so the clock was stopped until the snap and I felt the energy buzzing along the sidelines with every passing breath. The stands were wild, a thunderous rumble of *defense* chanted over and over.

The ball was snapped and Atlanta's QB, Allen, grabbed the ball. He turned to pass, looked up for a receiver, but our cornerbacks had them both covered. He spun, tried to find the shorter throw to the tight end, but as soon as he did, Cortland Knox dug through an opening in the offensive tackles.

"Look at that fucker go!" Davis shouted. His hand gripped the sleeve of my jersey.

God, that kid's energy was *infectious*.

Knox found Allen and tackled him, and oh... "The ball! The ball!" I was shouting, jumping along with Hall. The ball had popped out, and Knox snagged it. But the man didn't fall on it like he was supposed to. On the bounce, he scooped it up and started running.

Holy crap. For a dude as large as he was, he was *fast*, and the guy took off, ran five yards while our entire sideline screamed, "Kneel it! Kneel it!" We didn't need the big man rushing down the field. We were ahead in the game.

Knox covered the ball and started to take a knee right as the offensive tackles reached him. One landed on him. The other shoved his shoulder.

"Hell, yes! That's how you do it!" I shouted for Knox, our entire offense standing and cheering along with the defense.

The entire play lasted seven seconds, and I was strapping my chin straps to my helmet and running back out to the field.

Twenty-eight seconds to go, thirty-five seconds on the play clock. Game over.

We went out for the necessary snap, and I kneeled the ball. As I stood, my gaze drifted through the stands.

"See?" I held the ball in the air for Davis and gestured to the stands. "Just like high school."

"Better than!" He slapped the back of my helmet and trotted off the field.

He was right. He'd had another incredible game, only dropping one pass and coming up with some I was pretty sure only made by the grace of God. He'd been double-covered all day, but that hadn't stopped him, and it hadn't stopped me from trying to get it to him. He might be a rookie, but for a deep receiver, he was still the guy I trusted the most.

I hustled toward the center of the field, waving in the vicinity where Jasper was. I rarely saw him after games until I came out of the locker room. Another reason why Selma's display during our first preseason game had pissed me off. After telling the coaches and other players I could find a good game and grabbing a quick chat with Allen, we headed back to the locker room, where I stripped out of my gear, showered, and spent a few minutes loosening my muscles on a bike before getting dressed into the suit I'd had to wear to the game.

Now that the game was over, I was only focused on one thing and one thing only.

Family dinner, where Eden would be meeting up with us.

Outside the locker room, Jasper called for me, and I turned, saw him at my dad's side before he ran to me.

"Good job today!" He flung his arms around me.

"Couldn't have done it without you cheering for me, kiddo." I set him on his feet, and he went running straight to our kicker's kids. Samson had four, the oldest was eight and the youngest was two. Jasper occasionally spent half of the game hanging out with them and the other kids in the family room if he didn't want to watch the whole game.

"Hey, Marley," I said.

"Hi." Her smile was faint, not nearly the boisterous smile or congratulations I was used to. I bent to give her a hug and she stiffened.

"You okay?"

I pulled back and dropped my arms. My mom's brow furrowed.

"I'd like to leave," she said and started walking away. I wasn't even sure if she knew where she was going right then, and I pulled up next to my mom while Dad grabbed Jasper. "She okay?"

"I don't know. She was fine during the game. I think. Maybe she's tired?"

"Maybe." Or she was forgetting what just happened.

"Hey, Marley," I called out, and she stopped. I jogged up to her and grinned. She still had that fake smile on her face, but it wasn't one I was used to seeing. "You ready to get back home and grab Eden before dinner?"

"Oh? Is she in town? That girl, so precious. I've missed her so much since she left for school."

She didn't remember…and as she smiled that fake, barely there smile, reality slammed into my chest with the force of an Atlanta tackle I'd already taken.

I cleared my throat.

"Yeah, Marley. She's here. Eating dinner with us."

This was what Eden had meant when she said she was starting to forget things.

And the doctor had told her once that started happening, the rest would follow soon after.

I'd just never thought she'd forget me, or my games. She'd stiffened in my hug because she didn't know who I was, and she had no idea she'd just watched me lead to a victory.

# CHAPTER 34
## EDEN

"See you later!" Nora called out, her arm lifted in the air.

"Thanks again for coming!" I waved back.

Nora slipped into the passenger seat and Sarah started the car. They'd known Marley was going to today's game, Cole insisting on it before it was too late. When I mentioned it to Nora earlier in the week, she said she and Sarah would come over, as long a I made my queso dip again.

This time, they also brought tacos and refried beans from one of the food trucks and margarita mix and tequila. Marley's coffee table looked prepped for the Super Bowl instead of the first home game of the season.

We watched the game, cheered on Cole and the rest of his team to victory and this time when they scanned the crowd and landed on his family, I not only smiled because Marley was there, waving down at the field where Cole had to be, but because the seat on the other side of Jasper was empty.

I hadn't told Cole I'd been worried Selma would show up and put on a happy face for the game. He didn't need my worries, my stupid jealousy distracting him from anything else, but it *did* make me smile when she didn't show. Whatever her parents had said to her must have worked because Cole had said the other night, she'd remained bearable.

I wasn't so certain she wasn't gearing up to do something to me, but fortunately, as I'd spent more time venturing into town, going to Frank's and the brewery one night and to volunteer at BarkTown, I'd never once run into her. I'd even swung by a salon to grab their pricing sheet and schedule an upcoming appointment I'd need soon. I'd walked the streets of downtown and popped into a few antique shops. Still, no sign of Selma.

I was adjusting to Cole being gone more, I was finding ways to get out on my own and feel comfortable in Marysville again, and I was even starting to make some friends.

Nora and Sarah's offer to come to Marley's so I wouldn't be alone was hopefully proof of that.

Outside of Marley's slow decline, I was noticing more and more— like the morning I came down to the kitchen to find her staring at the coffee with an empty expression as she turned to me, flinched, like maybe she didn't know who *I* was and said, "I'm not sure how to use it. Is it new?"

No. Her thirty-year-old coffee pot was most definitely not new.

"I'll show you," I'd said, thinking quick on my feet and remembering Melanie's words not to make forgetful moments a big deal.

They could scare her, and they'd come and go with increasing frequency but so far, she hadn't seemed to have forgotten anything *too* major. I was still holding out hope she'd be there for Christmas. I was already making plans to decorate earlier and give her the best Christmas she'd ever had.

Wasn't quite so sure how I'd pull it off, but she deserved one more year celebrating her favorite season and I was determined to make it happen.

I was in the kitchen, washing the rest of the dishes and cleaning up after Nora and Sarah's visit when my phone buzzed with a text.

**Home in five. Coming?**

*I'll be there.*

Nerves hit as I smoothed out the tank top I bought. In truth, I'd bought four different Nashville Steel tops but considering it was definitely still summer weather, I was plenty warm in the cutoff denim shorts and tank I'd thrown on to watch the game. In my dresser was a sweatshirt, short sleeve and long sleeve shirt supporting Cole's team. Nothing with his number, I wasn't presumptuous. I figured showing up like this would make him smile enough even if he'd be dressed in his typical suit when he arrived. But like last time I went there for dinner, I didn't doubt he'd strip out of those clothes and throw on something more comfortable too.

After using the bathroom and running my hands through my hair, I slid into a pair of my black Birkenstock sandals, grabbed my purse at the door and locked it on my way out.

Dave's old, blue Ford pickup rumbled up the driveway right as I reached their front porch, so I leaned my shoulder against one of the beams.

Cole hopped out first, slamming the door and waved hello before opening up the front passenger door. He held Marley's hand and helped her down and repeated the help to Kate who'd sat in the back.

"Hello," Marley said, as Kate came up next to her and cupped Marley's elbow gently in her hand. "Did you have fun?"

"Cole won, so I was happy. Nora and Sarah came over to watch the game with me."

Her brows furrowed. "Good. That's good."

I stepped back while Kate helped her up the stairs and inside.

"Does she not know who they are?" I asked Dave.

"Had a long day, probably tired. Seemed for a minute there earlier though she didn't recognize Cole, and when he asked if she was excited to get back to you for dinner, she was excited you were in town."

"Oh." Excitement from the win of the game diminished with the news. "She forgot how to make coffee the other day."

Dave settled his arm over my shoulders and pulled me to his side. "Getting old isn't a walk in the park. We knew this was coming."

"Yeah, but now that it's happening, it feels like I'm staring down a runaway train."

"Probably gonna be as painful as getting hit by one when she's gone too, even though we all see it coming. Doesn't mean she's not worth enjoying while she's still with us. Got myself a feelin' there's a lot of wisdom left in that head of hers if we keep paying attention."

I allowed him to walk me inside where Kate was already in the kitchen, getting dinner ready.

Dave was right. On all accounts. We knew her end was near but that didn't make the goodbye coming less painful. I took a moment to watch Marley gather the vegetables for the salad as Kate handed them to her and got to work cleaning and chopping them. Enjoyed the warmth of their home they'd re-welcomed me into without so much as a blink and the quiet conversation Kate and Marley were having.

She'd be gone soon, and I'd spent enough time away. It was time to enjoy her as much as I possibly could.

————

"Cole," I rasped his name against his throat as he moved deep inside of me. Slowly, with powerful thrusts. I planted my feet on the mattress so the bed didn't squeak.

I'd walked Marley back to the house earlier and sent Cole a text once she was asleep. He was spending the night with me, while Jasper had a sleepover with his parents. Tomorrow was Labor Day. Cole had to go in for an easy practice and game film, and he was dropping Jasper off at Selma's so they could have the day together.

As soon as he stepped inside Marley's house earlier, he'd taken the remote control from my hand, turned the television off, and taken my hand and led me upstairs where he promptly divested me of my clothes, whispering about how much seeing me in the short shorts and wearing the Steel shirt had him hard all dinner long.

With how quickly he started turning me on, I'd expected the rest of our time together to be as fierce, but as soon as he'd slipped me out of my clothes and shucked off his own shorts and shirt, he'd laid me out on the bed and taken his damn time.

I'd climaxed twice before Cole slid inside of me, glancing at where our bodies connected until he was fully sheathed inside of me. I had my hands at his shoulder, and in his short hair at the back of his neck, my breaths ragged and my muscles already aching in a pleasured way while he continued to move, pulling out so slowly he dragged against my most sensitive flesh before thrusting back inside. Every deep thrust of him tore a quiet plea from my mouth for more as the heat of another orgasm grew inside me. This was not the hard and frantic sex we'd done before, but there was more passion. The strength of his body against mine, the scrape of his chest over my nipples and breasts as he moved. He tore my hands off his body, gripped them in his and shoved them to the mattress next to my head.

"Finish for me, Eden. Get there. Let me feel you when I'm deep inside you."

Oh gracious. I couldn't hold back. And I rasped his name as the tightness inside me spiraled, coiled tighter where I knew the explosion would be mind-numbingly beautiful.

"There we go. Good girl," he grunted, and like that, the spiral flared out, ignited my veins and seized my chest along with my core and I came, biting down on his shoulder to stay quiet while I shattered beneath him.

He came moments later, throbbing deep inside of me, and he fused his mouth to mine and kissed me through the lingering aftershocks.

"I love you," I whispered, and the words flew out so quick I couldn't take them back if I wanted to.

Cole stilled on top of me, pushed up enough so our noses brushed and smirked. "Yeah?"

I swallowed my fear and my nerves and everything holding me back. Dave was right earlier in more ways than about Marley. Life was too damn short.

And it was time I started living it.

I squeezed his hands still gripping mine and nodded. "Yeah, Cole. Always have."

"Damn glad to hear it." He kissed me, lips curled up into a smile and then trailed those full, soft and warm lips back to my ear. "Love you too. You know that, right? Always."

"I know."

His hands unpeeled from mine and he pushed up, bracing his arms. "As much as I'd love to stay like this forever I need to clean up. You want to use the bathroom first, though?"

"You go."

He climbed out of the bed with grace and strength without bothering to get dressed. The bathroom was right across the hall and while he took care of himself, I hurried out of bed and prodded as quietly as I could into Marley's bedroom. Her room smelled like roses and dust from lack of use, and I ignored the emptiness in it while I used her bathroom, cleaned myself and washed my hands.

Cole was already back in the bedroom when I returned, tugging on his boxer briefs. "Marley's bathroom?"

"Figured it'd be faster."

I slid back into the bed and Cole joined me, curling me against his chest while he lay on his back. His hand went to my hair, running through it before sliding his hand down my back and cupping my backside. "I missed you at the game today, you know. For years I'd always imagined what it'd be like to have you in the stands, cheering for me at one of my games, and today, seeing everyone else I loved there outside Graham and that empty seat, I wished you were in it. Tell me someday this season you'll come."

"I will." My hands went to his stomach, and I brushed my fingertips up and down. "I went to one of your games once."

His body stiffened beneath my touch, and his free hand cupped my chin, tilting my face so our eyes met. "What? When?"

"You weren't starting, but it was two years ago when you were playing in Tampa. I'd followed you. And I don't know…I knew you were going to be playing there so I went. I cried almost the entire game, watching you on the sidelines."

"Eden," he sighed my name and kissed my forehead. "I don't know whether to be pissed you never reached out, or thrilled to know one of my dreams came true without realizing it."

"For tonight, let's stick with thrilled?"

He chuckled and squeezed me to him. "Love you, Eden. Don't care right now how much time was wasted, just know when it comes to you, I never want to waste anymore."

That familiar taste of fear soured my throat before I swallowed it down. "Me either."

# CHAPTER 35
## COLE

"That's it. Nice toss, Jasper!" He gave a fist pump as his red bean bag fell into the hole.

Across the court from him, Davis, who was Jasper's partner in a corn hole game against his new friend, Archer and Archer's dad, Scott, cheered Jasper on.

Eden and I were at a nearby high-top table, hanging out with Nora who was off work on Saturdays, and Archer's mom, Cassy.

We were seven weeks into the season and on our bye week. Usually, I tried to head to wherever Graham was playing with Georgia, but today I was settling for hanging out at Buckin' Brews with a handful of my teammates coming out to cheer him on with me. The game wouldn't start for hours, but we were taking advantage of the comfortable fall-like weather, which meant the humidity dropped making the eight-five degrees bearable and enjoying the food trucks in the parking lot outside the corn hole area.

Word must have gotten out that Davis, Yeets, Cortland, and I were there because the back patio was beyond packed, and Nate had come over earlier to tell me he'd called in a friend for security and to act as a bouncer to keep track of the number of people there. I could feel the curious and excited stares, hear the murmured conversations when I'd walked past to use the restroom or grab a fresh round of drinks. What everyone didn't know was that if we were hanging out at Buckin' Brews, none of us minded the attention, or talking to fans.

Hell, Davis was more at home being the center of attention than he was avoiding it, and he hadn't bothered to mute his natural excitement every time one of Jasper's bags scored them points.

"I know you're from here," Cassy said. "So everyone obviously knows you, but do you get recognized a lot? Like when you're in Nashville or traveling?"

"Yeah, every once in a while, at the mall or something or when I'm out to eat, I can *feel* people looking at me, but you'd be surprised how few people want to come up and talk to us."

It happened less than I'd assumed it would being a pro athlete, and it was mostly kids which never bothered me. Adults tended to be more discreet in their recognition, catching a not-so-sly picture to show their friends. I'd been tagged in a few of those on social media, and when I caught them, gave them a quick like, maybe a comment and moved on.

"How are you liking Marysville?" Eden asked.

This was the first time Jasper and Archer hung out and when I'd called to see if Archer wanted to hang out with us at the brewery, thought his parents would not only feel more comfortable being included, but would like to get out and meet people. From what Jasper said, they hadn't met many people yet and since they lived on several acres, didn't have neighbors for Archer to play with daily.

She chuckled and spun her glass of beer in her hands. "It's a lot smaller than Indianapolis, that's for sure, but it's peaceful and that's what we wanted for Archer to grow up with. Besides, we're hoping with Scott's job in the city and the lower cost of living here, we can make our real dream of having a small working farm happen over the years."

"What kind of farm?"

"A small family farm. I'd like to focus on raising goats for FFA kids for showing at fairs, maybe for breeding, and we've already ordered our first batch of egg-laying chickens. Scott's building the coop right now so it's ready when they get here. It sounds silly, but I always had this dream of working a small-town farmer's market on the weekends, selling eggs and vegetables and herbs. I'm lucky enough I married a man who thinks my crazy dreams are worth following."

"Count me in for your first buyer with the eggs. And if you need help, I'm not so great with growing things, but I did do a short time job working with a vet who specializes in large breeds like cattle and horses and some goats. I might be able to help answer questions as you get started."

"Count me in, too," Nora said and raised her glass in Cassy's direction. "For help or research. For buying. Heck, I don't mind getting my hands dirty either if you want some help planting."

"That'd be wonderful. Thank you. We're going to wait and do most of the planting in the spring, but after the chicken coop is done our next step is to build a greenhouse. I'll take all the help I can get."

"Dad!"

I turned to Jasper, who was waving both his arms in the air. "What's up, kiddo?"

"We won! Your turn."

"Awww…is Mr. Hall too tired? Does he need a nap?"

Jasper laughed as well as the women at the table.

"Don't know about that, something tells me that kid could go all night," Nora muttered.

I cringed as the women laughed, especially Eden. "Enough of that." I pointed at them. "He's my teammate and like a little brother." Turning to Eden, I gave her a kiss on her cheek, it was soft and quick, but still enough to set her cheeks burning hot pink. "I'll be back later."

"Have fun," she said.

"What?" Nora asked as I walked away. "Like I'm wrong?"

Another round of laughter echoed from behind me while I shook off the disgusting visual Nora had put in my head.

We threw another few games of bags. Archer and Jasper got sick of it once Sarah showed up for another round of adoption events with her rescue animals. At one point, Nora and Eden and Cassy headed over there and spent time playing with the puppies and enjoying their time in the shade.

Mason Yeets and I kicked Cortland and Scott's asses, winning the first two games out of three, and eventually Jasper returned to the game area with Archer, ice cream cones magically appearing in their hands from somewhere and Nate following close behind them.

Nate's forehead carried worried lines and his gaze was skipping back and forth as he herded the kids in our direction.

"What's wrong?" I asked, heading their way.

Nate and I had taken a few years to get back to talking terms, longer until he liked me again, and while I didn't consider the guy a good friend, we did spend time together on occasion.

"Here." Nate dug into his pocket and pulled out some dollar bills. "How about you kids go grab some quarters and show your dad's friends how to play the old arcade games."

"We can?" Jasper grabbed the cash without hesitation. "Thanks!"

He and Archer took off, and I waited until they'd run to Cortland before turning back to Nate.

"What's going on?"

"Selma's here." His lip curled, and he glanced around again. "She and Kyleigh showed up a few minutes ago. My buddy, Jason, helping with security let me know but he had to let them in because we weren't at capacity."

"It'll be fine."

"Really? Because as soon as she saw you and your teammates, she scowled at the pretty little blonde at the table and took off around the back, but I can't find her."

That pretty little blonde he referred to was Cassy who was now at the table with Scott, munching on an order of nachos she'd grabbed.

"Shit. Keep an eye on Jasper?"

I had no doubt someone in the brewery had sent her a picture of me hanging out with Eden. We didn't go into town very much over the last few weeks and that was mostly because I was trying to avoid a situation like this.

"You got it."

"They weren't by the dogs?"

"Rescue event is closing up so unless Eden's helping load the dogs back in the volunteer's cars, I didn't see her, but Nora is out there taking down tents."

Odd. Wouldn't have surprised me if Eden had done just that, not wanting to be apart from the animals any longer than necessary. She mentioned last week she probably needed to start looking for a full-time job, but I knew she wouldn't make any decisions while Marley was still declining—which had happened much faster in the last six weeks than either of us could have predicted or imagined.

Eden had essentially quit helping at BarkTown three weeks ago and even now Melanie or one of her other nurses, usually Jodie, were always at the house with Eden and Marley. They were mostly there to help Marley bathe and use the restroom, and make sure she didn't wander away. Once they'd found her walking through the house naked because she hadn't remembered to get dressed after a bath and another time they found her in the backyard near the lake, ankle-deep in the water.

I headed out back to the dogs' play area and found Nora handing off a cloth grocery bag to a volunteer I didn't know.

"Hey. Have you seen Eden?"

"No. She told me she was going to use the bathroom. Why? Something wrong?"

"Nate said Selma was here, but he couldn't find either of them. Want me to go check?"

"I'll do it."

Nora's brows arched and her lips curved up. "You'll go search for them in the bathroom?"

"If I have to." Because if, for some reason, Selma had cornered her there for whatever ridiculous reason, I had no problem invading someone's privacy. Besides, there'd be stalls.

I hurried back inside, going around to the front of the brewery so I could check the parking lot, but Eden's dark hair she had up in a clip wasn't visible above any cars.

"Hey, man. Good luck next week." Considering he was at the front doors and as burly as one of my linebackers, I figured he was Jason, Nate's friend.

"Thanks, man. I'll need it." I gave him a fist pump. I wasn't wrong. Our next game was against Raleigh on their turf, and we were back one game so far in the standings to them. Beaux Hale would be bringing his team's A-game and I'd joked with Melanie that if she could somehow slip him the flu or something this coming week, I'd appreciate it.

The inside of the brewery was packed, not surprising given it was Saturday college football day, and I weaved through bodies, trying to keep my head down while also looking for Selma or Eden as I made my way to the back corner where the pool tables and restrooms were. There was a line, at least six women deep, and I said a quick prayer that phones didn't come out while I pushed by all of them.

As soon as I opened the door, Eden's voice was clear and sharp and angry, but she wasn't visible.

"You do that, Selma," she said. "Keep going for Cole. See how far that gets you."

"I'm his son's *mother*, that'll get me plenty."

"More than the ten grand he's already giving you?"

"Probably. Jasper some day is going to want his mom and dad *together* like all the other kids at school and I know Cole, he'll cave then. He won't want his son to be unhappy. Not like you'll make both of them."

I slammed the door so hard it banged into the wall behind me, and I found both women standing off facing each other around the corner from the mirrors and stalls where there was a sitting room. Thankfully, the rest of the women in the restroom were at least pretending to mind their own business and only a few raised their eyebrows at my appearance. "Anyone records this or lets anyone know I'm here and I'll sue," I threatened.

Normally, I wouldn't, but the last thing I needed was a social media shitstorm with said mother of my son in a public women's restroom.

The media would have a field day with it, especially the gossip sites.

The women I didn't know ducked their heads and scurried outside and I finally found Eden and Selma, standing off and glaring at each other.

Selma looked like she was going to blow a gasket at any moment.

Eden looked more amused than irritated or scared.

*That's my girl.*

"I think you haven't learned shit."

# CHAPTER 36
## EDEN

Of all the ways to end the best Saturday I'd had since I left Marysville, Selma tracking me down and following me into the bathroom and getting in my face as soon as I left a stall was not anywhere near my *Bingo!* card of possibilities.

Cole's voice was thick as he found us, hands thrown to his hips, and I had no doubt he was resisting the urge to strangle Selma and her irrational dreams.

As angry as I was, and as scared as I'd been when I first walked out of the stall and almost ran right into Selma's pinched-up, angry face, I was finding it difficult not to laugh.

Of all the things for him to overhear.

"Cole," Selma said and shot him a thousand-watt mega smile. "Hey. Eden and I were just talking."

"I heard. And I heard you still have your head full of bullshit."

"It's not bullshit." Her smile fell. "Someday—"

"Someday I'm going to marry the woman standing next to you and she's the *only* woman I'd ever marry," he cut her off abruptly, and my jaw dropped at his statement. "I'm not only going to marry Eden as soon as I can get her to agree to it, I'm going to plant babies inside her so Jasper can grow up in a house filled with brothers and sisters. She's going to move into my house, and she's going to be my wife. And Eden is the *only* woman I've ever wanted to marry, the only woman I've ever loved, so all this shit you have in your head, you need to take to a doctor to sort through, because I swear to God, you fill Jasper's head with any of this shit, not only am I going to be the one setting him straight, I'm going to take you back to court for creating a hostile environment for our child and I won't care frankly, if he ever sees you again. Eden and I will take care of him."

"I knew that was your plan," she hissed, and good-freaking hell.

"I'm not dealing with your brand of crazy anymore. Want to talk to me? Call my lawyer. Want to harass Eden? I'll slap a restraining order on you so damn fast your head will spin and no one in town will want anything to do with you."

"I get it," I said, and Selma's head whipped toward me, but in a way, I felt for her because she'd been holding onto the hope of Cole Buchanan for longer than I'd ever known her.

"Excuse me?"

"I get it—how much you love Cole." Even if her love was a twisted infatuation. "He's the best man I've ever met. He's an incredible dad. He's a good guy with morals that far supersede any normal human. He's talented, and he's sexy as hell, and he loves his family and everyone around him who's halfway decent. I get it, Selma, why you don't think you'll ever meet someone nearly as good as him because that'll be hard to find, but that doesn't mean you get to keep trying to claim a man who's made it clear he doesn't want you."

To my utter shock, her chin wobbled before she rolled her lips together. "You're not good enough for him."

She was right about that. "I don't think there's a woman on the planet who is. But I'm damn lucky he thinks I am."

"You are," Cole stated, and his voice was thick with as much emotion as mine was.

"I'll tell," Selma said. "I'll tell everyone that you two killed Hilary. He won't want you once you ruin his life."

"It won't be me doing that, it'll be you."

She shook her head.

"Go ahead," Cole said, and he stepped up toward my side. Selma turned his way, losing her persistence. "Tell everyone. Take it to the news. Frankly, I'm tired of everyone thinking I'm some damn perfect guy without any skeletons in my closet. You want to set them loose, set me free, go for it, but I'm pretty sure the media spin my team puts on it will only have me coming out looking like an angel, and you'll still be the cause of more headaches."

He turned to me and smiled. "Ready to go?"

"Yeah." I placed my hand in his. "I lived for seven years without this man, so I know how hard it is to want something you can't have, but now that I have him, I'm not letting go. Not for the mother of his son—not for anyone. You can keep causing problems, but the only one you're going to hurt in the long road is your son. Maybe think on that, Selma."

I turned my gaze to Cole and from the heat in his eyes, my declaration had meant as much to him as it had me.

He led me outside, and I ducked my head while the line of women watched us leave the bathroom. Selma didn't follow us, but I no longer cared about her.

We'd spent the last six weeks hiding out, awaiting whatever she had planned next and the truth of it was she was a woman who selfishly loved someone who simply didn't like her.

She could keep throwing her tantrums, keep causing public scenes, but I'd meant what I said.

I wasn't going anywhere and the only person she was hurting was Jasper.

I expected Cole to take me out back to his friends, but instead, he led me right outside.

"Shouldn't we get Jasper?" I asked when he beeped the locks on his truck.

"In a minute."

"Why?"

"Because I can't make out with you and kiss you the way I want to when he's around yet."

"Oh." I stumbled over rocks and laughed as Cole chuckled.

We reached his truck, but instead of getting inside like I expected, he backed me right up to the side of it. His hands cupped my face. "You were magnificent in there."

"I meant every word."

"Me too." He slammed his mouth to mine and pressed his hips to my body, pinning me against the truck with the weight of him like he was afraid to lose me, but there was no reason for him to be afraid.

Because I might not have realized it before I told Selma, but there was no way I was leaving this man.

Not now that I had him.

My phone buzzed in my back pocket, breaking our kiss, and when Cole pulled away, both of us gasped for breath while I dipped my hand behind me and grabbed my phone.

The name on the screen sent chills down my spine, evaporating all the heat Cole had stroked in a breath. "It's Melanie."

———

Dave and Kate were on the front porch when I arrived. While I talked to Melanie, Cole ushered me into his truck and ran around back to grab Jasper.

By the time he returned to the truck, I couldn't bother wiping tears off my cheeks, and as the truck pulled to a stop at the top of Marley's driveway, they started all over again.

Behind me, Jasper was silently crying as well and when Cole stopped the truck, he jumped out and ran straight to his grandma.

She fell to her knees as the weight of Jasper slammed into her body and Dave moved in close so she didn't fall backward on the porch.

"I'm sorry," Dave said as I came close, Cole appearing at my side and holding on to me. "Melanie said she was sleeping."

A sob tore through me, and I faltered in my step. Next to me, Cole wrapped his arm around me to keep me standing. "You've got this."

I didn't.

"I shouldn't have left her," I cried. "She was so quiet this morning. And didn't want to get out of bed. I should have known."

"You were doing what she wanted," Dave choked out, tears in his own eyes. "You were living."

While she was dying.

It wasn't fair, even if we'd known it was going to happen. "She was supposed to have one last Christmas."

"She'll celebrate it with Darryl for the first time in thirty years."

I laughed over another sob. She was with a full head of hair and probably ecstatic to see him while we were all miserable. Death was only horrible to the loved ones left behind, and I hadn't nearly enough time with her.

I needed more stories. More wisdom.

I needed Marley.

"Would you like me to call your mom?" Kate asked, hugging a still-crying Jasper with a sad smile on her face.

I nodded, unable to answer, but yeah…I wanted my mom. And my dad. "Thanks."

"Should we go see her?" Cole asked, and what a mess we all were because Cole didn't seem to be faring much better than the rest of us. "Say goodbye?"

I shook my head. I wasn't ready. Instead, I burrowed into Cole and threw my arms around his waist. His arms, strong and trembling with his own emotion, held me tight to him. "She wouldn't want this," he whispered.

"Tough. She doesn't always get what she wants."

"Yeah. She does."

I laughed, tears soaking his shirt and probably snot. Fine. Marley did always get what she wanted.

He held me for a few more minutes until I was able to soften the tears and wipe my ace. "You need a new shirt."

"I'll buy a thousand of them, so you don't have to worry about how much you cry on them."

The door opened, and Melanie stood behind the screen door. Her eyes were equally red, and for a moment, I was surprised. She was used to this. She had to see it often, but seeing her genuine emotion made me like her so much better.

"Keep Jasper out here," Cole said quietly. His dad agreed and then I was being guided inside the house I'd grown to love so much that it would never be the same again.

"I'm sorry," Melanie whispered. "I'm so sorry for your loss. I know she meant a lot to you both, but if it brings you any comfort, know she's no longer suffering."

I knew that. Knew how hard the last several months were for her on her good days and in her good moments.

"Thank you." She gave us another sad smile and stepped farther back, giving us a moment.

I headed toward her room, the hallway blurring in front of me and behind me was the soft thump of Cole's sneakers following. When I reached her doorway, Melanie called my name.

"Yes?"

"Before her nap, she asked for some paper and a box. They're on her nightstand. I believe she left it for you."

God…how much harder could I cry?

With bravery I absolutely didn't feel, I stepped into Marley's room. The blinds were opened enough to let the outside sunshine in but the lights in her room were off. She was tucked beneath her favorite floral quilt, gray hair around her face, and I froze so suddenly Cole stepped into me, his chest to my back. I reached back and squeezed his hand.

"She looks like she's still sleeping." He stepped forward, moving me with him. "I don't know how to say goodbye to her. Not after all the time I ignored her and wasn't here for her."

"You were here when it mattered. Came when she asked."

It wasn't enough. There was never enough I could do for her.

I collapsed onto the side of the bed, sitting down, and I took her hand in mine. She was cooling, and her hand was frail and her skin already pale, but I brought it to my cheek, felt her soft skin against mine one more time.

Next to me, Cole picked up the piece of paper, but I was so focused on memorizing every single one of Marley's features, every softened wrinkle, every strand of hair, and every age spot I didn't notice until I heard him chuckling.

"Sorry," he said, but there was a smile on his face, and he handed me the paper. "You should read this."

"I don't want to."

"It'll help."

Nothing would, but with wet fingers and shaking hands, I took the paper.

Tears blurred the faint, jilted writing, and I wiped my tears off on my arm so I could see them better.

. . .

*The box is for your running shoes. Put them away and never look at them again.*

*Marry him. Start a family. Have all the adventures you ever dreamed of. Live with no regrets and a lot of laughter.*

*Love with all of your heart. It's large enough for everyone—I've seen it.*

*Most of all, be happy.*

*Love you-*
*Marley*

*PS. Told you I'm always right.*

I couldn't help it. Like Cole, I barked out a laugh and wiped more snot from my nose. "She said she wanted me with you, and I told her she was wrong, that there never was an us. She told me not to lie to her. Then I called her stubborn. She said it wasn't stubbornness if she was right."

"Marley was the smartest woman alive."

"Yeah." I smiled up at Cole, and then bent down and gave her a kiss.

We stayed in her room until the ambulance came and then we joined Jasper out back, so he didn't have to see them remove her body, but even then, as much as it hurt, there was also quiet laughter, stories we shared with him, and stories Kate and Dave joined in on.

In the end, our pain was replaced with a quiet, soothing peace.

We all hurt now that she was gone, but we were all better than we'd been because we had a chance to have her in our lives.

Me, especially.

"Come on," Cole said to me, taking my hand in his once the ambulance was gone and the nurses had left. "Let's go home."

*Home.*

I smiled down at Jasper, up at Cole. "Sounds perfect."

<h1 style="text-align:center">EPILOGUE</h1>

EDEN

"Jasper! Your mom is here! Come on, buddy!"

"Coming, Eden!"

He trampled down the stairs as loud as a herd of elephants, and almost knocked me off my feet as he threw his arms around me. "Have a good weekend, okay?"

"Will do! Bye, Dad!"

Selma stood at the front of her SUV in Cole's driveway and gave me a wave.

I had no idea what happened to Selma after that day in the bathroom. I didn't know if she'd been hit with a wave of guilt that while she was cornering me to get me away from Cole, Marley was dying and that was a wake-up call, or if her parents had another brutal talk with her after word of her behavior reached them. Word around town was her parents told her to get her butt into therapy or she'd lose any inheritance they'd ever promised her. Maybe, she finally realized the truth that she'd never have Cole and started trying to move on. I assumed Cole moving me into his house the night Marley died gave her a speed course on that reality. He refused to let me stay at Marley's house alone so he took me to his, and after that first night, I'd never wanted to return to Marley's house. Or Florida.

Shortly after Marley's funeral in October, Selma put her house on the market and before it sold, she'd moved to Nashville.

She switched to the labor and delivery floor, getting a day shift.

She and Cole reworked their custody arrangement. We had Jasper with us during the week to make getting him to school easier and she had him on weekends. Because of that, Cole gave her more time with him during holidays and a few extra weeks during the summer. Surprising both of us, she hadn't asked for an increase in her child support. She and I didn't get along, and she never came to the door to let us know she was there, but if I was the one who sent Jasper to her, she'd give me a wave before whisking Jasper away.

I closed the door to stop Bongo from sitting there and whining like he did every time Jasper left and gave him a good rubdown. "It's okay, big guy. You'll have too much fun at BarkTown to miss him while we're all gone."

Cole came around the corner of the kitchen, bottle of water in hand and a smile on his face. He was already dressed in his travel clothes, his suit and tie, and it was a shame he had to get to the airport because every time he put on a suit, I wanted to strip it right off him.

"Everything packed up and ready to go?"

"Yep. My plane lands an hour after yours and I've already gotten confirmation from the concierge service."

Cole was preparing to fly to Dallas for his first ever Thanksgiving Day game start. I was meeting him there, flying commercial while he flew with his team. The game wasn't until Thursday, but Jasper didn't have school all week, so I was heading out today with him where I'd join him in the hotel while he had practice tomorrow and after his game on Thursday, we were flying out to spend the weekend in the Dominican Republic.

He prowled toward me with that look in his eyes that made my toes curl and didn't stop until he had his hand at my lower back, was pulling my body toward him and his mouth descended on mine. "Have I told you today how excited I am to marry you?"

I laughed against his mouth. "Only once before our shower and again during."

"Good. Because I don't want you to forget."

He slid a ring on my finger last weekend, on the one-month anniversary of Marley's death. The ring wasn't an extravagant diamond. It was a two-carat ruby ring Darryl had given Marley on their twentieth anniversary. She'd bequeathed it to Cole in her will, along with a note that said, *"You'll know what to do with this."*

Every time I caught a glimpse of it, I laughed, knowing how happy she was with herself for being so right about Cole and me. We were getting married once his season was done, eloping to the Caribbean with only a handful of friends, including Jasper, my parents, and his brother, Graham.

As far as his season, he and Raleigh were tied for first in their division. Both were having incredible seasons, each only losing one game, Raleigh to Nashville in their first match up with the second coming up to be played right after Christmas. That game would probably decide who ended up as the division champions if you went by what the announcers kept saying every weekend.

I was pulling for Nashville and now proudly sat at every home game wearing Cole's jersey next to Jasper with his parents behind us.

"We need to get going," I reminded him as his hand drifted from my lower back down to cup my backside.

"I have a few minutes yet."

A flutter of excitement rolled through me. "And what do you plan on doing with those few minutes?"

"Eat my dessert first."

He crouched, grabbed my ass, and lifted me. I squealed in surprise and was quickly plopped down on the kitchen counter where Cole was already working to shimmy down my underwear from beneath my dress and stepped in between my spread legs.

"Lie back."

His hand came to my chest, and he lowered me down, so I was spread out on the counter, toes curled around the cool marble.

Cole didn't waste time, sliding his hands up my inner thighs, finding me already wet and ready for him. I always was. Every time the man walked into the room, I couldn't wait to get him alone, and this time was no different. He kissed me while his fingers slipped inside and slid his mouth down my body, plucking my nipples with his other hand while he worked me into a frenzy, quickly, powerfully, and by the time he settled his mouth at my sex, I was dripping, shaking for him and I could do nothing except slap my hands on the counter and cry out his name while he sucked my clit and used his fingers.

"Fuck, you're delicious," he muttered, sucking the taste of me off him.

"You're so good at that."

I laughed, and he helped me redress, smoothed out my dress as I sat up.

"We need to go."

"You can walk with that?" I pointed to his bulge.

"I have no doubts you'll take care of me once we get to the hotel."

He was right. Absolutely, I would.

But better than what the hotel would bring was the fact Cole knew I wouldn't just take care of him there, I was committed to living out every single one of Marley's last wishes for me.

To love him with my entire heart, to have a life of laughter, and absolutely no regrets.

And I'd honor those last words of hers until my own dying breath.

***

THANK YOU for reading Sneak Attack. I hope you loved Cole and Eden's journey to find love! Davis and Maggie's story, Time Out, is now available, and I hope you love their story just as much! Download here: https://amzn.to/3ily4ZS

Want to be the first to know about any new releases or sales? Subscribe to my newsletter! As a thank you, you'll receive a FREE ebook! bit.ly/3nC4exd

# THANK YOU

HUGE thank you to Nina and all the incredible women at Valentine PR for throwing your full enthusiasm and support behind me and these books. I've loved working with you and can't wait to see what the future brings us.

Ellie and Virginia, as always, thanks for putting up with my mess and spit-shining each manuscript until it sparkles. Thank you especially during this crazy time in our world for your flexibility and your extra hard work.

Shannon, you're the best. Always. Forever. Your talent is astounding and I'm thankful I can call you a friend.

To my Sweeties! I love you ladies and your excitement for my books!

To all the bloggers who devote their time and passion into reading books, book tours, release events, leaving reviews, promoting and pimping – you are all rockstars! Thank you for all the love over the years.

My family— I love you all to the moon and back. I don't know what I would do without you in my corner, cheering me on every step of the way. Your support is everything to me and I love you all with all of my heart.

To my girl crew— Tamara, Lauren, Niccole, Cassy, and Bree. What would I do without you ladies? Thank you for blessing me with your friendships. My life is a hundred times better with y'all in it, and a gazillion times more entertaining! To the SteelP! May we forever reign.

And last but definitely not least – to you, the reader. I'm blown away with every release how much you adore my books. You have made my dream a reality and I hope I can cheer you on with yours. Please don't forget to leave reviews on Goodreads or whichever retailer you've purchased this copy from. It helps us so much!

# ABOUT THE AUTHOR

Stacey Lynn likes her coffee with a dash of sugar, her heroes with a side of bossy, and her wine a deep shade of red.

The author of over forty romance novels, many of which have been best-selling titles, she loves being able to turn her vivid imagination into a career that brings entertainment and joy to her readers. Focused on sports romance and emotional, small-town romance, she also loves stretching herself in different genres.

Born in Texas and raised in the Midwest, she now makes her home in North Carolina and loves all things Southern. Together with her ultimate tall, dark, and handsome hero, she has four children. Her life is a chaotic mess that fights with her Type-A, list-making, neurotically organized preferences and she wouldn't have it any other way.

Subscribe to her newsletter so you can stay up to date on all her new releases. www.staceylynnbooks.com

# OTHER BOOKS BY STACEY LYNN

**<u>Las Vegas Vipers ~hockey romance</u>**

Final Shot (free on all retailers)

Game Changer

Dream Maker

Rule Breaker

Shot Taker

Goal Chaser

Secret Keeper

**<u>Ice Kings Series ~hockey romance</u>**

Playing With Fire (free on all retailers)

Playing To Win

Scoring Off The Ice

Hooked One Her

Hard Checked

Fighting Dirty

**<u>The Rough Riders Series ~football romance</u>**

Dirty Player

Filthy Player

Wicked Player

Cocky Player

<u>Love and Lies Duet ~angsty slow burn, romance</u>

<u>All the Ugly Things</u>

<u>All the Beautiful Things</u>

<u>Love and Honor Duet ~angsty, romantic suspense</u>

<u>Twisted Hearts</u>

<u>Unraveled Love</u>

**Love In The Heartland ~small town romance**

Captivated By You

This Time Around

Long Road Home

Before We Fell

**Crazy Love Series ~small town romance**

Fake Wife

Knocked Up

28 Dates

Weekend Fling

**The Fireside Series ~small town romance**

His to Love

His to Protect

His to Cherish

His to Seduce

**Tangled Love Series ~erotic romance**

Entice

Embrace

Enflame

**The Luminous Series ~BDSM romance**

Dominate Me

Crave Me

Long For Me

**Just One Series ~rockstar romance**

Just One Song

Just One Week

Just One Regret

Just One Moment

**The Nordic Lords Series ~MC romance**

Point of Return

Point of Redemption

Point of Freedom

Point of Surrender

## Standalones

Remembering Us

Don't Lie To Me – billionaire romance

Try Me – A Don't Lie To Me Novella

www.ingramcontent.com/pod-product-compliance
Lightning Source LLC
Chambersburg PA
CBHW020134310726
48970CB00006B/1867